THE VALOR OF VALHALLA

THE TIDES OF NIRVANA

ALSO BY
MARTIN KEARNS

The Valor of Valhalla Series

Beneath the Veil

The Sands of Akhirah

Coming Soon

Kinder: Nightmares and Plaintive Hauntings

from Beneath the Veil

Ω
3

THE VALOR OF VALHALLA

THE TIDES OF NIRVANA

MARTIN KEARNS

NEW YORK, USA

Martin Kearns
New York, USA
www.readkearns.com

"The world is full of stories, and from birth to death, we are all living our own mythologies."

Ω

"God is a metaphor for that which transcends all levels of intellectual thought."

– Joseph Campbell

Ω
3

THE VALOR OF VALHALLA

THE TIDES OF NIRVANA

PART ONE

DISSENT

CHAPTER 1
ABADDON

An elevated platform carried the 6 train over 173rd Street in the Bronx and shielded Keyana from the sky. Twilight sprinkled light over the concrete, and she hurried to make it home before full dark. It wasn't supernatural entities she rushed from, though some found their homes in the cities and were often of the type to be a mite cleverer than those that roamed the woods of the suburbs and upstate beyond.

It was the people she wished to avoid. Malice spread like ink in a bowl of water, and the fluid of civility became more tainted by the day. It was as though the revelation of inhuman entities gave a license for people to abandon their own.

Crime rose, and Keyana didn't like the feel of her work attire while out on the streets.

A solution to her far commute would have been to keep her apartment in Riverdale, but her mother needed help at the home that swaddled Keyana through her childhood, and she wasn't the type to shy away from returning the favor of caretaking—even in the face of excited calls to social events one only gets to enjoy for that limited time when the orbits of youth and financial stability briefly merge in their transits.

She turned off Westchester Avenue and slowed her pace to quiet her footfalls. Fifty feet later, she keyed into the small house and walked inside to her first order of business, which was always to draw the curtains and hide the ugly bars beyond her windows. Those bars made her feel exposed when she was a child, but Keyana was thankful for each one these days.

"Baby girl?" her mother called from the living room.

Lady Perez, that's what the kids on and around her block had called Keyana's mother for decades. Time moved forward, as we perceive it to do whether we like it or not, and the kids grew older. Some would leave their section of the Bronx, as Keyana had done, and some would stay to become matriarchs or patriarchs of the area and glean respect from those who sat the stoops and made mischief up and down the streets. Keyana's momma had maintained infamy as one who fed the neighborhood children ice pops in August, spent top dollar on Halloween candy in October, and always made sure her leftovers from the Thanksgiving feast found their way to elderly widows or kids. This continued on until the tech age sapped people's attentions from their local communities to the far more alluring global reels and influencers. Lady Perez maintained her status only in the whispers of some who remembered the bygone era of community living as it was before.

"Yes, Momma, it's me," Keyana said as she unzipped her boots. The home wasn't exactly a time capsule, but the decor hadn't much changed over the years. The carpet and the walls were the same she'd scored with crayons as a child, but her mother sat in front of a large flat-screen TV Keyana had purchased after she'd worked her first office job for a few months.

A constant barrage of news cycles streaming through the television made her wish she hadn't.

"That's no good for you, Momma," Keyana said. "Turn it off while I make you supper."

"I already ate, baby," Lady Perez said and used her toe to give the TV tray in front of her easy chair a little push, showcasing the empty plastic container.

"Too many preservatives in that, we talked about this," Keyana said as she collected the container. "These are for emergencies. I have frozen dinners you should be using."

"That white bean mash nonsense? Please, Key, let me enjoy the last few years I have."

"I guess that means I'll be finding a stash of candy around here again."

"No. I've been good. It hurts my feet when I eat that anymore. Everything I love hurts me now."

"I don't hurt you, Momma."

They bantered and passed the evening as the surrounding borough transitioned from its daylight persona to a nocturnal vibrancy. Lady Perez discussed the happenings of the world, and Keyana could only convince her to keep the television news reels muted while they spoke.

Images of the ocean frequented the screen, but Lady Perez wasn't so interested in talking about the monster that hid beneath the waves. Keyana had thought it odd that little was done to discuss the earthquakes tormenting the Caribbean nations and mainland Florida. The intensity of the tremors was meager, with few reaching a six on the famed Richter scale, but the shaking proved a frequent reminder that something was amiss.

A watermark read "*Pulse24 News*" and changed locations

as the broadcast transitioned between warring nations and those with burgeoning conflict. The closed-captioned text revealed which side America had taken up support for in each respective conflict. Keyana snapped Lady Perez's attention long enough to remind her of upcoming appointments and important events, but her mother's eyes would always drift back to the television screen. Should she have been parenting a teenager, she assumed she would have the same problem but with a smartphone.

"I have to go tonight, Momma. Don't forget to defrost the container tomorrow morning so you can eat a proper dinner."

They hugged and Keyana left the little home, made her way to the train, and quickly boarded one heading back into Manhattan. The car appeared normal, and she took her attention off of her immediate surroundings to watch the city fly by from the elevated tracks. The signs for Longwood Ave slipped past, and she returned from her daze as a man took the seat next to her. Keyana didn't look directly at him—any native New Yorker would approve—but the air in the car had shifted and she glanced at the few others in the train. They shifted in their positions and many moved toward the other end of the train.

Keyana glanced to the window and glimpsed the man next to her. He wore a light suit and fedora hat. Something that may have been more fitting in the sixties than today, but his visage was crinkled in the reflection, giving her little more than the image of something hanging from his mouth, like an idle cigarette.

She waited a few beats before shifting her weight to exit as the train stopped. She'd hop out and walk down the platform to reenter in another car. A tried-and-true trick she preferred over exiting the train car for another while it was in motion. It was a less conspicuous way to make space between herself and any uncanny people one might see on the NYC subway.

As the train pulled into the eventual stop before it would cross the Harlem River and enter Manhattan, the man placed his leg out and across the aisle, blocking her in. Keyana had no choice now but to look up and see what she was dealing with.

A normal occurrence might have shown her a pervert or someone strung out and looking for an easy mark to rob, but the man next to her appeared almost exactly as his reflection in the window. His facial features were melted, and the cigarette she had observed didn't hang out of the man's mouth, but was attached to it as if an appendage that waggled in the air.

She glanced down. Options were limited, and she hadn't found one before he reached into the inside pocket of his jacket. His hand moved and the sound of a slurry being pushed around filled the car. He pulled a lighter covered in scummy ooze that coated halfway to his elbow. Despite the viscous liquid, the lighter, a bronze flint wheel by the look of it, produced a broad flame and he touched it to his appendage, setting it alight.

The train eased to a stop and Keyana jumped to her feet and leaped over the man's leg, but evil is swift, and he stood to block her path. A seam split his midsection wide, revealing a gaping carnivorous mouth stretching from stem to stern. Keyana stood mute and rooted to the floor; a mouse in the face of a sphinx cat.

Keyana heard hurried footfalls behind the monster and the telltale sound of a bag colliding with it. She sprang to the doors and looked back to see a middle-aged woman in sweats and a Champion hoodie. The good Samaritan gained her feet and stumbled toward the exit. As the speakers issued their telltale directive—*Mind the Closing Doors, Please*—Keyana saw the creature grasp the woman's foot and pull its gaping mouth atop her.

She dared not look back again after hopping out of the train and promptly left the platform. She issued no call to law enforcement, but simply opened an app on her phone to log the encounter and describe the victim of the attack, so, perhaps, any family or friends might know what fate had befallen her savior.

Ω

He comes to people who are lost. He, once the great bright thing, now the tramp in the darkness.

Lilith had no hope of bending him to her wiles. She, the woman who'd raged against the framework of creation, again pinioned below a glass ceiling.

The cavern radiated her cries, her anguish elevated by understanding mortality.

"Don't rush," Flueric said. "We simply can't hurry the new messiah. It wouldn't do."

Shadow cloaked him as he watched her torment, his burning smile the sole feature in a murky outline of him, as though his darkness was of a different nature.

She raked the soil with her nails. "Take it away."

"No, dear woman. This is the favor. The pain is the most important part, after all. Be happy for yourself. You are a true mother."

Lilith screamed as the hot claws of her unborn raked her womb. None, not even Asmodeus, had burned as fiercely within her.

"That's it." Flueric approached, flipping his pocket watch in his hand before cracking it open. "Time is growing short. Perhaps it would be prudent for me to give you a hand." He folded his sleeve to the elbow and placed his hand on her writhing belly. Lilith's eyes rolled wildly and Flueric frowned at her. "Oh, it's much less fun when you are hoping for death," he said while sliding a clawed finger down her belly. "In any event, I'll have to make do with what I have."

Lilith's wail faltered into a sigh, and her body fell limp to the floor as Flueric lifted a writhing mass from her.

"There now, don't worry," Flueric cooed. "Let's take you to get something to eat, yes?" He looked a last time at the once-proud mother of demons and spat into the growing pool of blood surrounding her, leaving a lasting sizzle.

She felt the life Rose had imbued within her—*a gift*, the girl had said. It ran from her veins and, though weakened, boiled with rage at the unfairness of it all. Darkness consumed her and silence prevailed. At least for a small time, until the whisper of slippered feet crept upon her.

A crone and one abnormally large and sassy toad stood beside Lilith. "Princess, quick work is called for. Bring earth, and plenty of it."

The toad croaked in affirmation and hopped a few feet away to pull soil into its mouth.

"Not so pithy here, bleeding in muck," Baba Yaga said. "There's life in you yet. Let's see what it shall bring."

Princess hopped to the witch's side and sloughed a pile of sodden earth on the floor. The witch winked at her frog and received a frown in return. "Now, now, dear. You're helping in the good work. More of this and you'll be back in gowns and heels before the next worm moon."

Baba Yaga went to work, turning the earthen slurry over in Lilith's spilled blood while Princess formed small balls from it and stacked them nearby. They tended to Lilith's wounds until dawn crept upon them from behind the surrounding hills.

Ω

"Is it still out there?" Meriel asked.

"Not sure. Let's stay quiet." Ben sat by the flap of their tent and peeked through a small opening to scan the trees. Nothing.

The Taconic mountain trails were sunlit and clear of debris as they'd hiked through that day. Meriel had pointed out rattlesnake skins among the rocks, and they'd taken care with where they stepped, but those had been the only perils on a scenic hike. The couple had grown familiar with the near outdoors in the area, or so they'd thought, and stepping on an unsuspecting serpent or twisting an ankle had been their chief worry. Until the sun set.

"I felt it, Ben. It was in here. Look at my leg." Meriel had her nylon pants hiked up to show angry red impressions on her calf. An angry reaction and prelude to the hand-shaped bruise to come in a few hours.

"The flap was zipped shut. Is there a rip in the tent?" Ben asked.

Meriel slid around the exterior in search of an opening when its shriek tore through the trees. Their eyes locked and Meriel sidled close to Ben. They listened and felt the pounding of their hearts as something crashed through the surrounding foliage. Meriel wasn't sure she could take much more. She recalled chastising her older sister for panicking all the time. *Panic is what kills you. Remember that and keep your head.* Meriel herself had taken after their grandmother, a staunch believer in her own grit, but the forest had a way of disrobing people of their bravery.

Ben's eyes crept back to the opening and the foliage moved as a dark shape crashed through to enter the small clearing where they'd thought to make camp. Its lithe body stilled and stretched to its full height under clouds bright with the light of a gibbous moon. The same they'd sat under as they ate their dinner before retiring to make love at hiker's midnight among a chorus of crickets and katydids. The insects had gone now, demonstrating a wisdom earned by existing lower on the food chain.

A twig snapped some distance away, and the thing cocked its head and crouched onto all fours. The moon shone through, and Ben saw it. An image he'd known as a child from the books at his library where he'd pass his time between school and home.

"What is it?" Meriel whispered.

"I… It's a satyr, I think. Or something that looks like one," Ben whispered.

Its head turned back to the tent with shoulders tilting as though it was planning to leap upon them. He pushed Meriel behind him and prepared to fight the thing with his Leatherman knife before another twig snapped. This one much closer than before. The creature turned its head to the sound and sniffed the air, and Ben let out the breath he'd been holding when it skulked off into the underbrush.

The young lovers held one another as time passed, bringing calm to their nerves. When the silence proved lasting, they dared to prepare items to defend themselves.

Meriel gasped at the sounds of a struggle in the distance followed by smaller disturbances that drew near. Ben spied animals fleeing from their dens in the opposite direction of the chaos.

Meriel buried her face in her hands, and Ben held her while they waited for it to end. He lifted her chin and said, "Open your eyes." She did—to see orange light as it danced on the tent.

"That's a fire, Ben. We have to leave," she said.

"I know." The surrounding hills and mountains were dry of late and, while the woods weren't exactly a tinderbox, a fire could surround them in a hurry. "Leave the tent. Let's grab our bags and try to get to the trail."

They moved with all the silence of modern people while in the mountains at night, replacing branches from their path and ducking under those too large to bend. The crashing had ended, and their movements were all the more conspicuous without the sounds of insects to dampen them.

"There's no smoke and I don't see firelight anymore," Meriel said.

"I think we will be okay, but it's a good idea to keep our headlamps off."

They traveled on in darkness until the tree line broke, revealing their path. The car rested cold and useless seven miles and three summits worth of trekking away to the south. But before they could begin what Ben knew was going to be a harrowing experience, Meriel grabbed his arm. Ahead of them, standing dead center in the path, was a silhouette. Both froze, at the mercy of their genetic fight-or-flight response, and neither dared breathe until a light switched on and they were exposed.

It was Ben who screamed first.

Ω

Leonard unlocked the doors to the van, and Chelsea hopped inside. "Did you find it?" Leonard asked.

"Yes, it was pretty deep in the mountains," Chelsea said. "Looks like it had stalked a couple of hikers out there. Don't worry, though. It didn't get them before—"

"—*we* got it," Dodd said, startling Leonard to jump in his seat.

Chelsea scowled at Dodd's mischievous grin beyond the driver's side window. "One of these days that little habit of scaring people is going to get you a broken nose."

"Couldn't imagine it could get any worse, this old knob's already been broken twice," Dodd said. "Sorry, Leonard. Meant to give ya a thrill, not stop your heart, buddy."

"It's fine," Leonard said looking back to Chelsea. "I'm just glad there weren't any casualties."

"If you don't count some deer and the cattle from the farmer who called us, looks like we're clear of any, yeah."

Meriel and Ben emerged from the trailhead and stopped short of walking over. Leonard recognized the daze in their eyes. He was intimately aware of how they felt after having been confronted by a supernatural being.

"Are you guys going to be okay?" Chelsea called.

Meriel nodded and guided Ben to their car.

"They're pretty shaken up. That thing was a mean

customer. Had a little bit of the old intelligence left in its eyes, too. I think it was playing with them before having its midnight snack."

Leonard thought of Lilith's feral children. A scant few with personas remained, but most had perished in the battle in Virginia. Her most recent brood, which he'd surmised she'd rushed to ensure her victory, were subpar compared to the creatures she'd born that became legends of yore. It hadn't worked out for her, and they were left with various cryptids roaming the country.

"Get in, Dodd, let's get out of here and to a warm bed," Chelsea said.

"Get into the what?" Dodd said.

"I swear, Brendan, if you make me say it again, I'm going to brain you."

"Hop into the Mystery Machine, Detective," Leonard said.

Dodd's smile returned. "Will do."

"You're always bailing him out of trouble, and he is always playing tricks on you," Chelsea said.

"I never had a big brother," Leonard said. "I kind of like the pitch and catch."

During the drive through winding roads, Chelsea asked Dodd how he'd dispatched the creature.

"It heard me coming," he said. "Damned thing tried to stalk me. Worked out well because I didn't have to fight it near the hikers. I played lame in the woods, like I was hurt. It crept up behind, and I grabbed it from the brush. Tall lanky thing, with a really pretty coat on it. I used some of my fire inside to turn it to charcoal. Sorry to say you won't be getting a new blanket for Christmas this year."

"That's fine," Chelsea said. "I still haven't gotten over imp socks."

Leonard turned the dial on the radio. "That's only three this month, guys. Down from seven last month and eleven the month before that. I think the cleanup is working."

"I have a feeling there will be tall tales to investigate for years to come," Dodd said from the back.

Chelsea bopped her head to a Blondie song. "Eager to put this spooky business behind us?" she asked Leonard.

"Not really. I like the adventure of it, and I get to use my knowledge for a practical purpose. That's not something I thought I'd ever be able to do."

"Don't worry, when we're all done, Chelse will keep you in the house. Wouldn't feel right without you there," Dodd said, as if sensing something from Leonard's mind.

Leonard smiled and aimed the van south down Route 7 toward Connecticut.

"I get the feeling we're in an interlude," Chelsea said.

"Don't go talking like that. Every time something big goes down, I end up being crippled," Dodd said.

"You don't move like a cripple anymore," Leonard said.

"That reminds me," Chelsea said as she produced a bottle of pills from her pocket and tossed them to Dodd in the back. "It's time for your meds."

"How have the whispers been?" Leonard asked with keen interest in the entity clawing at Dodd's psyche.

"Quiet lately. I think whatever Rose did to me has helped to keep it tamped down. I can still feel it crawling behind my thoughts, but it isn't weighing on me like it used to." Dodd downed his three purple pills dry. "I'm not even sure I need to take these anymore."

"Don't get ahead of yourself. David is pretty sure you can be cured of that thing. Until then, you take the purple pills."

"Luckily, there aren't any side effects," Leonard said. "A perk we probably wouldn't have without Sam tweaking the recipe for us." They hadn't heard from Samael or Freja since a few days following Virginia. Chelsea was happy to have them gone given David and Rose's circumstances, but Leonard felt the silence was ominous.

As if on cue, Dodd asked, "How are the kids holding up?"

"They're due back home soon. Rose wants to finish helping with the agricultural issues in Judea."

"Still hasn't rained there?"

"Not a drop. Even she is having trouble keeping food growing."

"Has David found any luck rekindling his power?" Leonard asked.

Chelsea turned the radio off and sighed. "He hasn't been very forthcoming. I know he hasn't *lost* it, per se. The way he puts it, it's like trying to hold a flopping fish without gloves. Feels scattered, he says."

"I think we've all been since this whole thing began," Leonard said. "I have panic attacks at night thinking about how much bigger reality is than we believed."

"Existence, you mean," Chelsea said. "And it *is* heavy, Leonard. But we can handle it if we stick together."

Chelsea reached her hand and took Leonard's as they drove south toward home. Dodd's snores filled the cabin, and Leonard and Chelsea waited for the sounds of struggle as he batted away the ifrit as he slept.

Ω

An arid wind blew from the west and rustled a patch of thirsty Saint Augustine grass on a small plot of land where David and Rose stayed. Rose left early in the morning to see to the wheat and barley crops. David found himself in a familiar vista where he'd taken to watching the work of the farmers and feeling the quiet wind. He strove for stability, and the rock upon which he perched graced him with just that, though it refused to whisper its secrets to him.

Flueric's attack had left him sectioned, he knew, and the firm progress he'd been making to understand his power and purpose was now just beyond his fingertips. Odin's appearance had allowed for him to collect his mind and strength, but they were separate, and he knew this was part of his adversary's designs.

David had grown to dislike being manipulated. A trait he'd come to know by watching his mother refuse the yokes of any man or task she deemed unworthy. He admired her for it. In his own life, graced as it was before he'd been plunged into the Hudson, there wasn't need for shirking the will of others. This had been subject to change as of late, and the boy had realized the board he'd been placed upon—a pivotal piece in some grander scheme.

On his rock, bathed in sunlight, David mused about removing the board and taking his place in the player's seat rather than a rook on the board. The answers were slow to come despite advice from Azazel and Iblis, and the stakes were too high for revelations that traveled at a snail's pace.

A change in the wind opened David's eyes, and he watched Rose as she used her gift to help this land yield the bounty it was holding back. Drought and fire had become endemic to the world, allowing famine to bare its fangs. People wanted, and David had become wise enough to know that want led to war. The turmoil was only enhanced by the presence of Leviathan. Though staked firmly to the ocean floor, her existence was known to the wider world. Knowledge that shook its collective sanity. Zealous and charismatic people spun public perception to their whims at every opportunity, and David could feel the machinations of carnage glut with the fear and the anger of many.

"Did you have a fruitful conversation with Azazel?" David asked. "Or was it Iblis you needed to talk to first?"

Michael slid down from a precipice above David and came to a rest on the ground behind. "I don't have use for the fallen."

David smiled. "I think you're coming to realize that their situation is a bit more dynamic than that. Bravado is wasted with me, Archistragos. I'm familiar with your opinions and respect them."

"Likewise, flattery is wasted on me, Nephilim."

"I think you know my existence has meaning beyond the old labels. We are in a new era, whether you like it or not, one that calls for a fresh perspective."

"Too much time with philosophers has the pup speaking like a sage," Michael said. His form was of a man dressed in loose linens befitting the current climate, and his wings were hidden as he walked amongst the men of Judea. "Wisdom takes time to cultivate. You would be all the wiser to remember that when considering my words."

"I hope you understand I am not your enemy," David said. "Despite you having decided to annihilate me when the Host had a chance."

A wind blew dry earth through the air before the angel

replied. "You'd be wiser still to understand that we can still eliminate you."

"I don't think you have the votes in favor for that course anymore. Not given recent events, and I'm sure, despite your very scary muscles, you understand the cost to you would be pretty severe if you tried." David opened his hand and fire danced upon it until his will formed it into a ball of plasma by his added energy and understanding of his power. "I'm not so ignorant anymore."

"You flaunt knowledge we've held since our creation. Do you expect me to be impressed?"

"Yes," David said. "And you are. Why else would you have come to me?"

"I've come because you've loosed the serpent upon the world, and Lucifer himself revels unchecked. I've come because the creator has remained silent."

"Have you finally decided to work together against them?"

"We have not determined that. Our course is to deliberate."

David looked to the clouds and watched as the sun's strength gave energy to the winds that pushed them.

"You are considering destroying the earth, aren't you?"

"A calamity not unlike the flood has been considered, yes. And no, your opinion on the matter will not be considered."

"For a guy who is known for his brawn, you have an elegant way of telling me to go fuck myself."

"There is a charm to your moxie, David Dolan." Michael bared his teeth in a smile. "I should like to fight you someday to test your words against your mettle. If you find yourself in league with the light bearer, all the better."

"I know a very bloodthirsty Mongolian who can be my corner man, if we ever do."

Michael turned to leave. "Measure your actions well in the coming days. They may tip the scales and alter the future."

"The future of mankind?"

"No, the future of existence."

With that, the archangel stepped away, leaving David alone with the dust and the wind. David inhaled deeply to smell its aroma before leaping from his rock toward the small house he and Rose had made their temporary home. Iblis sat on the ground out front as he whittled a branch from an olive tree.

"How was your chat with our guest?" he asked.

"Not the peachy sort, that one," David said.

"He'd have been a lot less agreeable if your strength wasn't as considerable as it is," Iblis replied. "A real proponent of *might for right*, that one."

"He doesn't seem to have a lot of respect for the three of us."

"More for Azazel and you than me. He'd wipe me from the ground in an instant if he were allowed. Michael revels in his station as the hammer. I'm only lucky for the fact that he requires orders to act on nails such as me. At least he used to. It's when he understands he has his own free will, like Uriel did, that we are in trouble."

"I think he's too conservative for that. Acting of his own accord is a radical course, and he rages against the radical," David said.

"True," Iblis said.

"He came with a warning or a veiled threat. I'm not quite sure. Either way, the Host is in play again. Maybe they'll come down and destroy Leviathan."

"Doubtful. Leviathan was handcrafted by the creator for

a purpose. To end a creation from his hand is blasphemy of the highest order."

"What's dear old dad think?"

"Best you go and speak to him. I don't do well with games of telephone. Things get lost in translation, you know."

"Are you making a spear out of that?" David asked.

"The symbolism isn't lost on you, then?"

"I was thinking irony, but I'll leave you to it." David climbed the stairs and entered the home. Devoid of furniture by design, the home offered little in the way of comfort, except for the small stove. Around it were meager chairs where the four of them would sit and speak at length on various topics. Rose often held court with her whimsical views, and it was clear Azazel and Iblis had found her charming. As David entered, Azazel sat alone with his tea.

"Is this cup for me?" David asked.

"I prepared it for Michael."

David lifted the cup and drank, filling with the aroma of cardamom. "Doesn't like tea?"

"One of the few of us who doesn't, it seems," Azazel said. "I think he prefers to live without pleasantries. He finds his joy in conflict, which is a conundrum for him, as his station is largely to prevent it."

"He would like to fight me, I can tell."

"He would, and mostly because he believes he might lose."

"They're not clued in to my current situation. It took me months to prepare the trick I used to impress him."

"Thankfully true. I don't enjoy the idea of them acting unilaterally without orders."

"Like you did?"

"…Yes."

David swirled the dregs of his tea, and Iblis came inside to tend the fire.

"It's time for you to leave," Iblis said.

"Off to the bottom of the basin to fend off the big snake?" David asked.

"No. That serpent is primordial. It takes far more than brawn and some cursory knowledge of creation to shatter a pillar of existence. And if you could, what then? The pillar supports something, after all. We may not be privy to what, but it's safe to assume you'd destroy us all should you kill Leviathan."

David nodded and looked to the door moments before Rose entered. She crossed the room and embraced Iblis and Azazel before taking up David's hand. "How are the menfolk faring?"

"Not one to be found in here. Nor women, truth be told," Iblis said.

"I still count myself as human," David said.

"Samesies," Rose said.

David kissed her hand and turned soft eyes on her. "They're telling me it's time to go, but I don't know where."

"You might not have a date, but I do," Rose said. "A rendezvous with other non-ladies that's come due."

Azazel stood and brandished his wings. A sight that never lost its novelty on David. He enjoyed how the color bathed Rose in a lavender hue. "David, you should go east for now. Take your journey to a special man. Iblis, have you found Yehuda?"

"Not quite, but I am reasonably sure he's in Puri."

"That's in India, David," Rose said.

"Thanks. I was afraid I'd sound dumb if I asked," David said.

"And what can I glean from a human that I wouldn't from, let's say, a celestial tutor?"

Azazel pulled a feather from his wing and handed it to David. "Don't make the mistake of assuming human enlightenment is any less significant than any other being's," he said. "Here, take this to Yehuda and ask him for help."

"Oh, you're buddies with this guy?" David asked.

"You could say everything is," Iblis chimed. "Rose, would you like to have us organize travel for you? I've become very proficient at finding good prices." Rose smiled at the jinn and turned to the window as the sound of beating wings descended on the home. "No thanks, here's my ride now."

Ω

Blakely and Barbara sat at the newly installed conference table in the All Century headquarters.

"A triangle? What's he trying to do, break all our necks with this setup?"

"It's made from the finest Bubinga," Blakely said as he tapped the wood. "It makes a statement, no doubt."

"And what might that be?"

"That we are prospering."

"It's so we can't look one another in the eyes," Robert Wilson said as he took up his seat at the table. "Nothing Flueric does is without calculation. I should know."

He was right, Barbara knew. As the chief financial officer of All Century, Robert was significantly more in the know than she or Blakely. Robert had intimate knowledge about the developments of the UHovas while they were in the dark.

A revelation that rattled Barbara's belief in her security within the company.

"Any clue as to why we've all been called?" Barbara asked. "A bit out of the blue, this meeting."

"I know enough not to ask questions," Robert said.

The double doors on the opposite side of the room opened, and Flueric entered from his office with another man. Barbara tried to give Blakely a cursory glance to see his reaction. *I'll be damned. He was right, we can't look at each other.*

"Welcome, everyone. I trust the long days and nights haven't left you too sapped for a fruitful get-together," Flueric said as the members of the board stood for his appearance. "Please, sit. We have a few important topics to explore." Flueric chose to run the meeting on his feet with his hands on the table, as he always did. The man remained beside him. Barbara didn't enjoy his all too familiar charismatic smile.

"Gemma, how are our media holdings looking?" Flueric asked.

"Well. Very well, in fact. We have controlling stakes in most print markets in the US, as well as considerable leverage in twenty-four hour and local news broadcasts, including Pulse24," she said.

"It cost us quite a lot of our nut, boss. I hope there's a way to recoup the losses to research and development," Robert said.

Flueric looked down the line of faces to Robert Wilson's place tag then darted his eyes to the man. "You seem to be under the impression we are operating under the same framework as before *the event.* That's no longer the case, Robert. I assumed you'd be savvy enough to understand this."

The man beside Flueric laughed and wagged his finger at

Wilson. "Tsk tsk, Bobby. Tsk tsk," he said. "The game board has changed, and you should know, because All Century is what changed it. The world moves fast. Faster now than ever. We will be twice as swift. For example, we have seeded the nomenclature for Leviathan as Species 0 to the media. We are controlling the narrative so the government can't get enough traction to hamstring us on what happened in Virginia. It wouldn't be in their best interests, anyway. They'll look incompetent, and any punishment coming our way will be doled out painfully by the justice department. By then, we will control everything."

"And who is the esteemed gentlemen who joins us?" Blakely asked. Barbara didn't know if it was stupidity or the sheer volume of the balls on the man that allowed for him to question Flueric. He'd grown a lot bolder since their chat in the coffee shop in Virginia. More distant as well.

"Ladies and gentlemen, please welcome Muriel Abaddon to the table," Flueric said and stepped back from the preeminent corner. "He will serve as the new CEO of All Century from hereon." Abaddon took up his spot and placed his hands on the table where Flueric's had been.

This place is a fucking zoo, Barbara thought.

Abaddon turned to look at her, and she blanched. "How are things on the ground, Barbara?"

"Um, well, we are making significant progress garnering our following using social media. We have three separate facilities abroad working to spread our message and preliminary numbers of zealous followers are encouraging."

"How encouraging?" Abaddon asked.

Flueric's smile broadened.

"We have reliable estimates at ten thousand members

domestically and millions more abroad. Though those are substantially more in number, they aren't as thoroughly trained. Not that it's a concern—we have pockets in nearly every nation on Earth and can mobilize people given a small amount of lead time," Blakely said, saving Barbara from Abaddon's attention.

"Be ready to roll out astroturfing campaigns shortly," Abaddon said. "I want to test the mobility of these people."

Barbara could read the writing on the wall. Something big was coming.

"Something big *is* coming, everyone. And we will need the hearts and minds of the world to foster it," Flueric said.

"Where will you be, since you are stepping down?" Robert asked.

"Oh, I'll be here and there. I might even be hiding under your bed if you fail to check, Mr. Wilson." Flueric straightened his already immaculate tie knot. "Always acting for the interests of the company but without the yoke of my old title. Don't you worry."

Barbara found the declaration decidedly worrisome.

CHAPTER 2
YEHUDA

Lilith's eyes fluttered open to the low light of a cabin. She glanced over the drying plants and various tools to muddle and tincture.

"You live," Baba Yaga said. "What a treat that is, right, Princess?"

The toad made a derisive throaty gunk.

"Don't go getting jealous on me now, little girly. You'll always be the apple of my eye." The witch issued a cackle that bounded through the interior of her hut and caused it to shiver as it resettled itself.

"Why did you save me?" Lilith asked. "I know Rhea's opinion of me and mine, and it isn't flattering."

"You don't know more than what I make at a squat, succubus, and you'd do well to get that lined up right in your brain."

Lilith sat up and inspected her belly. The skin had mended around a brown scar where no stitching was clear. She ran her fingers over it and stared, perplexed, at the blear of soil left on them.

"You are nearly whole. Feel free to stand and move about. T'will be good for you. The human heart needs stimulation. Something you will no doubt have been getting used to, yes?"

Lilith swung her bare feet to the floor and stood. She was impressed at the stability of her body after such a calamitous delivery. "That little nebby made sure I'd never be whole again."

"Never been called a nebby before," Rose said as she entered the cabin with handfuls of roots. "Must be a foreign insult."

"Aye, British it is," Baba Yaga said. "I remember it well from my days harassing Arthur on the great isle, back when legends steeped the lands in virtue."

Lilith pulled herself back into a corner and bumped her head on a shelf.

"Relax. We don't mean you harm. Wouldn't make much sense to heal you just to kill you, would it?"

"I wouldn't be so sure, little thorn," Baba Yaga smiled. "There's always the example of the pit of despair."

Lilith gritted her teeth. "You took everything I had, you *evil* little bitch. Everything I fought so hard to gain."

"That's a more modern insult, to be sure," Baba Yaga said.

Rose placed the roots on the table and approached Lilith. "Your body, you mean?"

Lilith clenched her fists.

"It's unpleasant, isn't it?" Rose asked in a whisper. "To have it taken from you, I mean."

"Maybe I should take to calling you *great* thorn," Baba Yaga said and shuffled between them. "Any way you shake the stick, she has a point. By my eyes, I see you two as more or less square now."

Lilith looked away to Princess, who wore a toad's smile, before pulling up her skirt to plop on the bed. "What do you two want with me? To make me into a salamander or something? If so, get on with it."

"I have wonderful familiar already, and Rose is far too kind to take on such companions. I'll leave it to my apprentice to explain your circumstance."

Rose pulled a chair to the wooden table and began peeling layers from the roots and shaved them into various bowls. "I have a proposition for you."

"How self righteous you are to think to ask anything of me—" Lilith said.

"You are projecting again, and despite Baba Yaga's opinion, I don't think we are quite square. Your son took me, disgraced me, and burned me alive. All for nothing more than feeling he was entitled to do it to accomplish *your* goals. And what did you do? You let him. Maybe even ordered it." Rose looked to Lilith, and she felt the familiar fear that had enshrouded her that night. "We are not even steven. Not yet. Not by a long shot."

"Easy girl," Baba Yaga said. "I won't condone any scuffles in this cabin."

"I don't mean any harm to come to you," Rose said, acknowledging the witch without taking her eyes from Lilith. "But I do need something from you."

"And you expect me to bow to your whims just because you didn't let me bleed out on the cold stone?"

"No, I think you'll help me because I'm going to bring you home," Rose said. "Back to Eden."

Ω

Leonard adjusted his glasses between key taps at his computer as he worked.

"What's the latest, Lenny?" Dodd asked as he laid a sandwich and glass of milk on the table.

He'd taken to looking after Leonard as he toiled at the computer. "He doesn't eat for hours while he's on that thing," he'd told Chelsea, and while he had a certain amount of respect for the work ethic involved in what Leonard was doing, he knew it wasn't healthy.

"The rumblings about some impending catastrophe are spreading all over. To the untrained eye, it's just memes and jokes online, but that's one layer of it. The news is showing the world ramping up their military productions, and nationalism is spreading too." Leonard took a swig from his milk, and Dodd smiled. "The zeitgeist is being groomed, Detective, and it doesn't bode well."

"What can we do on our end?"

"There's little doubt that All Century is behind it. As to what we can do, well, I'm not quite sure."

"Chelsea's taking a nap, but if she was in here, I'd bet she would say we should march right into their headquarters and shake the foolishness out of 'em."

"Probably. A less direct approach is likely better, but we don't have the infrastructure to combat this stuff. Even the existing QAnon nonsense is dying out in lieu of this stuff. They're saying the world will end if we don't fight, but what they're telling us to fight against is basically each other. Woke versus conservative, Japanese versus Chinese, Russia versus NATO, the US versus just about everybody and nobody all at once—it's exhausting."

"I'd wager its exhausting by design. Keep people good

and angry but unable to focus. Not a new tactic, but it looks like they've injected it with steroids."

"The existence and evolution of the internet has. I do know of one avenue available to us. There were two people at the containers holding the HOVAS in Virginia. I think we should go speak to them."

"Are you sure they were even people?"

Leonard thought of the man and woman holding tablets at the containers during the conflict. The look of surprise and fear more notable in the eyes of one than the other.

"Oh yes, Barbara Cole and Blakely Sullivan. Both real people with real pasts. I recognized their reluctance in the situation. There's no better evidence I need to tell me they are human than that."

"I'm not sure anybody who works for that organization is going to be willing to pull a Benedict Arnold at this stage of the game. It's pretty clear what's going on."

"I wouldn't be so sure. People get indoctrinated, sure, but there are others who are just trying to scrape through and make a living. I'd like to at least see."

"Of course. We can try to make contact and go from there," Dodd said. "I'm reasonably sure they are already well aware of us if you have them in your sights. That may help."

"They're aware of us. I've kept them off our network, but there are other methods of surveillance I can't control. Satellite for one. I'd bet they keep tabs on us as best they can to ensure David is under wraps."

"Think Chelsea would go for using a decoy van?"

"You just want a second mystery machine to play with."

"But this one can be all-terrain, and we can put on armored panels! Is that such a bad thing?"

Leonard smiled and picked up his plate. "No. No, it's not."

Ω

David gazed at the Jagganath temple towering above him and surveyed the Hindu faithful coming and going. The air about holy sites felt heavy with holy reverence and the diligence of belief, and this was no exception. The Hindu pantheon eluded David more than most others due partially to the vastness of it. He had no doubt that the veiled world contained a version of each and every deity being worshipped here and wondered at their opinions of Flueric's dark works. India would not be spared in a global conflict, after all, and there were rumblings of China's desire to conquer the whole southern portion of Asia as imperialistic fervor ramped up in the East.

The wind pushed from the north, causing people to look to the dhwaja, a flag atop the temple. It fluttered in the opposite direction of the facing wind, seemingly in defiance of the laws of nature, and pilgrims pulled close to their collars as they observed the phenomenon. David took his leave of the landmark. His business was in a meager dwelling, and the way by foot along the grand road revealed a city teaming with culture. Dwellings abutted the streets where many stalls had been erected for the peddling of wares to pilgrims and tourists. David waved off solicitations and smiled at passersby until he was clear of the popular swell. A side street led him to the sub district of Duttatota, where his destination nestled amidst the scent of the Bay of Bengal. He hefted a tarnished door knocker in the shape of an elephant and let it fall three times.

"Please, come in," came a gruff voice.

David raised an eyebrow and entered through the door

with no lock to be seen. "Hello, sir," David greeted using the Odia language. "May I introduce myself?"

"Sure," Yehuda replied in English. "That's a real cordial way to say hi."

David produced Azazel's feather and placed it on a table beside where Yehuda sat on a square mat. "I'm David Dolan. Who and what I am is a bit of a long story, but I need your help."

"It's a short story, considering all things, and it looks like most of it will go unwritten."

David smiled. "Ah, you're one of those cryptic guys. I know a man on a boat who you'd just love to meet."

"Kharon the ferryman and I are buddies. Once upon a time, he guided me through the murk to the far shores beneath the veil."

"And yet you're here on Earth."

"You made it, didn't you? There and back again…"

"Yeah, and it wasn't easy," David said and sat on the floor across from Yehuda, conjuring a smile from the man whose features didn't fit quite what David had expected. Yehuda was older, with dark skin that ran smooth without the creases that come at the cost of acquiring wisdom. His arms and legs showed tattoos of words in many languages from around the globe, and his tough beard and long white hair gave the feeling of something between a biker and a sage. If put to the question of where Yehuda was from, David couldn't have guessed.

"Not much worth doing is, David Dolan of the long and winding tale."

"I suppose not." David surveyed the single room home. The spartan interior reminded him of what Brahman had tried to achieve in Gaza, but this lacked the artifice of the tycoon's design. "May I call you Yehuda? That's what Azazel said your name is."

"You may call me that, if you'd like. Humans have a need to understand, and they place names and labels to guide them. I was without a name for most of my existence. I only gained one when I became human."

David wondered at this and felt an understanding, though it was well farther than he'd cared to travel for in order to fully grasp it. "I am here because I was fractured, somehow. My mind and body feel separate. Do you think you can help me?"

"I know about your problem. Someone came and told me. Powerful and wise sort."

"Was he a bit cyclopean in nature?"

Yehuda smiled. "One eye and vision almost as keen as mine. Fancy that. A great irony hiding a sneaky truth about existence." The man uncrossed his legs and stood to reveal his great height and mass. Memories of Bulwyf crossed David's mind. "Come, if you would."

David stood and followed him into the corner of the room, where a small table held a box he wasn't sure was there when he entered the abode.

"Open it, but be ready to see before you do."

"I've had about as many revelations as I have years on this earth, Mr. Yehuda. I'm not sure more knowledge is going to help me at this point."

"Measured in small doses and given time to steep, knowledge is a key to happiness. You've had the veil wrenched from your eyes quickly, but try to muster some courage. A good lot of people have come nearly as far as you without wise teachers, and your journey requires less ignorance than theirs."

David lifted the box and opened it to see a small mirror, a cylinder, and a spring housing. *Another music box.* He grasped the lever and turned to hear a melodic tune unlike anything he'd experienced before. Even Uriel's version sounded decidedly different from the notes that graced his ears.

"Look at yourself and see."

David glanced to his reflection. He was a boy. A man. An old man. He saw dust swirl where his reflection had just peered at him, and then ashes. There came a splendid light, and he expected to see a star become born, but lying on the floor and surrounded in darkness was a baby. It looked at David and he knew they were the same, yet this baby had eyes the hue of Azazel's wings.

The process wound itself through the growth and decay until the ashes swirled and the music box completed its last note. Then, he wound the crank and began again and again and again. This iteration of him felt courageous, and the next him was a woman. Another seemed to have a glimmer of greed in its eyes, but most were more like him than not.

"They all exist concurrently. You are not the only you. Do you see?" Yehuda said.

David looked within himself and felt at the pang of fracture that resided deep within his belly. "Have I been cut off from them?"

"Yes, in a manner of speaking. You've been isolated from a great branching connection that connects and completes all of the Davids in other realities and they you."

David needed little explanation of what Yehuda may have been alluding to. String theory, alternate dimensions, a multiverse. It had long been posited that similar variations of existence grew alongside our own.

"This would mean there are more versions of the angels and gods," David said.

"It would, in most cases."

"And more of you."

"No. There are some things that are universal. I am a one-of-a-kind thing."

David pondered this as he watched the hundredth version of him and stopped the crank.

"I could tell, you know. I could tell that you were something different. On another level."

"And I was carved from you. Ponder that mystery another time, though. We still have some work to do."

Ω

The sky, a canopy of sulfurous fire and smoke, bore down on her as she ran to escape. She could hear them coming behind her and didn't dare turn to see what evil closed the gap. The sounds of claws scraping asphalt ushered her on, and she looked along the sides of the residential street to see ticky-tacky homes with no doors or windows to provide sanctuary in this suburban hellmire.

I've got base! a child's voice sang.

The street came to an abrupt end at a cul-de-sac where a large Victorian home stood in dominance of the others. Barbara could feel the hot breath of something on her back, and she pressed forward even faster to leap the rock wall surrounding the home. This entryway was barred by an ornate door, and she smashed into it—only to be flung back. She pounded the door with her fists and her eyes closed, expecting to be torn to shreds by abominations or roasted alive by the sky, which now dropped liquid fire to the street. She gasped as the door opened and a glimmer of hope was snatched away by the glowing red eyes of the man in the foyer. Flueric smiled down on her, his figure contorted and gaunt. She stepped backward from his outstretched hand and felt the clutches of thousands of claws and mouths tear into her skin.

Barbara woke up in a tangle of blankets and sheets.

The cool breeze sifting through a cracked window in her bedroom did little to stop her from being covered in a cold sweat. Her home was nestled in the woods just sixty miles away from one of the most densely populated cities in the world. Hidden from the lights and embraced in solitude, yet close enough for convenient travel. She rubbed the cool sweat from her forehead and wondered at why she hadn't just taken to a luxury apartment in New York like Blakely. It would be nice not to feel isolated in a moment like this. She pulled her duvet up over her chest in an effort to ward off the cold and lay there, as one does after the mind has reeled through a phantasmagoria.

Sleep had almost returned when she heard the clicking.

Her brain told her it was the central air cycling on, but then she remembered it was powered off. Denial couldn't ward off the fact that the sound was coming from outside and getting louder. The last dregs of muddled sleep left her as her adrenaline peaked again, and Barbara realized she heard something scraping the siding of her house. She sat up and looked to the window—a side slider, opened just three inches to the capacity of the child-safety locks.

A voice rose from deep within her, the one that is dormant until peril is close. She swung her feet from the bed and rushed to the window to slam it shut only to find four tiny fingers curled around the edge. What remained was veiled by the curtains she'd drawn to ward off the sun and allow her to sleep past first light. She backed away, unsure whether or not she still found herself in a dream.

A single eye glowed against the sliver of blackness and narrowed on her.

She fled from the room and closed the door behind. The hallway felt ominous, and she flicked on lights as she fled down the hall to an office where she barricaded herself. It was here where she spent the night, listening to the unnamed things jitter from within her home. As time passed, she regretted leaving her cell phone in her bedroom. She picked up a wireless phone and strained to remember Blakely's number and then screamed as it vibrated in her hand. The jittering grew louder, and the office door rattled in its frame, but the lock and chair she'd wedged beneath the doorknob held. A light showed *unknown caller*. Barbara answered.

"You are in danger," a calm voice informed her.

"Who is this?"

"My name is Leonard, but we can talk about that later. For now, do you have anything in that room that's metal? Something that will ring when you tap it with anything hard?"

Barbara considered the name and took the caller's advice to think more on it later. If he was willing to help, she'd worry about who he was later. She moved to the small desk in the room and ripped a metal leg from the cheap pressboard wood, toppling the furniture and sending its contents across the floor. A triton letter opener from All Century with the words *Transforming the World for a Better Tomorrow* etched on the handle lay at her feet, and she retrieved it.

"I've got something. What now?"

"Tap the metal three times. Wait a second, then tap twice. Repeat that until help gets there." The line went dead.

Barbara dropped the phone and sat on the floor with the leg in her lap. She heard the creatures working on the door methodically and wondered at their prowess. She couldn't be sure, but it sounded like they were cutting the Sheetrock around the frame.

She tapped the leg three times, waited a beat, then twice more. The sound of the creatures working paused briefly, but it didn't take long for the sounds to resume again in earnest. It wasn't enough; she knew. Her grasp on the leg stifled the vibrations and muffled the sound. Barbara placed the metal leg on the floor, propped it up with a plastic tape holder from the desk, and resumed the ritual. The ring issued much louder, and the creatures stopped. Jittering talk came through low, and it sounded as if they were less frenzied.

She continued the rhythmic notes and let her mind drift to the caller. Leonard Barlowe came to mind. She'd known he was at the incident in Virginia, but how could he have isolated her as a person of importance from All Century? She should be worried about being confronted by the enemy, but she couldn't help but wonder at him calling to offer aid. Flueric explained that all members of David's party were to be treated with the greatest of caution and contact with them was forbidden, but desperate times called for desperate measures, and she wasn't keen on dealing with a home invasion by a variant of Lilith's children by herself. Especially now, after they'd been left to roam like wild animals.

The sounds of screeching intensified all at once, and Barbara realized she had mistaken the order of taps on the metal leg while her thoughts wandered. She heard the sounds of sawing increase and saw the molding of the doorframe begin to fall away from the wall. Concentrating on the task at hand, she continued the rhythmic taps, but the creatures didn't respond—as if they'd awakened from a charm and realized the trick.

Her only protection rattled loose in its frame and the chair lost its purchase under the knob, clattering to the floor just before the door fell outward into the hallway. Darkness lay behind small red eyes as her doom peered inside.

She grasped the letter opener and table leg and resisted the urge to cry out. Working for Flueric always carried with it the risk of a grizzly end, she knew, but staring it in the face was nearly too much to bear. She thought of her mother, whom she used her wealth to care for as she battled late-stage dementia, and the niece named primary beneficiary of a trust so she could attend the best schools money could offer when she came of age. Little gestures to launder blood money and trick herself into believing she wasn't poisoning the fields of the earth at the behest of a monster.

The eyes, so eager to consume her before their mouths took their turn, turned to the stairs as hurried footsteps ascended. There was a time when such creatures would have fled at the approach of another party, but these had been born feral. The eyes turned to confront whoever stood before them in the hall, and small screeches and chirps changed to the telltale growls of animals guarding their prey.

Barbara shielded her eyes as the hall erupted in an orange light and the creatures screamed. She heard the sounds of a scuffle and smelled her carpet burning.

When she dared a glance, she saw the doorway clear of her aggressors and smoldering embers littering the ground. A small tug to her side attracted her attention, and she glanced over to see a goblin. The light betrayed its mystery, and she felt relief at seeing it unmasked before it leaped upon her and sank its teeth into her chest just below the collarbone. She gasped, unsure if this was actually real before her body took the controls from her mind and she stabbed the thing with her letter opener, but it would not relent.

The unshakable feeling of what it was like to be consumed by a predator rose in her and she became frenzied, slamming the goblin with the leg upon its head and using her other hand to stab it. The melee distracted her from the approach of a large man who reached down and grasped the creature's head in his hand.

"That's enough now," he said in a fatherly tone. His hand glowed with fire, and the creature's mouth slacked as it released her. Barbara felt warmth flow down her chest and stomach. When she reached up to explore the wound, she was glad the thing hadn't ripped its mouthful of her bosom from her body.

"Brendan Dodd?" Barbara said in a daze as she used her legs to scoot back from him.

He concentrated, and the glow from his hand filled the creature's body before it withered to ember and scattered throughout the room.

"Barbara Cole," Dodd said as he looked at her.

Chelsea stepped into the room with Leonard.

"Finally learning that you can't just reach into Pandora's box without the lid blowing off?" Chelsea asked.

"Let's get her out of here. She's bleeding badly," Leonard said.

"We have the kit in the van with quick clot in it," Chelsea said. "She'll be fine. It's not more than she deserves, anyway."

Barbara felt herself slipping into unconsciousness as Dodd lifted her from the floor and turned to leave the room. She remembered feeling grateful for how warm he felt before she slid into darkness.

Ω

Abaddon walked the property of Flueric's home in Amagansett and surveyed the pristine landscaping that was commonplace in the Hamptons. He smiled out at the Atlantic, wondering at how the serpent fared. No doubt she thrashed and writhed beneath the waves to undo her binding so she could finally realize her utmost desire to surface and consume.

What exactly she craved, Abaddon did not know, but her lust for the desires and hopes of humans was the thing of legend. He knew deep within himself that she had craved little else since people had been molded.

He strolled to the tall grass, where guinea fowl roamed, and stopped at their nests. The eggs were many, and many had hatched, giving way to small chicks that pecked the ground of the new world they'd been born into. The feeling resonated. He, just given entrance to this world by his father, remembered the realm beyond. Born of the natural order and set in place to stand in contrast to creation. His charge was to stem progress from growing unchecked, and Abaddon existed bathed in light.

That was, until the siren's call to change reality consumed him, as it did many others, and he chose a fresh path. Flueric's path. They fell, the lot of them, and he worked to the whims of his new leader ever since. Now, born again, he reveled in the possibilities of this era.

A chick chirped in alarm as he lifted it from the ground. "There's a great many of you here, and no hawks or foxes to remind you to look up," he said, holding it to his eyes. The hens lifted their heads at its distress, and Abaddon looked at them while squeezing it to increase its cries. "You should have kept them closer."

"Delighting in the torture of animals is a sign of psychopathy in humans," Flueric said. He'd come up the path from the beach and looked relaxed in his tan linen suit.

Abaddon looked at him. "Is that what I am now, a human?"

"Hardly. But you will have to continue to make them believe so. Hearts and minds, Abaddon. Don't forget."

"I haven't. They love me, don't worry. Who would have thought such a brash approach to my greatness would be enough to win over so many."

"What's your plan for the others that aren't so enamored with your persona?"

"They work in my favor as well. We are dividing them. What better than to pit one side against the other?"

"I've used this tactic before. It starts great wars and sends souls to the river, but we aren't here to annihilate anymore. We need their favor to win the endgame. It's the wind in our sails."

"Fair point," Abaddon said as he kneeled and lifted another chick to hold them akimbo before him. "I'll deliver them some more *truths* with small twists. I think that'll serve as enough to ignite their rage."

"When that occurs, we advance. The prize is everything," Flueric said and smiled to the sky. "Should you falter, we lose it all. Don't forget your role."

Abaddon squeezed the chicks until their soft bodies crushed in his palms, and he dropped them to the ground where all but some hens pecked at their lifeless bodies. "I won't forget. But there's no harm in having some fun along the way."

Flueric smiled and walked off toward the house to tend to his part of their plot. Abaddon crouched to retrieve eggs from the tall grass. His mouth gaped, and he leaned his head back to crush his handfuls and feast on their spoils.

CHAPTER 3
UNMASKED

"There is no returning to the garden, naive girl. No power in creation will convince Raphael to lift his sword for my return. This edict was passed down after I refused to reenter when the host first pursued me," Lilith said as she and Rose moved through the trees to a clearing and found the remains of the charred building.

"I don't plan to convince him to *let* us do anything," Rose said, switching to a somber tone. "Do you know where we are?"

Lilith look around them and inhaled deeply. She recognized the odor of the foliage. "You've taken us back to where Asmodeus and I took up arms against you."

"The Hudson Valley," Rose said. "I'm glad you recognize it from the smell. There's hope for you yet." She pointed to the burned cabin. "This is where your son took my life."

Lilith pivoted and crossed her hand to grasp her own arm. "So it's to be here where you kill me. Seems fitting."

"Drop the bravado. We are here because there may be something that will help us find Eden."

"I've told you. There are precious few who know the location of the garden, and only one of whom traverses this realm."

"Raphael, yes. The only archangel with access. But, did you know he was here with Michael and Uriel?"

"Taken to measure David for his annihilation?"

"That's my take, yeah," Rose said. "It was a foregone conclusion for Michael, from what I've heard, but Raphael came along to observe on behalf of the rest of the archangels."

"It was already too late by then. David had realized his power," Lilith said. "It never would have happened if Asmodeus had followed my orders." Lilith realized she was glorifying the topic of David being murdered and paused before she looked Rose in the eyes. "I never planned for him to torture you, you know."

Rose avoided the topic. "Do you know why David is so strong? No half-breed has ever been on par with the members of the host before. Azazel said so."

"No. He is more powerful than we had ever imagined. It defies all the logic found in the history of the Nephilim."

"Then maybe he isn't a Nephilim. There's still some mystery to it. Even our celestial friends haven't exactly been forthcoming about how David was conceived."

Lilith thought about this and looked at the cabin. She wondered at the girl's willingness to share information.

She really isn't planning on killing me?

"You have every right to my life, yet you show me kindness. Why? And don't preach some biblical logic to me like *turn the other cheek*. I've seen few follow the actual teachings of that book."

Rose gazed long at Lilith, and the mother of demons felt

the weight of her potential smother her. *Where did this girl come from?*

"You aren't exactly acting from a place of pure evil, like Flueric. The way I see it, you had a bad shake. The stories say you were told to submit, and you wouldn't. Your recourse was to run, and once banished, you steeped in vengeful thoughts, looking to burn the whole thing to the ground. I kind of get it." Rose placed her hands on the ground and Lilith watched as vines of Virginia creeper wound through the remains of the cabin and covered it from view. "This way," Rose said.

Lilith followed her to the small hill that looked down on the burned grass and wreckage. She glanced about and saw signs of deep impressions and extravagant growth in the grass. "He stood here," Lilith said. "Raphael's presence is always followed by bountiful growth."

"A side effect of his proximity to the garden," Rose said. "Not the same way I affect growth. His has cosmic roots."

"Power born from creation. Far more powerful and less chaotic than Rhea's," Lilith said.

"Rhea's power is in the same tier, I assure you," Rose said. "Life is as powerful a part of creation as the churning flames of the angels."

Lilith sneered. "If you say so."

The trees above rustled, and Lilith noted the lack of wind. Both she and Rose heard the whispers at the same time.

She will kill you.

Trust no one.

They'll burn you for what you've done.

"I hear it too. Don't listen," Rose said.

"Can you tell which tree it is coming from?"

"No. They don't speak to me, I just help them grow," Rose said. "Can you sense it? It's likely one of your children."

Lilith felt pressure in her head and realized she had grown angry.

"I can't sense nor command them any longer."

"Then we were right. They've all gone feral."

"There may be some that retain their consciousness. I couldn't imagine Tchakyen becoming mindless, or…" Lilith trailed off.

"You have a point," Rose said. "Stay put, I'm going to move into the trees there."

"What purpose does that serve?"

"Bait," Rose said.

"I knew I shouldn't trust you!" Lilith said.

Rose shrugged and receded into the greenery, leaving no sign of her presence.

Lilith realized she'd been assaulted with subliminal messages from her child the whole time and wondered if that caused her outburst. This thing reminded her of something. A special child that tormented the Ojibwe, the Saulteaux, the Cree, the Naskapi, and the Innu tribes to the northwest. *It can't be here. Not this far south.*

She raked the surrounding trees for a sign and found a pair of glossy eyes the size of saucers peering at her from twenty feet in the air. They narrowed on her.

"Atchen, I command you, come out!"

The creature flinched as though slapped across the face. The branches parted and it unfolded its long supine limbs from their hiding places before skulking out on all fours. Lilith wondered at how well it must have been eating given its impossible size. She'd never known one to grow to such proportions.

"Come to your mother," Lilith commanded. It approached with a bowed head, and Lilith felt reassured, but there was a sinister quality to how its ghoulish face peered at her. A trick. Offering a glimmer of hope before burying a victim in despair. Its favorite game.

Lilith stepped backward, a sign of weakness that differentiated predators from their prey, and it reached for her before balking and turning to growl at something behind.

Lilith fled to the trees at the first opportunity before daring a glance back.

She watched as vines entangled the limbs of what was once a creation she took great pride in. Despite this, a relief filled her as it was pulled to the ground while it thrashed against its bonds.

"I can't will the living to do my bidding, but I can ask," Rose said. Lilith knew she was speaking to her. "Sometimes my requests are ignored, and as I get better at listening, I can feel the contempt of the flora toward me. As if they hold me responsible for the lack of unity between the living things on this planet. Then there are times like now, when I can support the growth of something as seemingly harmless as five-leafed vines and they support me. It's a real rush." Rose walked upon the wendigo, bent to place something on the creature's exposed belly, and then skipped away. "You'll return to the earth now, with a little help from this white oak."

The seed glowed briefly before springing to a sapling and burying roots within Lilith's child. It wailed, offended to have been placed in the same desperate circumstance as so many of its previous victims. Lilith watched the hatred leak from its eyes as roots tendrilled through its body and into the earth.

A remarkable tree spread its branches and spun a trunk

over the creature using its substance to reach even greater proportions than any other in these woods. Passersby would observe it in awe for hundreds of years. A very perceptive few might pull their collars close as a chill crawled up their spine. The memories held by the grass and trees would be passed down through countless generations.

A memory of evil staining this soil in a tiny grove near the Hudson River.

Ω

Barbara blinked her bleary eyes to daylight as it filtered through sheer curtains. She knew a guest room when she saw one from riding out periods of time in various homes during her twenties. This fit the bill right down to a tchotchke-littered bedside table. Voices vibrated through the air vents, and she closed her eyes again. Her home had been ransacked, and she was under the plush duvet of the enemy. How mind-numbingly inconvenient.

A cursory glance around revealed that her own nightclothes were not in the area, and she continued to regret having left her cell behind when she fled. She waited and even dozed from the firm grip of comfort the room afforded.

"She's up," Leonard called down the hall as he pushed the door open. He gave a triple tap knock to signal his entry as if she had the choice of receiving him. "How is your wound feeling?"

"I hadn't even thought of it until you reminded me," Barbara said, pushing herself up to a seated position. "Just a dull ache."

"Their teeth are like razors," Leonard said. "Clean cuts

like that have a weird way of not hurting all that much until they start to heal. It will probably itch soon." He walked to a dresser and inspected a bottle of salve. "We can put more of this on, if you'd like. It's basically priced up petroleum jelly, but it should help."

"Were you the one who hiked up my shirt to rub that on?" Barbara asked, defensive at first but enjoying his face as he turned red.

"No such luck there, tramp," Chelsea said as she entered with a breakfast tray. "I took care of tending to your little bite."

Dodd ducked through the doorway last, and Barbara wondered at how the man seemed so gentle and imposing at the same time.

"Well, I guess the first question in a hostage situation is to ask what you plan to do with me," Barbara said.

"Hostage?" Leonard asked.

"She's more deluded than I thought," Chelsea said. "Probably thinks we plan to ransom her."

Dodd tossed her phone onto the bed. "You're not being held against your will. We came to get you, sure, but we've been doing that all over the valley for the past few months. Those critters running around off the leash are causing trouble."

"They aren't our doing," Barbara said. "All Century never had sway over those things."

"But you knew about them and had the means to stop them, didn't you?" Chelsea said. "Not enough profit in that for you, though."

"It's not just about money. The company is leveraging change on a worldwide scale. I wouldn't expect you to understand," Barbara said and scooped her phone into her hand but kept her attention on the three cohorts of David. She'd very much like to see him, if for nothing more than the novelty. His reputation had spread through All Century by way of hushed whispers after he had been observed standing toe-to-toe with Flueric.

"I understand enough to know your choices quite literally bit you in the ass last night," Chelsea said. Barbara grimaced as she ran her hand down her leg and felt a sharp pang. "That's right. I didn't just have to bandage up your chest."

Leonard cleared his throat. "Detective Dodd and Chelsea Dolan are good people, Barbara. Dodd having gone to your room to get your phone for you should lend credibility to that."

"Or he was snooping around the house for information, and he handed off my phone to you to try and lift info. Then you guys rehearsed your little Stockholm syndrome play to get me to feel comfortable enough to chat."

"Far from it. We have all the information we'd ever need about All Century, and that's partly because Flueric isn't bothering to hide anything. It's actually pretty much the opposite. He's brandishing the true intentions of that company far and wide to help divide up the scared and witless from those others who don't much like unkempt globalization and warmongering. It's pretty clear he aims to divide and conquer."

"So, why am I here?"

"Because it doesn't sit right with us to just watch you die," Dodd said.

"And how did you know I was in danger?"

"We were tracking that group of goblins for weeks. Yours wasn't the first house they attacked," Leonard said.

"They devoured a family of five a few days before, not that you'd care about those poor souls," Chelsea said. "But we'd be lying if we didn't say we were looking to talk to you and the other one."

"Blakely?" Barbara asked.

"Yes," Leonard said. "You're right about our knowledge of your organization, but what we don't know are Flueric's plans with the Leviathan."

"What makes you think that sociopath lets us know the inner workings of his mind?"

"You'd have to be human to be a sociopath, based on the entomology of the word," Chelsea said as she adjusted the statues of Osiris and Set on the dresser. "He exists from outside our society."

Barbara opened her mouth and then closed it. She looked at the wall as though it held an image only she could see.

"You can't tell us you didn't know," Dodd said.

"We all know he's *something*. We whisper about it when off site, but never on the grounds of any All Century property. He has ears everywhere and a single word against him means swift punishment. The word he uses is annihilation."

"And you still choose to work for him," Chelsea said. "Pitiful."

"I've had about enough of your self-righteous mouth. Not all of us have the means to get a fancy degree and run off to the cradle of civilization for trysts," Barbara said.

Chelsea laughed. "You're a still too green to get under my skin, little love, but high marks for the effort."

"I've known plenty of kids from the street who never chose to sell junk for their payday because they saw the havoc it wreaked on their communities. Don't think a sob story is going to earn our pity," Dodd said. His expression of neutrality had faded into one of disappointment.

"How's the leg, Brendan?"

"I go by Dodd around here, *Barb*."

"Fine. How's the leg, *Dodd*?"

"You know damned well how it is."

"Exactly. That's what I signed up for. The medical research that was curing cancer and cerebral palsy and dementia and polio and, hell, I don't know, erectile dysfunction. It was a miracle in a jar, guys. Once I got good at the moving and shaking, I moved up. That's how things work. At first, I thought it was Piper trying to get into my pants, but that would require that guy to be aroused by anything other than power. No, it was my lack of attachments to anybody who might compromise me and my ability to get shit done."

"And the side effects?" Dodd asked

"Didn't know about them at first. Not until condos started to burn down, and that didn't begin until they really ramped up the dosage."

"Yeah, to make supernatural soldiers to wage war against an invisible enemy."

"The enemy isn't invisible either. At first, it was for mercenary work overseas, and then the supernatural stuff started and Flueric laid his plans bare. By then, we'd been in denial so long and Blakely and I were committed—no, trapped. Even if he won't admit it."

"I'm not surprised Flueric would threaten you if you tried to leave," Leonard said.

"He didn't have to. Only so many colleagues can fall from high windows or drown before you start to connect the dots," Barbara said.

"You can connect those dots, but ignore the obvious signs of maleficence for years?" Chelsea swept her hand through the air and pointed her finger at Leonard, who flinched. "And you better not get soft on her for those doe eyes, Leonard. She's no better than that demon who sucked the life out of babies before Rose dealt with her."

It was Leonard's turn to open his mouth and then think better of saying anything.

"Rose? Didn't she die? And are you talking about Lilith? She's been annihilated?"

Leonard noted Barbara's choice to not say "die" for the mother of demons. "There's plenty you don't know. We'd like to share what we've experienced and learned in exchange for information about Flueric. It's pretty clear you aren't on his side for any reason other than being trapped. We can untrap you."

"It's not that easy, he's—"

"We know. He's the devil."

Ω

Freja and Samael arrived at the mead hall of Valhalla flanked by Valkyrie. The resident warriors did little to hide their keen interest in the presence of an angel with obsidian wings and the commander of the forces the horn routinely called on them to clash with. Some even sidled close to the Valkyrie, as if they had imaginings of testing their mettle against the famous warriors. Or perhaps their intentions were more cordial.

Mist clutched Freja's mace and she hissed to send a group scrambling back to the doors, and the party laughed. Samael wondered if they'd be laughing had the warriors been clad in armor and held arms themselves. He supposed they would. The Valkyrie were made for more than ferrying souls, after all. Warrior elites who would cause him to break more than a small sweat should he choose to test them.

Sarena met them at the entrance and bowed deeply at the feet of the goddess. "My Lady Freja, to what do we owe this great honor?"

"I understand Odin has returned," Freja said, motioning for her to rise. "We come to have an audience."

"I'll inform the All-Father," Sarena said and ran off.

"I remember taking her soul from the ashes of the pyre set by the English in that traitorous ordeal. It's odd to see her continue on here instead of going to that other place for resolution," Samael said.

"A great injustice was done to her by her own countrymen. Men she saved. Sarena certainly belongs here to work that out of her soul."

"And why doesn't she break bread at a table in your hall at Fólkvangr?"

"Odin found her to be far too intriguing. I couldn't argue for her, and it was his turn anyway. We don't always get the ones we want."

"Interesting. A shame, really. You two seem very similar."

Freja looked about the hall. The number of warriors had dwindled, and she knew it wasn't because of any era of prolonged peace. Great wars had paused in the realm of the living and reduced the opportunity for warriors to die a valorous death, but she knew this wasn't the entire reason. The numbers in Fólkvangr had thinned as well, and here their long tables lacked the great bowls and trays of limitless food, which affected the revelry one would so often observe within the halls. Change had come to this place that had remained changeless for thousands of years, signifying to the warriors that they were on the precipice of some unknown future.

"You're thinking of it, too?" Samael asked.

"Yes. They're merging more quickly."

"And the phenomenon is the same in Fólkvangr?"

Freja nodded her affirmation. "Many of those damned souls from the colds of Helheim are merging as well. It is accelerating."

"I can't help but think these things are all connected."

"That may be. The serpent's absence, perhaps?"

Before Samael could offer an answer, Sarena returned and motioned for them to come across the hall. They followed through the doors, and the sounds of merriment and revel faded behind them as they once did for David as he walked these corridors. Freja lifted her hand to touch the golden arm of the warrior statue as they passed, and they ventured beyond Bulwyf's chamber, unsure if he still inhabited them or had become one with another warrior altogether.

Beyond and up an ornate staircase, seemingly as wide as the hall itself, they found the doors to Odin's chamber. Sarena didn't bother announcing them, an act Samael regretted, given the artistry of the iron door knockers shaped for Grendel and the monster's storied mother.

They entered to the sounds of a single raven, and Samael spied either Huginn or Muninn, based on the size and keen eyes of the bird. He knew the ravens numbered far more than two, and that the wise old god employed a vast web of spies for his needs. The sight of the bird reminded him of the old stories, and he felt comfort from the ancient familiarity.

"It took you quite some time to come," Odin said from beside his large throne. Freja felt her own envy for the chair carved from the world tree, Yggdrasil, but Odin had given more than she was willing to for its seat.

"We've been busy," Samael said and flourished his wings, to the delight of the raven, who returned the gesture.

"Jormungandr remains skewered to the depths, but we can't tarry. She won't hold that place forever," Odin said as he greeted Freja with an embrace that included all the clangs and scrapes of armor. "How fares the boy?"

"He is finding himself. Azazel and Iblis have guided him as much as they can, but he's stunted from Flueric's attack," Freja said. "He may never recover."

Samael took Odin's gloved hand next and was impressed by the power radiating from the old god. There weren't many he considered close to his equal or more, but this old god felt different from the others.

"David is lucky you were here to save him. We hadn't expected your aid," Samael said.

Odin's eye glowed from within a broad helm, and Samael wished he could see his face. A luxury like so many others that's taken for granted until you cannot access it.

"Circumstances led me to return." Odin nodded to Sarena. "My warriors informed me of the happenings I wasn't already privy to. It was bold of you to use them without my blessing."

"We gave your blessing, All-Father," Sarena said with her head bowed. Odin looked to her for a long period before turning back. "They've found quite a champion in the boy. It's admirable to see one galvanize so many. Reminiscent of the great but young Alexander of Greece."

"Now isn't the time to ruminate on history," Freja said as

she approached Odin's throne and ran her fingers along the wood grain. "Samael's host feels we are on the precipice of a monumental shift, and I agree. The circumstances *here* have certainly changed."

"Yes, they have," Odin said, referring to the increased rate of merging warriors.

"We wonder if your keen insight could be lent. Perhaps you saw something of this when you hung from the tree?" Samael asked.

Odin looked to Sarena and dismissed her with a wave of his hand. She exited and pulled the doors closed behind her.

"I know what brings the calamity but never the outcome. It makes my foresight more a curse than a boon. I do feel the future rests on both the boy and the girl. Celestials in human form. Humans should be the saviors of humanity, after all—"

"Quite the romantic notion," Freja said.

"The deck has been stacked against them. If there was a grand plan for the judgment of humanity, it appears to have been perverted by Flueric and much of humanity by proxy," Samael said.

"And your champion had an answer to this?" Odin asked.

"I assume you refer to Uriel. No, Uriel did not have plans to do more than foster David and Rose and let them act on their own. That much seems clear now." The dark angel clothed himself in his wings and walked the perimeter of the chamber in a display of frustration Freja found interesting for the dark angel.

"There is concern that the creator will be displeased with how much meddling has been done already," Freja said. "It's rather taboo, you know, to influence or act without the direct blessing and all."

"Then leave the humans to it," Odin said.

"We believe creation itself rests on the outcome of humanity. It's not so simple as that," Samael said.

"If that is the case, then the time has come for them to be tested. Let them endeavor to pass and earn their future," Odin said.

"Perhaps we are being tested as well."

"Gungnir will soon come loose from the ocean floor, and I will not endeavor to provoke or skewer the beast again. Humanity has all it needs to win this battle. They will rise or they will fall, and we with them."

"It's not that simple if we allow the other side to tamper with them and divide them so they stand no chance at all," Samael said.

"Do you have so little belief in Rose and David?"

"The girl is fragile, and the boy is fractured," Samael said, uncloaking his wings and walking toward the door. "They're hobbled in the face of a malice our mightiest won't confront."

Samael left, and Freja sighed. "He worries because he knows them best of all. Samael dreads their failure not just for existence, but for they themselves."

Odin shifted to remove his helm, and Freja reached out to stop him. "There's no need. I know who you are, All-Father."

The sound of the horn vibrated through the hall, and Odin hefted an axe of incomprehensible proportions. "Shall we go out and give the warriors a thrill, like older times?"

Freja smiled and stalked through the doors to find her Fólkvangr on the fields.

Odin's eye radiated light as he stalked to the door. It faltered and flickered blue for an instant before returning once again to a scarlet crimson as he followed Freja to the fields.

Ω

David and Yehuda took their tea together and enjoyed watching the sun lower over the vast expanse of the Bay of Bengal.

"Flueric used his giant tuning fork to resonate some disruption between my connection to my other selves," David said.

"Yes, something like that," Yehuda replied.

"Yet I can still feel Rose. She was just in danger, and I could feel her peril. We've been like this since she returned."

"Since she found out she is a seed of Rhea, you mean? She simply turned on a switch and reached a similar tier as you. These things come with certain cognitive benefits. Surely you noticed this connection prior to your fall. It is often attributed to true love or being one's soulmate. Two halves of the same whole."

"Then why can't I feel my other selves any longer?"

"You're quite clever, David. Stop asking the questions, open your eyes to the answers. There is no fast lane to enlightenment. It doesn't work this way," Yehuda said in a tone close to frustration.

David understood his meaning. He and Rose were in the same reality, for one, and they were very in tune to one another. These were likely reasons for their connected emotions and even small communication. "I don't think I'll be finding any enlightenment using a long journey or meditating under a lotus tree, boss. We're under something of a time crunch."

"You'll find your way."

"And if I don't?"

"We will lose."

"You think of it in terms of winning or losing, too?"

"Very much, yes."

"And what happens if we lose?"

"Servitude, despair, and annihilation."

Hearing the circumstance doled out in such a way caused David to feel a panic in his gut he hadn't known since being a child—a time when many circumstances feel critical.

"Sip your tea, David. Find your calm."

"I should have guessed you could read my thoughts."

"I cannot. It doesn't take a psychic to feel disquiet graduate to dread. Any empathetic person might know your pain in this moment. It was a heavy truth you received. Take some time with it."

David stood and left the abode. He walked to the nearby water and watched as the light faded behind the horizon despite stretching its last rays to their limit. The sunset felt inevitable. He thought of the organized forces of darkness and the scattered remnants of good who could feel it coming but seemed so frail in the shadow.

We can't push back the dark. The light is going to fail.

He let the idea out of its forbidden box he'd created for it since being so easily cast aside by Flueric. As far as he could tell, nothing could stand in the way of that fallen light bearer. Perhaps Yehuda, but things weren't so simple, and he was acutely aware of that as well. It had to be him and Rose to unite humanity and defang the false idol.

He watched shooting stars streak across the sky and felt the earth rotate, closed his eyes and imagined the slowly changing constellations. It would be a gift to turn to stone and doze through a great surge in time. The night sky would be changed when he broke free from his rest, and the world would be entirely different from the one he knew. A luxury of the gods and angels, to be sure, and one he, as a human, could never allow himself to indulge in. It was the way of humanity to experience life in measured doses, cruel in their small size.

A group of teenagers came to play in the surf. They danced and crashed into the waves, and the braver ones swam out into the twilit waters. Their youth balked at the dangers of such a thing. Worry was a meddlesome task for their bridled elders.

David observed until a boy found himself clutched in the riptide and pulled farther than even his weighted ignorance would normally allow.

He walked toward the group to say in Odia, "There is a bull shark in those waters. I've seen it here night after night, feeding close. Your friend is in danger."

The youths would have looked to him, perplexed to see an American speaking their dialect. Then they would act. But David never reached the small party.

The smallest in the group was the first to dive into the surf, and the other two weren't long to find their bravery.

David watched as they reached their friend and pulled him outside of the ripping tides before all four made a mad dash for the shoreline. Darkness came on in full, and David had receded back to see them panting onshore, all the while ignorant to the dark shadow swimming in the waters they'd just been immersed within.

He left the beach and returned after some manner of wandering to find Yehuda exactly as he'd left him.

"I don't think I'll ever be whole again," David said.

"Might it be that the person you were yesterday is not the person you are meant to be tomorrow?"

"Yesterday I was strong."

Yehuda smiled and closed his eyes.

"The weak can't save anyone," David said.

"At least you deem them worthy."

"There is nothing that isn't worth saving."

Ω

The great serpent raged against its bonds and thrashed upon the ocean floor. She grew in size and in strength. It was no mystery to her. This realm held great nourishment, a likely reason for her having been barred after millions of years roaming its seas.

This energy felt different from those times. There was more of it, and it radiated from the people to be certain, but it had changed from being tinged with mystery to having been steeped in anger and want. Leviathan felt the glut over time until the difference became imperceptible to her as she changed to match it.

Gungnir held firm to the bedrock of the North American tectonic plate, and she cursed the meddling god who had pinned her so close to what she craved. She perceived time not as moving slowly or quickly. It was all one moment of unkempt agony. The slow progression of seconds to centuries was something she'd grown numb to during her long imprisonment in Valhalla.

She grew.

She waited.

She raged.

CHAPTER 4
THE FIRE RISES

Blakely had been to Barbara's house and called a top tier survey team to the site. The company's official position had been that she was devoured by rogue creatures running rampant in the area. He was shocked to see her number appear on his phone, and he quickly opened a tracking app before answering.

"Barbara?" he asked.

"You must be in a tizzy if you're not using your stock *this is Blakely* salutation," Barbara said.

It sounded like her, but his tracker was giving him nothing on her location, and he felt suspicious.

"Calling from beyond the grave like some Stephen King short story?" he asked.

"Not so artfully crafted a tale, I'm afraid. At least not yet. I'm with some… familiar people, Blakely. They're willing to bring me to you, or you can pick me up."

"The ones aligned to the asset David?" Blakely asked.

"The very same," Barbara said.

"You're on speaker. Please refrain from referring to my

son as one of your little experiments, Mr. Blakely, or I'll have my boyfriend burn your mouth shut," Chelsea said.

"Best tread lightly, son. I'm not one to disappoint my lady," Dodd said.

"Will you speak to him?" Barbara asked, and Blakely heard the shuffle as the phone passed to another. A skilled eye may have noticed Barbara's sleight of hand as she passed it.

"This is Leonard. We don't mind if you come directly here to pick her up. We're well aware you know Chelsea's address and have been doing your best to keep tabs on us," Leonard said.

"Why abduct her just to turn her over?" Blakely asked.

"We didn't. We saved her when you and your company couldn't have cared less that she was about to die. A high-level board member at All Century with security measures at home? It reeks of negligence." He paused and looked at Barbara. "Or worse."

This wasn't the sheepish Leonard she'd observed in the footage from the nearby All Century facility. She was glad he'd looked away before she felt her face flush.

"I don't appreciate the implication," Blakely said.

Barbara leaned to the right and placed a tracking tag from her phone inside of a duffel bag beside the bed. The exposed button-up T-shirts made it a safe bet the bag was Leonard's.

"Why? You should know you're expendable to them just like she is," Leonard said. "Either way, you can come get her."

"How do I know it's safe?" Blakely asked.

"Oh, shut up, you shit head, and get over here. I don't have my wallet to call a ride, and I'm not bumming thirty dollars from the *Dolans* to get home," Barbara called, conveying the abrupt anger that comes from disappointment. Blakely was no white knight. This she knew. But she thought of him as her friend. His attitude toward her situation made her feel that her assessment of their relationship was left of center.

There was a pause before, "Roger that, Barb."

The line died.

"He won't be stupid enough to call some group of storm troopers to come here with him, will he?" Chelsea asked. "I don't want the HOA on my case."

"Doubtful. I'm sure we have tech and teams designed to deal with something on the scale of Dodd, but I doubt they want the exposure. And, like you said, they probably don't care if I die here in your house. There are plenty of shit-heels looking to take my place, and they've probably got a lot more glimmer left in their eyes than I have."

"I'm sorry if you had your feelings hurt, but I'm not sorry you seem to be getting the point. All Century is not where you should be putting your faith," Leonard said.

"I'm not exactly sure a kid who is barely past drinking age is much better."

"You're not that daft," Chelsea said. "You know David is much more than that, or dear leader Flueric wouldn't have spent so much time and money on hobbling him."

Barbara thought about Chelsea's assessment and knew she was correct. The HOVAS program had been sold to other countries, but mostly to smaller nations without the means to upkeep them and all under the rule of a micro-dictator or some such warlord equivalent. Their real deployment had been on US soil, and there was no further development or ramp up in production after the catastrophic losses they'd seen in Virginia. All signs pointed to the actual plan of releasing the Leviathan and defeating or crippling David. And both had been realized.

"And don't leave out Rose. She's undergone quite a little growth spurt herself."

"Yeah, you mentioned her earlier, and I still can't figure out how she's alive, but I guess nothing is off the table these days," Barbara said. "Mind giving me some privacy to change my clothes? I don't want to give Blakely a glimpse of my goods if I can avoid it."

Dodd and Leonard moved to leave, but Chelsea stayed. "The boys will go, but I want to have a chat with you. Woman to woman."

"I'd really rather you didn't."

"And I really don't give a good goddamn what you'd rather," Chelsea said. "And don't worry about me watching while you change. I've seen shelves stocked with better goods in my time, and I'm not looking to appraise yours."

"Damn, you've sure got an edge," Barbara said.

"Watching assholes try to destroy the world and nearly losing my kids will do that," Chelsea said. "If it was up to me, you'd be dead right now. I won't hide that fact. I think Brendan would probably have had more of a crisis of conscience about it, but he might have let you be torn to shreds as well. You're only alive right now because Leonard sees potential in you."

"He's the smart one after all," Barbara said as she pulled a pair of leggings up over bruised skin.

"That's right. He's gifted and he has a good heart. I recommend you thank your lucky stars he was here for you and change your ways," Chelsea said.

"That all?"

"Yeah, that's all," Chelsea said and left the room.

Barbara finished dressing and looked outside to see if anything was amiss. Nothing but a picturesque view of suburban life verging on rural looked back at her. She waited and watched the road for an hour, and then cursed Blakely. She knew he wasn't working in Manhattan right now, and the facility in Connecticut was just a few miles away.

Barbara stared at the brass doorknob. *Screw it*, she thought and opened the door to descend the stairs. She was surprised to find Leonard reaching to knock.

"Listening to ladies dress, Leonard?" Barbara said. "I thought your kinks would be a little bit techier than that."

He blushed and Barbara thought his glasses might fog up. She almost felt bad for teasing him.

"I came to have a word before you left," Leonard said. "You should stay in touch with me. I mean, us."

"And why would I do something like that?"

"Because you're going to need help again, and so will we."

Barbara looked at him for a minute and then stood on her toes and gave him a kiss just long enough to make her stomach feel light. "I like the Clark Kent look, but you should lose the glasses sometime and show us how you play Superman," she said as she descended the stairs, resisting the urge to look back at his expression.

Blakely's knock came as she entered the same room where Asmodeus had dismantled their worlds in what felt like another life.

Dodd opened the door, and Barbara enjoyed seeing her cohort's fear in the shadow of the big man who'd saved her.

"Thank you," was all she said as she walked out.

"Thank you? That seems a lot like cavorting with the enemy, Barbara," Blakely said.

"Hardly. They weren't lying about saving me," Barbara said. "Let's go to what's left of the facility and debrief."

"Nobody has asked for one," Blakely said. "Everyone is surprisingly nonchalant about your circumstance and finding out you were alive."

"Almost like they already knew—"

Ω

Abaddon entered his town car and settled into the leather seats. His driver was a retiree named Fred, originally from Long Island. He had taken the job to keep his pockets full enough to live comfortably into his golden years and understood the protocol to stay quiet and hear nothing. Abaddon relished the silence, not for the joy or comfort it may afford, but for the obedience and discomfort it lent to Fred. Now and again, he might say something in passing to the man—something implying Abaddon knew well the subtle details of Fred's life.

How's Katherine handling the twins? It's difficult when they toddle around like they are. Head on a swivel 24/7 and all.

A bloom of dread rose within Fred, who knew, just as everyone else who spent any span of time in his presence, that Abaddon was something inhuman.

It's not always easy being a granddad. The knees don't hold up, eh, Fred? Try taking them to the park down in Ridgefield to run them around a bit. It takes the strain off you and puts it on them.

The subtle details the newly minted CEO of All Century knew were not specific to just his driver. He'd share an anecdote with his publicist about her hairdresser and drop a sly smile or a nugget of advice about his assistant's pernil recipe with a quick wink. The reaction was always the same. A smile to veil their fear of him. But fear breeds obedience and fosters effort, both things Abaddon required.

Fred pulled up to a press junket on the stone steps of the All Century headquarters in Midtown Manhattan and put the car in park. "I'll get the door, Fred. You just drive off and spend a little time at the big toy store on 42nd Street. There's a big birthday coming up." For once, Abaddon didn't look at Fred's expression. No such time for a tasty morsel today. He had an important announcement to deliver.

"Sir, your speech and notes." Abaddon took the papers and brushed past the young man to stalk up the stairs. He took up residence at the podium and surveyed the crowd below before putting on his plaster smile.

"Good morning, everyone. I'm sure some of you are wondering why All Century has called for this press conference, but I'm certain the vast majority of you already know. We are living in unprecedented times. Not only have we seen evidence of the paranormal during the last two years, but we've learned that what lies on the other side of the curtain is quite dangerous. Couple that with conflicts beginning around the world, and we have a recipe for catastrophe of cataclysmic proportions."

He looked upon the reporters and onlookers who held their breath as he spoke and gestured to the sky.

"Where is our savior? There's one in every story, yes? The clouds should be parting for a white knight to emerge and deliver us from evil, yet here we are, cowering in the shadow. I'm here to proclaim my newly minted appointment as the CEO of All Century, certainly that, but more to bring you a message. We can't wait for a hero to save us, because there are no heroes. You've been lied to. Mankind has only their own mettle to rely on. This is a lesson you knew during darker times and with that notion people banded into nations representing their individual selves and tested their might against one another for thousands of years. And what did you learn? That only the strong persevere. Those who can take, should take, and those who cannot stand up to the might of their enemies are doomed to be absorbed into them. This is the way of things."

Those in the crowd with signs reading sentiments such as *Deliver Us!* or *God Punishes Infidels* showed signs of losing their fervor. No applause broke out between Abaddon's pauses, yet he showed no sign of discomfort. His public relations people continued to motion for him to read his speech, which he'd ignored since beginning.

"And what does the mightiest nation in the world do when confronted with the impossible?"

A shout from the crowd carried to the podium. *We step up!* Abaddon's smile broadened.

"That's right. And All Century is right here to usher our great nation into the next phase of American history. Our tech is being spread to our allies around the world so they may fend off the barbarians at their gates. The cost to them is little more than allegiance to us. Anything short of that, and they can fight their own battles."

Cheers rose louder from within the crowd as Abaddon's fervor rose.

"On the home front, we step into an age of medical advancement without precedent. Our procedures and technology have cured paralysis, cerebral palsy, dementia—a groundbreaking cancer drug is all but on the market yet being held up at the FDA. I say if they don't push it through within a week, you walk right up to their doors and let them know what you think about them playing with your lives!"

Chants of *Storm the FDA, Storm the FDA, Storm the FDA* came over the heads of the press at the front right on cue, for Abaddon had seen to crisis actors being planted in the crowd. There'd be more and more need for them as time went on. He'd installed a special wing of the public relations department that had no other role than grooming thousands for the task. A wing that answered only to him.

"And you can be a part of our mission, yes you can. Our stock prices are still affordable, but they won't be for long. Buy, buy, buy, and enjoy the dividends due to you as All Century not only steps up the security of your nation but also fattens your coffers."

More cheers rose from the crowd, and Abaddon could feel the eyes on him as his image was streamed throughout the world.

"Take note of the senators and states who are working with us. When the time comes to go to the ballot box, cast your votes for those who remember that might for right is the only way to salvation. If you do, you'll have High Output Variant Attack Soldiers manning our army to ensure we never have to worry about our borders. There's a plan in place for civilian variations of the HOVAS to put an end to the creatures that wait to suck the life out of your loved ones."

The cheers reached a fevered pitch, and Abaddon's pride swelled. He was certain his speech would have worked without stacking the deck by seeding the crowd with agents, but Flueric had insisted. This moment needed to hit big, and lucky for him, it had.

"Let All Century bring our country to the pinnacle. Greater than any empire that has spanned the globe before!"

With that, he abandoned the podium and descended the stairs.

Reporters shouted questions.

What is your stance on allegations that your technology is being used in genocide in Pakistan?

Where did you come from? Nobody can find a history of your education or employment.

There are allegations that All Century has information on the Species 0. Why won't you tell the public what is going on under the water?

Cameras flashed upon him as he walked by unfazed. Later, those who were not so enamored with his speech would say it was like he'd merged Machiavelli and Mussolini. Many would notice that no matter from which angle you looked at an image of Abaddon, it appeared he was looking directly back at you.

Ω

David continued checking in with Chelsea, Dodd, and Rose during his time with Yehuda. The wise man held no technology within his apartments, and the embassy and consulates were far off from Puri, or Odisha, leaving David no option but to travel to a local hotel for these accommodations. On some occasions, David would call Iblis to gain insight into the happenings of the world abroad.

"War is looming, David. One on a scale that will make your generation understand the stakes at play during the previous world wars," Iblis said.

David rocked a chair back and forth, hearing the static that tagged along with their analogue phone connection.

"It feels very manufactured," David said. "The timing, I mean."

"No doubt. Brahman may be dead, but his role was to set the dominoes in such a way that they'd cascade in this manner once pushed."

"And what does Azazel plan to do?"

"He watches. It's his role."

"And the Host will stand by as Flueric pushes civilization to the brink of nuclear Armageddon?"

"Their movements are harder to predict, given the mute Seraphs, but I'd wager they'd simply watch humanity falter, yes," Iblis said.

David could hear the sadness in the jinn's voice. Iblis's kind were known for not having fealty to humanity and perhaps even hating them, but Iblis himself had seen some manner of reformation from his time with Azazel. David could sense his sorrow at the idea that mankind might be on the brink of blasting themselves back to the bronze age or worse.

"And how has your time with Yehuda been?" Iblis asked.

"He doles out his teachings in measured doses, and we don't have tons of time," David said and paused. "The more I work with him, the more I'm convinced I won't figure out how to fix myself."

"Maybe being fixed was never what you were supposed to strive for in the first place," Iblis said.

"You two would get along great."

"Our previous encounters weren't very genial, but I've changed quite a bit since those times."

"I have a distinct feeling that he probably hasn't."

"Well, you seem to be learning something worth knowing out there," Iblis said. "Where will you go once you've finished?"

"Not sure. I guess that all depends on what my role in all this should be," David said.

The two discussed more aspects of All Century and the rise of their new icon before ending the call. David returned to Yehuda as the afternoon broke for the evening.

"A storm is brewing and churns the waters of the Bay of Bengal. Do you feel it?" Yehuda asked.

"Yes, it is a cyclone. They've named it Khao."

"Do you feel its presence looming on the horizon?"

"Yes."

"Then your power serves you well enough for you to feel earth. This is good."

"I can still feel the weight of the murky veil and the movements of the dark actors at play," David said. "That hasn't changed."

"Focus on the tides," Yehuda said. "The water rises and recedes at the whims of the moon's presence. We know gravity is at play, but mankind's understanding of that force is no deeper than cause and effect. You are the same."

David considered this and sat to rest his mind and marinate on the wise man's words. He strained to feel the movement of the world around him at first before relaxing and giving up his efforts to force an epiphany.

"Good," Yehuda said. "Simply be."

$$\Omega$$

Chelsea turned the garden soil and planted lavender seeds on the outskirts of her vegetable garden. The ashes Dodd provided far exceeded any concoction of fertilizer and compost she'd ever used. At first, she enjoyed the boon in growth, but it somewhat trivialized what had once been an ornate dance between her and nature.

She hated Dodd's circumstance to her core and stopped just short of wishing his past crippled state upon him. They'd both known the large man, now pushing into his latter fifties, would have made nothing close to a full recovery from such an injury. Brendan had put on a brave face about it all, but it ate at him. He needed his mind and mobility to help look after Ramirez's family, for one, and he wanted a fairytale relationship with his new love. Not to force her into the role of patient and caretaker.

Regardless, there was an insidious presence within him, and Chelsea could see his mind drift to it when it scratched at the locked door, barring it from Brendan's mind. The ifrit were lamentations of rage and regret, and All Century had found a way to use the energy from fallen angels to yoke them to host bodies before they could be released upon death. The entities allowed for amazing attributes, sure, but the cost was a very pissed off dervish of fire that often delighted in bringing pain and torture to the living. Not exactly the roommate one wanted inside of their mind.

The wind shifted behind her, and Chelsea heard the telltale sound of feet touching earth from above.

"I wondered if we would be seeing you again," Chelsea said, turning to see Samael put away his obsidian wings.

"I once told Detective Dodd as we parted ways that he should always expect to see me at least once more."

"It's possible that he didn't understand back then, but he probably does now."

"I know that you unravel such word play rather easily, Chelsea Dolan," Samael said. "You've all fared well. This is good."

"Keeping tabs on us from on high?"

"Yes and no. I have my ear to the ground for large rumblings. We really aren't supposed to meddle with you to near the extent we have."

"I have a distinct feeling the rulebook has been put aside. One good example being that I was impregnated by an angel. That sort of thing has a bit of an antediluvian vibe, right, Sam?"

"Yes, Chelsea, it does." Samael walked over to inspect Chelsea's garden and noticed her intent gaze as he lifted a squash from the soil. "Please don't tell me you are afraid it will turn to ash the second I touch it. You've seen me carry a person before, and they didn't perish."

"It's hard for my mind to conceive you as an ally, Sam. For Pete's sake, you're the grim reaper."

"Am I so grim? I hadn't ever thought of myself that way. I have anger at times, more now than before, to be sure. But I do resent the idea of humans feeling dread at the idea of death. It's just a step in the natural order of things."

"No, you're not grim," Chelsea said and dropped her trowel to take off her gloves. "You are considerate and inquisitive and wonderful. I'm sorry if I hurt your feelings." Chelsea reached to take his hand.

"You are very considerate," Samael said as he allowed Chelsea to guide him into her home.

"What brings you to us again?"

"Be at ease, there is nothing pressing," Samael said as he took up a chair and watched Chelsea set the tea kettle atop a flame to boil.

"I'd be lying if I said I wasn't nervous," Chelsea said.

"I'm here because—" Samael went silent and Chelsea turned to him again.

"Are you alright, Sam?"

"I am. It's you I worry over. All of you."

"Leonard and Dodd are fine, and you probably are more aware of how David and Rose are than I am at this point."

"It's not that. It's the state of things," Samael said. "You've quite an adversary to overcome, and you aren't going to receive any help from the Host. In fact, they may well hinder your efforts."

"We will manage. Haven't we always?"

"No. No, you haven't. You're well aware things have gotten so bad as to almost wipe you out."

"Yes, that's true, I suppose. But here we are. I have a distinct feeling we will remain, too."

"It's odd to see you with such optimism, Chelsea," Sam said as he took a mug of tea from her. "You so often chastise us and beware some imminent doom."

"I'm worrying over my loved ones. It's different from worrying over annihilation. To you, they are pieces on the board for a grander scheme. But Sam, to me, they are all that matters in your vast eternity. My Armageddon comes if I ever lose them."

Samael sipped his tea and considered this as he gazed out of the window. Chelsea couldn't help but be stricken by his poise and the sheer power emanating from this being as he calmly sat in her meager home.

"I'm choosing to meddle some more, Chelsea. Would you find that agreeable?"

"Not if it means you'll go the way of Uriel."

"It may."

"Well, then I suppose it's your choice, Sam. But have you watched the news lately? We may not be worth saving at this point."

"There's always been avarice. It leads to conflict."

"This feels more grievous, and I think you know what I mean."

"I do, but never forget the invisible hands pushing your kind to these places. On your own, there would be far less death and despair."

"We shouldn't be so susceptible to the wiles of bad actors. It's a moot point, and I feel we should take accountability for our own greed."

"This mindset of yours is shared by a great many, Chelsea Dolan, and is all the proof I need to validate stepping in on your behalf," Samael said as he took a last sip of tea.

"So you came for reassurance, Sam?"

"Yes. I came for that and for another reason."

"What's that?" Chelsea asked, opening the door as she sensed her time with the angel was coming to a close.

"I find you comforting," Samael said and embraced her before walking outside. Chelsea had no idea how long she stood at the open door looking after him as he flew off, but she was all too aware her mouth had hung open the entire time.

Ω

Lilith followed Rose back into Baba Yaga's hut after hearing the girl recite the telltale rhyme to command the thing to sit.

"Did you rustle up anything, ladies?" Baba Yaga asked.

"Nothing left there of Raphael," Rose said.

Lilith took a seat on the bed and put her head in her hand. "Why do you keep this dusty house of yours, witch? Surely by now you have grown to know faster modes of transportation."

"Why, it's my home, that should be reason enough," Baba Yaga said and turned to her cauldron pot upon the fire. "Rose, dear, would you please remind that harlot to watch the way she speaks to me, lest I turn her into a salamander for this stew?"

Rose turned to Lilith. "Have you eaten? You get cranky when you're hungry, and you always forget since becoming a mortal."

Lilith glanced to Baba Yaga and opened her mouth to speak, but she saw Princess in the corner eyeing her and thought better of it. "What is there to have?"

"I'll get us some fruit. It'll do the trick until we get a chance for a proper meal," Rose said.

"Aye, tonight's stew will be hearty indeed," Baba Yaga said as she waved her hand in the air.

The house of brown took off, and once airborne, there wasn't any feeling of motion—a subtle trait that Lilith found interesting. She considered it magic and retracted her previous statement about the house. It was likely the old crone could enhance its speed with her magic.

"Where are we going?" Lilith asked as a means of extending an olive branch. The sort that required chipping away at an icy block for delivery.

"Nowhere of import. Best not to stay idle in one place overlong."

"Lilith," Rose said. "The feather idea was a bust, but we aren't completely in the dark just yet. Leonard mentioned that quote from Genesis about Eden being the source of the four tributaries, but there may be a shroud hiding the entrance, like with Azazel's tomb. Do you have any idea about it?"

Lilith smiled and turned herself to face both Rose and Baba Yaga, who'd craned her neck to peak over her shoulder at the Rose's utterance.

"I was born in Eden, it's true. The garden isn't a metaphor for the realm of the living nor is it someplace beneath the veil. It is, in fact, accessible from your world. I do not know what angelic entity spoke to whomever first wrote Genesis, but I can guarantee whichever it was wasn't referring to rivers in Egypt or Mesopotamia or Armenia or Disneyland either. The 'rivers' jargon is pointing to something important, which may very well be a veiled metaphor of sorts. I also believe that finding the garden's entrance will not be enough to enter. We will need special key to cross into it. Even if we do, we will meet the guardian, and he will destroy us with the flat affect he has always worn."

"Raphael—" Rose said.

"Yes. He who sent the three to drag me back from the Red Sea after I fled."

"And why did you leave absolute paradise?" Baba Yaga asked.

"Paradise is subjective to treatment. I was made second and would always come second. Adam himself asserted his claim over me like he was my owner, not my partner. Would you, a woman of such great strength, have stayed?"

"Presumably not. I'd likely have been far less capable as a youth, much like Rose here was not so long ago, but I'd imagine Adam would have found his death at my hands instead."

"There is no death for those born in Eden unless otherwise ordained, like after he was expelled. Besides, I was weak before," Lilith said as she turned to inspect the contents of the jars on a shelf by the door. "It takes time for hatred to transform into strength. Time and treachery."

"When you left, was it an easy transition to the veiled world?" Rose asked.

"Yes. All I had to do was walk toward the boundary, and I simply flipped over to here."

"I don't suppose where you landed would be much help to us these days," Baba Yaga said.

"No. I landed in separate places each time I left. The first time having been dragged back at the whim of the creator."

"I'm guessing free will was in full effect with us from creation, and whatever plan was in store required us to make certain decisions. Ones that didn't quite line up to the first humans," Rose said.

"And you are a human, little harlot," Baba Yaga added. "No longer so well steeped as you were and laid bare like the rest. Rose delivering life to you wouldn't have worked if your vessel was otherwise designed."

Lilith knew this to be true, but she hated the idea of it. She'd spent nearly the entirety of her existence separating herself from, and delivering torment to, Adam's kin.

"Baba Yaga, can we head toward New York? I want to see if Leonard and Chelsea can help us isolate a few details, and if Lilith's idea of the metaphor in Genesis rings true, he may help us to know where to start looking."

"No harm in steering here or there, since nowhere is where we were headed," Baba Yaga said.

Once again, Lilith felt no shift in the house's movement and wondered at whether it flew through the sky at all. The celestial beings and other entities from the veiled world were imbued with, or had discovered, various means to harness the power of creation that mankind was only beginning to scratch the surface of. Lilith pondered Baba Yaga's surface appearance as a witch. The monster hiding in the Slavic woods, as it had been whispered amongst those who lived on the periphery. It appeared she was far older and mysterious than a mere demigod. Rose had revealed that both women were seeds of Rhea, the primordial mother and product of sky and earth. A powerful combination to have in one's family tree.

Leonard sat outside of Chelsea's home, enjoying the midday sun, when Baba Yaga's hut landed in the yard and flexed its wings before settling. His initial reaction to stand and flee brought a smile to Lilith as she observed him from a window.

"He's a flighty one, our Leonard," Rose said. "Be gentle with him."

Lilith kept the man in her stare and felt a familiar pang in her chest. "Don't worry. I won't devour the handsome genius."

Baba Yaga once again peered over her shoulder to watch the girl as she left the hut and approached Leonard.

"Did we scare you?" Rose asked.

"I mean, it's not every day a giant hybrid chicken house comes at you out of nowhere," Leonard said while scratching the back of his head. "We weren't expecting you."

"I know, but we haven't been as successful as we'd hoped," Rose said as Chelsea and Dodd came out of the house to join them.

"Not one but two interesting visitors today," Chelsea said. "But you're always the best surprise. Even when you were little."

She and Rose embraced, and Chelsea released her after seeing Lilith and Baba Yaga approach from the lawn.

The six stood together in the sun between the two respective houses, one lifting a leg to scratch its other. Dodd broke the silence. "It's a pleasure to meet Rose's mentor. We can't thank you enough for guiding her back to us."

The witch smiled and enjoyed a courteous gesture from both Chelsea and Leonard. Lilith felt only an icy silence from Chelsea and looked to Leonard, who cast his eyes downward and put his hands in his pockets.

"I'm sure you're all hungry," Chelsea said. "Let me fix you some lunch."

"We've a stew on," Baba Yaga said. "It'll be ready before the hour turns."

Chelsea opened her mouth and then closed it again.

Rose slapped her hands on her upper thighs in the manner a Southerner might to change the subject. "Lunch and some conversation. Just what the doctor ordered."

The unlikely band arranged themselves at an outdoor table after Dodd plucked the umbrella from the middle, and Chelsea served up an assortment of cold beverages to the group. Lilith took up a cup of iced tea and Leonard observed as she emptied her glass, filled it again, and then held it close to her chest with both hands. Baba Yaga produced a root that reminded the researcher of ginger, but the shape wasn't quite right and the interior was bile green in lieu of the vibrant yellow one would expect. She shaved slivers into a glass of iced water and let them steep while she ferried herself back and forth to the house.

"We aren't worried the neighbors will start asking questions, Chelse?" Dodd inquired.

"There's a thinny on it," Rose said. "That's what Baba Yaga calls them anyway. People outside of our little sphere will only see a trick of the light. If someone peers too long, they may make out an odd outline, but a nauseous sensation causes them to inevitably look away."

Baba Yaga returned with an ornate serving bowl steaming with stew, and Dodd salivated at the smell. With their bowls full of food, they settled in to discuss the garden.

"We have some luck on our side. Lilith has been to the garden, but on both occasions when she reentered it, she was brought by members of the Host, so she has no knowledge of the four rivers," Rose said.

"And I didn't see any rivers when we crossed over in either location," Lilith said

"There's also the interesting matter of there having been an entrance from two separate locations," Rose said. "It seems it doesn't matter where you are when you open the entrance to Eden."

"There was water present both times I was taken, if that matters," Lilith mentioned as she took another sip of her iced tea and spooned a hearty helping of the stew that nearly matched Dodd's.

"So we have that and the concept of the four river heads from the book of Genesis, and that's all?" Chelsea asked as she pushed the stew around her bowl and eyed Baba Yaga.

"Yup, that's where we stand," Rose said.

"The four river heads have been spoken of and dissected for centuries. It's clear that each has a separate origin and thus a single spring from Eden doesn't actually make them up," Chelsea said.

"Euphrates, the Tigris, the Gihon, and the Pishon," Leonard said. "If I'm not mistaken, the Pishon is all but dried up in modern Kuwait these days."

"I'm thinking it's a riddle," Dodd said, wiping his mouth. "This is delicious, by the way. What's in here?"

"Best I keep my recipes a secret," Baba Yaga said. "Likely the same as the true nature of those rivers. It keeps the topic spicy, eh?" She gave a short, cracked laugh before bringing more stew to her mouth.

Chelsea gently dropped her spoon and inspected what she had originally assumed were potatoes. After giving up on those, she looked at what she guessed was rabbit meat, as it was delicate and small without seeming to have been overly chopped. Now she wondered.

"You've a mighty appetite for a jinn," Baba Yaga said. "I've never seen one so ravenous. I'll treat you to one fine detail about my cooking. The quality of meat may never matter as long as one has the perfect knife for carving."

Dodd nodded at the tidbit of information and skirted the subject to keep Chelsea from throwing up her lunch. "I've always had an enormous appetite because I ain't no jinn. Just a normal man who ran into some interesting circumstances. I suppose it isn't a surprise that you would know there's a fiery monster in me—"

"Ifrit," Leonard said out of impulse.

"—yeah, that. But I've got it pretty well tamped down."

"Mmmmmmmh." The sound issued from the woman, and nobody prompted her for more as she dived back into her stew.

"Well, what are four things that would stem from the garden?" Chelsea asked.

"Hard to say," Rose said. "First we should consider what the garden actually is."

They all looked to Lilith, who frowned back at them. "What?" she asked.

"You're the only one who has been, and if it is obvious to me, it should be within grasp for you," Baba Yaga said. "Don't play coy with us. I won't remind you again that you are only graced with this opportunity at life by the whims of that girl there." She pointed a spoon across the table to Rose. "I have a bad habit of losing my patience and letting my spells fly, harlot. Consider ye warned."

The gravity of Baba Yaga's statement was undercut by Chelsea's inability to stifle her laugh. Lilith's scowl deepened.

"The garden is a cradle. You all imagine it as an infinite grove of fruiting trees and bountiful animals in perfect symmetry and all blissful, and there is some truth to that, but it isn't synonymous with heaven. It's Eden. The beginning of life." Lilith barked her description as she spoke. "Within are the two trees more important than all others. One for knowledge, and one for life. There's been rumors of a fountain with mystical properties, but I never rinsed in its waters nor heard word one about it. Then again, I wasn't there overlong, was I?"

"She brings up a good point about it being the cradle of life," Leonard said. "If we are considering symbolic meaning, Eden may well be where life entered the equation of creation and that is its function."

Baba Yaga smiled at this.

"So what might be the four things that are required for life?" Dodd asked.

"Here, we'd need carbon, and oxygen," Leonard began.

"Bold of you to presume life only exists here on this floating orb," Baba Yaga said.

"That's a good point," Chelsea said. "I doubt it would be just four things we need for life on Earth."

"If there's anything I've learned through all this, it's that there is a genuine connection between cosmic power and biologic life," Rose said.

She looked up and locked eyes with Leonard as he had an epiphany.

"There are the four governing powers of the universe. At least, the four we know of," he said. "Gravity, electromagnetism, weak nuclear force, and strong nuclear force. These things hold together matter and without them there would be no life."

"And without rivers, there would be no life in the biblical deserts," Chelsea said.

"The idea holds water," Dodd quipped, and Chelsea smacked his arm without breaking stride.

"But we can't exactly harness these things and make a key," she continued. "They're infinitely difficult to even observe. Especially the strong nuclear force. It degenerates at a distance of one millionth of a hair's width."

"Aye, you won't catch lightning in a bottle, but you won't have to. You are privy by now to the avatars for sins and virtues, yes?" Baba Yaga asked, and Chelsea nodded with the vigor of someone who is at rapt attention. "Lucifer is Pride, Abaddon is Avarice, Beelzebub is gluttony, that gigantic serpent down in the sea—she is Envy. It's worth mentioning that her lust for all that humanity has been given and has earned will lead her to devour everything."

"That's why we aim to trap her in the garden, where the Host will have no choice but to deal with her," Rose said.

Baba Yaga nodded and looked into her water glass for some time before continuing. "There are representative items for other things in this universe. The angels hold the power of creation within them. The stars themselves. But the forces of the universe aren't given full persona forms, at least not all of them. These are laws that cannot be broken. The more knowledge one has of them, the more power and influence one can wield. Flueric may come to mind, yes?"

Leonard thought of Asmodeus and his relatively small place within the pantheon of beings they were dealing with. He'd only now made the connection between the demon's immaturity and his relative weakness among peers. Even David, recently imbued with celestial power, had very little trouble besting Lilith's favored son.

Baba Yaga continued, "These laws are represented within items, not beings. There are echoes of this in some traditions you've witnessed. Rose's heart was weighed against Ma'at's feather, which represents virtue. This was no accident, you see. The key to the garden is likely found in bringing these items together."

"Why didn't you just tell us this before instead of having the two of us run around looking for a useless feather?"

Baba Yaga, usually quick to silence Lilith's insolent remarks, merely smiled. "Perhaps it is that I am old and my wits are dull, or maybe I needed you all to put it together. It's a tricky thing to question the wiles of Fate and a foolish thing to question them."

"This is a fun theory and even my brain, which is definitely becoming dull, grasps the concept, but where would we look?" Dodd asked. "We don't even know what these things are."

"For most, I'll be of no help," Baba Yaga said. "But for one of the four, I am certain I know. The first river we shall find is the Tinker of the Nisse."

"The gnomes of Denmark?" Leonard asked.

"Aye, the same. Or the Nisse, as some call them. Kin to the Good Folk for others. It is they that have Tinker, which stitches together anything they may wish."

"The strong nuclear force, then," Chelsea said and grasped her glass. "I'll be damned."

"I'll look up flights. Things are getting bad around the world, and every minute that passes increases the risk that Leviathan will free herself," Dodd said.

"We have a quicker way," Rose said.

Leonard glanced up to Baba Yaga's house, and it gave a little curtsy. He smiled despite himself, but he filled with dread at the idea of entering it.

Chelsea, Dodd, and Leonard retreated into Chelsea's home to clean their messes and pack small bags before returning to the yard. Rose waited outside and gestured for them to climb the stairs and enter where Lilith and Baba Yaga waited. Chelsea wrinkled her nose at the well-organized mess she would be in as they traveled.

Leonard noted that there was a single large room. He'd have nowhere to burrow and hide if he became overstimulated. "I think I'll stay," he said.

"Are you sure?" Chelsea asked. "A chance to meet the Nisse won't come around very often."

"Tempting, but I have some ideas of things to work on here," Leonard said as he backed out of the door. "Be careful over there and reach out if you need help."

Lilith had a dour look upon her face at hearing Leonard bow out before Dodd sat on the foot of the bed opposite her and she bumped into the air. He smiled at her despite the scowl she favored him with.

"Off now, old chicken, to the land of the Danes," Baba Yaga said. The front door closed of its own accord, and the newcomers braced for a large shift that never came. Rose laughed at their exaggerated postures. "It takes some getting used to, and the ride won't be instantaneous, but it'll be much shorter than you'd think."

"Good, because I don't see a bathroom in this Airbnb, and my prostate ain't getting any smaller," Dodd said.

Baba Yaga threw the husk from a root she was working with across the room, and it landed in a cast-iron pot with a flourish.

"I don't suppose that's a magic chamber pot over there?" Dodd asked.

"That wouldn't do. We've only one pot. How else would we save the flavor for the stew?" Baba Yaga said.

Chelsea's jaw dropped, and the witch cackled as they made their way across the Atlantic.

PART TWO

ALL-FATHER

CHAPTER 5
RIP CORD

Grace Jordan elbowed her way to the front of the demonstration outside of All Century's Seattle offices. A sophomore at U Washington, she was no stranger to activism and had donated her time campaigning for various local and federal politicians since leaving her home in Kansas to attend school. Both her parents expressed a lack of thrill at her views, but she had whittled them down over time to where they were just happy to stop talking about current affairs within their home—a phenomenon which occurred in many households across the globe as normalcy became an echo of the past.

War breaking out in the country next door?

Let's watch something else.

Rampant starvation due to biblical drought?

Let's watch something else.

Monsters invading from the nether regions of reality?

Lock the door.

Hey, let's watch something else.

A velvet blanket of fatigue settled upon them with such

innocuous subtly it was nearly impossible to focus on what mattered. Unless you were like Grace, of course. She may have been overly focused upon it, growing ever angrier at All Century's plans to manipulate profit at the expense of lives and feeling insulted by just how transparent they were. Angrier still at everyone else's lack of urgency to stop them. As though nothing could be done to mobilize and stop these events.

Many of the protesters chanted, *Wages Are For Raises, Wages Aren't For War* and held up signs with similar sentiments. Grace saw familiar faces from grassroots social media campaigns who were standing out in the crowd and hurling insults to the towering building. One man held a handwritten drawing of a large snake that merely read, *We Know*. Despite the familiar outcries from those who were mostly of college age or just after, the crowds never surged to sizes one would hope to see in the face of tyranny. The likes of which didn't come from the monarchs they were taught to be leery of in secondary school. Modern tyranny was doled out by CEOs set behind hardwood desks in skyline offices.

Behind the man with the snake sign, from the bushes lining the park, emerged a person with a familiar face that Grace couldn't quite identify, as though a mystique had been cast upon him. He sidled up to the road and began crossing. Grace grew aware of the distinct feeling that he looked right at her as he moved, despite countless others being nearby. His odd shuffling movements and sloped grin made him stand out from others, but no one else reacted.

She moved up the stone steps of a small staircase to get closer to the group behind her when she heard a gasp cut through the chanting. Then another sound of alarm, and another. One leader of the protest with a microphone and speaker cried out, "What is that?" as he pointed out over the crowd in the opposite direction from where Grace had seen the other man. When she turned back, she saw a homeless person with an entirely unfamiliar face than the one that had scared the life out of her earlier. His clothes were ripped in identical spots, but a white beard dispelled any notion it was the same person. Unease climbed through her, from her legs and through her chest.

"You missed me," the man said from beside her. It was the grinning man's face on a man wearing chinos and a blank hoody. "I slipped right by you," he whispered.

Grace screamed, and others within the group echoed her cries as the same face appeared on others among the group. The protest unraveled into a scene of disarray as the activists broke off and ran while others attempted to understand what was happening. The stampede would crush many, and the police would take the brunt of the blame as Pulse24 ran a clip showing an officer use mace on a crowd from an entirely different demonstration than where Grace was in Seattle.

Above and within the confines of his ivory tower, Abaddon looked into a mirror perched atop a white Steinway piano, and his features blended and blurred within the dim light. His fingers danced upon the keys as he sowed discord and watched the people tear themselves apart.

Ω

David's work with Yehuda became a maddening mixture of meager progress and worry over being occupied here while the others endeavored elsewhere. He held a tertiary awareness of their progress through Rose, and she his, but this only enhanced his feeling of obsolescence.

"I have to leave soon," David said to Yehuda one morning as they walked the streets of Puri.

"This is true. You've made much progress, yet you still believe yourself broken?" Yehuda asked.

"Yes. I'm just not brimming with the power I had when I returned from Valhalla."

"You are. And you also have a treasure within you. The one you gained from your encounter with the serpent."

David thought of the sword inside of him.

"I wasn't able to wield the sword well even when I had full access to my power," David said.

"Do you think, based on the words of the serpent, that what you hold within you is just a sword?"

"Leviathan said it appeared differently depending on who saw it."

"This is partially true. It appears as what the observer truly desires. It has been in the hands of few, and found its way to Valhalla within the soul of a great hero who was gifted it during a time of turmoil. He, too, saw it as a sword. Of course the serpent felt its presence and coveted it more than all else, so she snatched it and remained coiled about it until you freed it from the stone once more."

"I hadn't considered it could have been in the hands of others before me," David said. "It feels like it's been in me all along. Like a song you recall from years ago that just fits neatly in your mind."

Yehuda smiled. "You've an interesting way of portraying things, especially feelings. I think you have grown firmer during our time together than you might understand. I'll miss speaking to you like this. It has always been the rarest of pleasures for me, since I came to be."

"You make it sound like we've done this before," David said.

Yehuda simply smiled and walked on in silence. He brought David back to the home they'd shared and paused at the door. "We have a visitor, one who excels at keeping his presence unknown. Do not be startled when you see him."

David did nothing to hide his surprise. It was true that he felt no celestial power present in the home, and this fact added to his feelings of waning power. He followed Yehuda inside.

"I see you are finally on holiday," Odin said. He stood at the rear of the room and his full armor appeared out of place with his surroundings. "I hope your rest has been fruitful."

"I wouldn't say I've been resting," David said.

Yehuda walked to Odin and embraced him before turning to David. "Do not feel as if taking a rest is an insult, David. It is necessary for us to grow."

"Why are you here?" David asked, knowing Odin's presence signified the end of his time with Yehuda. His tone belied an eagerness to jump back into the fray.

"Your time in my hall helped you understand yourself enough to face the serpent once. Your time here served a purpose much the same. I am here to tell you that you must face Jormungandr once more."

"Don't the stories say that your son is supposed to vanquish it?" David asked.

"The time for that has not yet come. We are not on the precipice of Ragnarok of the Eda. This is an unwritten chapter, David Dolan, and you must write the end."

"Well said." Yehuda removed himself and took up a place at his nearby table to scrawl upon a piece of parchment paper.

"I don't understand your involvement with me," David said. "Why didn't I see you when I was in Valhalla?"

"The answer is simple," Odin said. "I was not there."

"Where were you?" David asked. "Couldn't you have stopped this from happening in the first place?"

"This is a question that doesn't serve your task. You are here now. Look forward and take charge of your destiny or wilt like a grape in the sun. The decision is still yours, as was the one to attempt to save the boy in the river."

"Tim died because of the *meddling* of forces beyond the world of the living," David said. "If the other side had been in motion from the start, he'd be alive along with everyone else who drowned that night."

"Things are never as simple as that, and you have grown far too wise to cling to those notions," Odin said. "I bring up the boy because giving up your life to save him allowed you passage to Valhalla. It showed you have the heart required to walk among us. We need you to remember that now as you endeavor to stop the degradation of your kind into petty animals. Can you do that?"

David stared into the glowing eye of Odin. "I knew the broad strokes about you before all of this. A lot of people do, but Uriel gave a deeper glimpse into your suffering. It's a respectable thing, suffering for so long only to gain the wisdom to stave off the annihilation of our world—what you call Midgard. You remind me of my friend."

Yehuda paused in his scrawling and looked at Odin as if expecting what was to happen. The head of the Norse

Pantheon reached up and lifted his helm, revealing his face to David, who shook his head.

"I saw you disintegrate into light and vanish for annihilating Asmodeus. You can't be Uriel."

"I am not Uriel and yet I am. I am Zeus and I am others as well. We change, David, and it is humanity that guides this. A vast pool of consciousness that holds more sway over reality than you may know. As Odin, I oversaw the expansion of humans as they raided, murdered, stole, and expanded. A necessary step in their evolution, though a filthy one. As beliefs changed, so too did the pool of consciousness. My role as All-Father dwindled, and I was inducted into the Host as one of their own. This isn't the case for many, and especially not the archangels. But very few with consciousness are crafted solely for one purpose by the creator. As Uriel, I maintained my foresight and wisdom taken from the tree, but I lost all sight. I feel echoes of him, even now, but we are two separate skins upon the same frame."

Odin's eye changed from red to blue before David for the first time, and he saw Uriel's aura emanating from within, dispelling any remaining doubt about the old god's words. "I'm glad you weren't scrubbed from creation for what you did."

"It is not common for anything to be. A fundamental law prohibits it. Balance must be maintained, after all, to keep the pillars of creation firm. Though it is true, what Michael said. I should have been destroyed. I am uncertain as to why I remain."

"It's probably because the world is springing to war," David said. "Your action didn't end you, but had I done it… I would have been destroyed. Michael was hoping I would destroy Asmodeus and face that fate."

Odin nodded, and Yehuda completed his drawing.

"And who is he, then?" David asked as he pointed to Yehuda. "In this never-ending game of shifting names, I can't grasp it."

"He is likely the easiest to understand, but I'll leave you to figure it out. It is not the destination that is most important—"

"—but the journey," David finished. "Yes, you've said that to me before."

"I've no mead for our reunion."

"There's no fear I need it to take anymore. I'm just broken," David said.

"Better described as scrambled," Yehuda said and carried the paper to David. "You will find your center again. I am nearly certain of it."

"Nearly?" David asked.

"I've no prescient gift like Odin, despite what some believe," Yehuda said. "I am merely speaking upon my knowledge of you, and I am hopeful."

"And you?" David asked Odin. "Since you have the ability of foresight."

"My knowledge of events to occur is painted in broad strokes. The minutia, smaller matters, are unclear to me. It is why I'm here." He pointed to the map with a large, gloved finger, and David noted his hulking size and wondered if Uriel's smaller frame was inside of the armor or if his body had changed as well. "That will lead you to Vajra. He is close."

"And why do I need to visit Vajra?" David asked.

"He has a precious item you will need," Yehuda said. "The details will be made clear by your friends."

"I know a little. Rose is heading to grab something similar right now. I don't know the details, though. Broad strokes..."

Odin smiled as he replaced his helm on his head and said, "After you visit Vajra, find the serpent and regain my spear. You will require it as well."

"And what if I fail at Vajra?" David asked.

"Then you may sit back on holiday as the world you love is torn apart."

Ω

Barbara went about her business at All Century as though she had not experienced her ordeal. In reality, she only reported to work slightly later than she might have on a normal day, and those who endeavored around her were completely unaware.

"Hey, Barb," said Cathy, a friendly member of their human resources department. The existence of which always made Barbara laugh. What exactly does HR do in a company that's trying to take over the world?

Thus began the daily office banter she'd grown accustomed to.

"Hi, Cathy, how's the grandbaby?"

"Twelve pounds already, and she can sit up on her own!"

"Barbara, do you happen to know if the acquisition paperwork is done for our property in Uganda?"

"No, Niel, I'd ask Anthony about that. He's close to the project."

"Is there a plan for Raf's retirement party?"

"How come I always have to do this? It isn't even my job!"

"Where in the holy hell are the ACCO binding strips?"

"I really can't work late tomorrow night."

"Did you see the press conference?"

Barbara had not seen Abaddon speak, and she went to the bathroom, set up her VPN network, made sure she wasn't on All Century's Wi-Fi, and then pulled up YouTube. The stark nature of his speech was a bold approach, even for Flueric and Abaddon. They'd taken great care to remain in the shadows in the past, and the shift in dynamic signaled the beginning of an endgame plan none of them had been privy to. All Century was stepping beyond merely lobbying the government and meddling in international affairs and had now established itself as a war power masquerading as a savior. Take the mercenaries, their medical branches, control of media, influence over world leaders, and they were poised to do something big. What that was, she did not know.

Barbara emerged from the stall and jumped at Blakely, who waited for her.

"Hiding away and doing reconnaissance now?" he asked.

"Catching up on the speech is hardly recon, Blakely," she said. "I've been out of the loop."

He stayed silent for a beat too long. "What did you learn from them while they had you?"

"You make it sound so insidious. They saved my life and let me use a bed for a few hours. It's not that serious."

"I don't like it, Barb. Nobody of influence seems to care much, but it's awfully odd to me that they would care enough about you to even pull you out of the house. And how did they know about you in the first place?"

"I told you, they were tracking the pack of things that attacked my house." Barbara stalked away from Blakely and went to the sink. "I also told you that they found out about us in Virginia. They know you too, bub."

"I know. They've been careful in covering their steps, but hackers they ain't."

"*He* ain't. Leonard Barlowe is the tech guru on their squad." Barbara thought of him and how genuinely he spoke to her, in spite of the fact that they were on opposing sides of this conflict. She always had little belief in there being genuinely good people in the world but thought she may have stumbled upon one. Brendan Dodd came off as pretty virtuous at first glance, too, and Chelsea, despite her seething hatred of her, was likely also a good egg. She could not divulge her opinions on the matter to Blakely. Looked far too suspicious, but it was true.

"They've gone dark again, at any rate," Blakely said. "We lost them earlier this afternoon. All of 'em were home, and there hasn't been activity since. Barring some sort of suicide pact, they've flown the coop."

"Why are we still tracking them, anyway? At this point, can they really be anything more than a nuisance?"

Blakely's look belied his thoughts. She realized how bad that had sounded in retrospect.

"Their meddling resulted in the loss of billions in assets," he said.

"I'm almost positive that was always a part of Flueric's plan. The giant snake from some otherworldly portal, do you recall that?"

It was Blakely's turn to look away and heave a sigh. "Just keep your nose clean. You know as well as I do that the higher-ups don't need much cause to make people disappear."

"I appreciate your concern," Barbara said and left the restroom. She returned to her office and kept the door open so all who cared to could look inside and see her. Her fingers flew over the keyboard for a half hour before she paused to look at her phone and check the tracking tag she had placed in Leonard's bag. It had been a gamble that the bag was even his, but she'd assumed they'd been using that guest room for staging before they went on their little missions. It was also a gamble that Leonard would have taken the bag with him when he left.

The program opened, and she saw the last five pings from the tag.

4:32:04 PM EST - 41.5048° N, 73.9696° W
4:57:24 PM EST - *Unknown*
5:28:44 PM EST - *Unknown*
5:54:04 PM EST - *Unknown*
6:31:24 PM EST - 63.4177° N, 18.9974° W

Barbara had never seen the location from her tag come up as "Unknown." The rare occasion had occurred where the satellite would be offline, but in those instances, the system readout was simply that: *Offline*. Even then, it was only because of major solar storms slamming the earth with radiation. No such event occurred today.

She noted the sizable differences in the latitude and longitude of Chelsea's house and the most recent ping of the tracker. An internet search brought up Vik, Iceland as the location. Not even the Concorde could have gotten them to Vik in just under two hours, she knew, and that didn't even take into account the travel time to any airport they could have departed from. What the hell were they riding on?

The idea crossed her mind to bring this information to Blakely and send it up the line to show her allegiance to All

Century. The act of good faith should dispel any notions of where she stood. Yet, despite knowing this, and for reasons she couldn't quite understand, she closed the program and quietly returned to work.

Ω

Baba Yaga and Chelsea watched Dodd as he snored on the down mattress atop a frame any rustic decorator would have killed for.

"He's large, missus. That bed was carved straight out of buloke by a woodsman hundreds of years ago. It still may not hold," the witch said.

"What's the floor made of?" Lilith asked.

"Did you just tell a joke?" Rose asked from the corner, where she applied a salve to itchy spots behind Princess's head. The toad appeared quite grateful, with an expression of half-closed eyes and a lolling tongue.

Lilith shrugged, pleased with herself. Dodd made a choked gurgling sound and woke himself up with a gasp. He seemed surprised to see the women laughing at him.

"Are we close?" he asked.

"Soon to land, oh colossal one. Likely to arrive sometime before the witching hour. A boon for us."

Dodd rolled to his side and peaked over the edge to see Lilith sitting on the ground beside his bed, reading a book. "Whatcha got there?"

"It's a collection of stories entitled *Inferno*," she said. "Oddly enticing."

"Surprised you had the time to grab a book."

"Leonard left his bag in here before he left."

119

Dodd turned to Baba Yaga. "I don't know what this mattress is made from, but I'd do just about anything to get my hands on one just like it. Never slept so good in my life."

"Careful, Dodd. She may well take you up on that offer," Rose said.

"You're no fun, girly. No fun at all," Baba Yaga said with a cackle. "My stores of pickled pancreas have grown lean."

Chelsea gave a cross-eyed glance to the shelved jars of preserved organs and mimed gagging to Rose. She decided it was time to bring them back to the subject at hand. "Why is landing before the witching hour a good thing?"

"The Nisse will be active," Baba Yaga said, motioning for Rose to come closer to the group. "We will need to find one to follow if we hope to find the door to their city."

"Aren't they nearly impossible to find and track?" Chelsea asked.

"Aye, if you don't know where to look." She snapped her fingers to bring Lilith's attention from her book, and the woman sat up without a fuss. The mother of demons even looked the slightest bit interested. Perhaps because the Nisse were not counted amongst her children but born from separate origins, just as the shaitan and jinn. "Nisse will be at work around a farmstead where they find themselves needed. This holds true only if the Nisse have taken a liking to the farm. You'll know their work from that of humans by the telltale etchings they leave. Each has their own signature, you see, but they will look something like this." Baba Yaga took a paintbrush and jar filled with dark fluid from the shelf. She sat at the table, squinting at a paper, and made deliberate strokes that reminded Chelsea of watching planchette writing being performed in China. When Baba

Yaga finished, she held up the paper and pointed to the symbols. "Some examples, these."

"They look like cuneiform," Chelsea said, referring to the first form of written language once found in Mesopotamia.

"A shade older and lost to humans, as far as I know," Baba Yaga said, handing the paper to Rose to discern. She passed it off to Dodd, who took a glance and held it out for Lilith.

"We will land in the trees near some farmland, and you must go about in search of what's been recently mended. With luck, you'll find a symbol and then search the barn for the Nisse," she said. "Be wary of coming upon them at their work. They are flighty or fierce when interrupted, but in either event, catch him. Once in your hands, he will guide you to the door to be bartered for. It is common amongst them for this to occur, or once was."

"And we will ask for the Tinker in exchange?" Dodd asked.

"No, they will not part with it even for the life of one of their own. It is too precious to them," she said. "You will barter with them for entry. Once inside, you must find a way to get them to part with the Tinker."

"Do we have anything at all that can be an equivalent exchange?" Rose asked.

Baba Yaga frowned. "Only my house might entice them, and it likely isn't enough…" They felt the house of brown shudder. "And I will not part with it, as you may have guessed. You must find another way. Luck be with you that you've sharp wits." She nodded toward Dodd. "Even the big one."

He smiled triumphantly and gave a small bow, which Baba Yaga enjoyed.

The house issued a squawk that caused them all to crane

their necks toward the windows. At times, the scenery would be similar to what one might see outside of an airplane window during flight, and at others, it appeared as though they flew through dense fog where nothing outside was more discernible than a dream. Chelsea had commented on this phenomenon, and Rose mentioned the murk that she and David had become familiar with. Now met with a view more like the former, they could see a line of trees growing larger as the house dipped and flew alongside them before landing. It gave a dainty little sidestep inside of the forest for cover.

"Nimble little house," Dodd said. "Does it eat anything? I'd like to get it a treat."

"It does not eat, but enjoys compliments," Rose said. "You probably made its day by saying it was nimble."

Baba Yaga went to a door and opened it to reveal scores of trinkets and items. "Here, Rose," she said. "Take this and sprinkle some about if you find yourselves without luck. The Nisse will leave footprints in the powder." She handed Rose a cloth bag cinched tight with twine.

"We should split into two groups," Dodd said. "Rose with Chelsea, and Lilith with me and Baba Yaga."

"I'll not be coming on your venture, large man," Baba Yaga said.

Lilith wrinkled her nose and tossed her book at Leonard's bag. "And why don't you have to turn over stones looking for gnomes in the dark like we do?"

Baba Yaga's hands flashed, and a smell of rosemary and ozone filled the room. "Simply put, I've a poor relationship with the Nisse. Especially those gallivanting in Denmark."

Lilith leaned forward with a retort but found her lips cinched shut.

Rose understood what had happened. "Baba Yaga, she really should have her voice if we are going to work together out there."

"You'll make do."

"She should have taken the warnings seriously," Chelsea said, gesturing to Princess. "She's certainly seen what can happen if you don't."

The toad made a half hop in Chelsea's direction and croaked. Dodd couldn't be certain, but he thought he knew what the unfortunate creature may have been saying.

"Her voice will rise again with the morning sun. Until that time, enjoy her silence. Now go and find the Nisse so we can leave this land."

Chelsea noted the witch's discomfort and realized she may very well not be welcome here. "Let's go," she said and took Lilith's hand to pull her out. Rose and Dodd followed close behind. Once outside, the house rose upon its feet, shut the door, and backed deeper into the forest before crouching down to hide.

"Let's keep the same setup you suggested, Brendan," Chelsea said. "I work well with Rose, and you can simply annihilate that one if she gets up to no good."

"That's not really my MO, but I get the point," Dodd said.

They walked up a slight incline and looked out upon a moon-bathed view of a large farm among grazing fields, with another not far off in the distance. Rose pointed to the further one. "That one doesn't look equipped for raising animals. It may not take as long to search there."

"This one will have cattle, which means milk," Chelsea said. "The Nisse enjoy it, or so the legends say."

"I feel like moving my body a bit," Dodd said, shaking

out his legs and rolling his shoulders. "We will take the one that is further away."

"Sounds good to me," Rose said.

Lilith made an exaggerated gesture with her arms at the house, followed by some lewd ones with her hands, and Dodd hefted her upon his shoulders like a child. "Chelsea, whistle if you find one. That really loud one you do with the two fingers. If I spot one, I'll fire off some sparks."

Chelsea stood on her toes and gave him a kiss on the cheek. "Be careful."

"See you soon," he said. Dodd bounded away with Lilith as she raged and kicked her feet in the air.

Ω

Michael descended through the clouds and found purchase on the same beach David had recently used for his walks. The scenery proved useful for clearing one's head, and David's muddled mind benefited from the sound of the ocean. Crashing waves and the coming and going of all the people did not draw Michael, though, and the sounds of heavy footfalls soon made apparent his purpose.

"You seek an audience with me, standard bearer?" Odin said.

"It's answers I seek," Michael said. "And you'd be wise to provide them."

The storm named Khao neared the coast of Puri; a cyclone with winds to churn three-meter swells. Odin looked to the south and kneeled to feel the sand. A handful was all he needed to test the wind gusting ashore, and he used what remained to wash his gloves with grit.

"Come," he said and rose into the air. An impossible feat for most, lest you were a member of the Host.

Michael followed.

"The great snake coils in the waters far from here, and she grows stronger by the second. An enemy meant for the prison of your realm until such time as judgment be wrought on these souls. Yet, under your watch, she is loosed."

"I may not watch when I am not there," Odin said. "Jormungandr's escape is no blemish on my name. I also quite dislike thinking of my realm as a prison. I see it more as a proving ground."

Two ravens flanked the Norse god and briefly colluded as he flew ahead of Michael. The angel balked as the large birds departed. "Is there ever a foul purpose without your fingerprints on it, Odin?"

"You may not like me, taxiarch by the name Michael, but I'll remind you it is wise to use respect with those whom you will ask a favor."

"I ask no favors of your ilk," Michael said. "It is obedience to the one fount of all that I demand."

"Michael, you follow me into the storm without fear, knowing it is here above all other places in this realm that I am at the pinnacle of my strength. You've not once ever asked yourself why this is the case, nor what makes me who I am. You've never given a second thought to the existence of the other beings that some humans call gods. All you concern yourself with is your order and what has been passed to you from on high. A righteous way of living, to be sure, but erroneous in the broader context of our existence. Are you so mighty that you may bypass the strongest aspect creation has wrought: thought? Is your fiery sword mightier than the conjurations of the ever-lit mind?"

"I grew tired of being lectured long ago. Words do nothing to help me test my mettle. Let us see how your brawn matches up to mine."

"Fine," Odin said. "But remember that Tyr kneels in obedience to me, and wisdom has won more battles than any mighty arm could dream to."

Michael launched forward and flicked his wings open in a canopy to strike Odin with his feet. The acrobatic display gave the Norse god no cause to move, and he simply lifted his hand to catch the boots of his assailant, flicking them aside and turning his body to face the angel who had twisted his torso in the air to bring the point of his wing down on Odin's helm. The power of the blow sent him reeling through the wind, where he was swallowed by the cloud wall of the cyclone.

"Of course you'd choose to run and hide after a si—" Michael's words were cut short by an arc of lightning from the clouds to his breastplate. Another followed, searing his boots as he spun to avoid it, and from below, a heavily armored hand grasped his ankle and pulled him into Odin's knee.

"For one who hates words, you seem to have used too many," Odin said as he brought his gloved hand down on the angel. Michael barely raised his forearms in time to deflect the blow. "Or is it that you lack the right words to be effective with fewer?"

Michael used his free leg to kick the old god in the chest and leap backward from his grasp. His eyes flared with crimson ichor, and Odin responded in kind.

The angel smiled despite himself. Having not stretched his muscles in such a long time, Michael's true nature came to bear upon his adversary. He flexed his chest and relieved himself of his ornate armor plating to face an incoming bolt of lightning that left no sign of damage on his bare skin.

A cascade of funnel clouds surrounded him, but the angel dispersed them with a flick of his wings. Michael heaved himself toward the center of the storm with gritted teeth and billowed opposite the wind to match its onslaught.

Meteorologists who viewed Doppler radar readings would note the odd change from cyclonic winds to straight-line ones, and how the force of the storm appeared to be stalling or moving south for a few minutes.

"How can the root of your power measure to mine? I am made of the very embers of creation," he said. "You will tell me why the snake is loosed upon this world and what ill-plans you are enacting, remnant, or I will force upon you such misery and plight to make your time hanging from the great tree seem a pleasure."

Odin's smile hid behind his faceplate, but Michael could sense it through the wise god's words. "There is no torture great enough to sacrifice this world, standard bearer. I hung from the tree after casting my eye in Mimir's well and throwing myself upon Gungnir to feel all the pain of gravity's embrace. I then hanged from Yggdrasil, which you call the tree of knowledge. For nine days and nine nights I dwelt in a pit of misery you cannot begin to fathom, and for it I was gifted hands to cure the sick, power to calm storms, and dominion over arms. It is why my warriors may conjure the make of any weapon they choose as they battle for understanding in the fields of Valhalla. It is how their souls remain intact after countless deaths. All in service to the greater good of the creator's will," Odin said with the clouds dispersing behind him. "And what have you done with your great power? Stood vigil at a gate, too frightened to heave your influence upon the dire circumstances down here. I say *you* are the remnant, standard bearer. A remnant of heaven's might, once absolute, now gelded."

Michael raged toward Odin, and the mighty king of Norse gods crouched for his approach. "Tell me, do you have dominion over this weapon?" Michael screamed as he produced his fiery sword. The water in the surrounding air vanished at its heat, and the oceans boiled under their feet. Any stray wisps of cloud vanished, leaving a clear view of the setting sun and waxing moon above.

Odin stepped forward to grasp the weapon in his gloved hand.

"Your wisdom must be fading, All-Father—you've just sealed your fate."

Odin's arm disintegrated under the pressure and power of Michael's sword, but the angel's guard fell for the blow to land. With his other hand, Odin reached up and pulled a handful of the angel's feathers free and placed his foot on the creator's general to push himself away.

Michael remained still, panting in the air and considering what had occurred while Odin placed the feathers in a pouch at his side. His right arm, gone below the elbow, leaked an oily miasma into the air. "We live under the laws of equal exchange, Michael. You've taken my right arm. In exchange, I've liberated you of a handful of feathers. Though we didn't barter for the trade, it is in your favor, I'd say."

Odin turned his head to the water and emitted a whistle that raced across the waves. Sleipnir, the eight-legged horse known to serve as Odin's mount, emerged.

"Your scheming knows no bounds, wretch."

"If you would simply aid the people, there'd be no need to plot, but that is not our reality," Odin said as Sleipnir settled beneath him and made ready to fly off. "There are those who've taken up the courage to make a stand and choose a side. Have you considered the possibility of *that* being the creator's will?"

Michael, through with words, made ready to charge Odin and test Sleipnir's speed against his own. An unkindness of ravens emerged from the sky, flanked by the two larger Huginn and Muninn, who flew to Odin. The smaller birds encircled and harassed Michael, who batted them with his sword and cursed them.

Muninn grasped the pouch containing Michael's feathers and flew off in the confusion as Sleipnir raced toward the stalled storm in the south. By the time Michael flared his sword to turn the birds about him to cinder, Odin had fled and the angel stood alone.

CHAPTER 6
THE TINKER

Dodd leaped the exterior fence of the farm and trotted along the grazing fields. The soil here was rich, but the ground was littered with rocky protrusions from boulders far too large to move without great expense. He skipped among them like a child at play while Lilith beat his back with her tiny fists.

"Oh, come on. You can't tell me you aren't enjoying the ride a little," he said, putting her down.

She scowled at him and mimed a scream that made veins bulge from her forehead.

"I guess you couldn't tell me if you wanted to," he said, causing her rage to heighten. "Alright, take it easy. You're mortal now. You could give yourself a stroke."

Lilith turned her back to him and marched through the field toward where cattle grazed.

"You're no fun, but I guess I already knew that," Dodd said. "Being a vengeful witch lady and all."

Dodd let her go and circled around the field, checking the fence for recent repairs and finding none. He doubled back through in a question mark pattern to ensure he didn't miss any ground, and as he made his way, he saw Lilith had stopped at the cattle. She gently stroked the pelt of an old milking cow.

"Didn't figure you for an animal lover," Dodd said.

She turned to him, and he saw a forlorn look in her eyes.

"Did you ever stop to pet the cows when you were hellbent on killing everyone?" Dodd asked.

Lilith turned back to the cow, defanged, unable to snap a witty retort, ultimately defeated and at the mercy of those she had wronged. She thought about her past in the garden and her reasons for fleeing. She felt validated in them no matter how righteous the creator might be, but she had no interest in bending to the whims of *any* being. Her current cohort included.

Her time with them had made her lament on her actions after fleeing Eden. Being forced to devour the life and potential of newborns and littering the planet with children to terrorize Adam's kin was wrong. She knew that then, and she felt it now as she her mind had grown still and silent enough to listen to her now-beating heart.

To take the time to admit this to them was a bridge too far for her. Even through the kinship and friendliness Rose had shown her, she couldn't bear to utter the two words she knew she should to the girl who'd spared her life after she'd torn hers to shreds. Maybe that was the true reason Baba Yaga had muted her for the night—because she hadn't used her voice for that single utterance. Or maybe the old bitch just hated her. Either way, it shouldn't be so hard to utter just two words when they were justly called for. She thought of them as she ran her hand down the pelt of the cow.

I'm sorry.

Ω

"Rose," Chelsea whispered. "Is this something?"

Rose left the side of a well lined with worn stones and joined Chelsea at a small lean-to that covered firewood. The post was comprised of stripped and preserved Norway spruce wood with curious marks at the bottom.

"Cat scratches," Rose said. "Look here at the bottom." Rose pointed to the mound of dirt the cats were using as their litter box.

"Charming," Chelsea said. "Wait, do the cats hunt Nisse?"

"Not if they know what's good for them. Baba Yaga doesn't shy away from many things, but with all forms of the *good folk*, she takes great care. She told me the Nisse have been diluted in common folklore, and now they're equated as elves to be treated with at Christmas time, but I think they must be much more dangerous than you'd think at first glance."

Chelsea nodded. "There are legends of them killing livestock if wronged. Not many where they outright murder people like Lilith's children do, though. A more passive-aggressive folk than demons, I guess."

Rose kicked more dirt on top of the mound of cat droppings. "Let's check inside the barn."

Chelsea turned on her heel and marched toward the barn. It was built differently than what she might have expected from a dairy barn near where she lived in New York. There was no second story hayloft, and absent were the telltale doors that went along with them. The barn door rolled upon iron ball bearings but flowed smoothly, and both women crept inside.

Rose made her way through the darkness and relied on

moonlight shining through slats in the boards to guide her. Chelsea found her older eyes had far more trouble, and she felt around in the darkness for any etchings in the wood before kicking a pig trough with her shin.

"Shit!" she hissed as something in the trough tumbled around.

Rose heard and crept nearer before sprinkling seeds on the earthen floor of the barn and placing her hands upon them. Vines sprang from the ground and quickly covered the trough in a canopy.

"Did you get one?" Chelsea asked as she peered through the top at two glowing yellow eyes. The cat inside issued a mew, and Rose gushed.

"Good kitty," she said and pulled a hole in the vines for the cat to leave.

They searched on through the moonlit night.

Ω

Barbara packed up her things and locked her office. She had made a habit of working later than most of the others at All Century, but tonight was extreme, even for her. The others peeled off in the midafternoon and walked to their respective homes on the property. Many would put the finishing touches on their nightcaps about now and get ready to nestle into cozy beds to rest for a new day.

Barbara's cozy bed did not entice her in the slightest. The idea of returning to her home revolted her after the intrusion of feral goblins, and she had put in extra hours to build courage for the ordeal. Her plan now was to find a local hotel and spend the night. Tomorrow, she could go off and find clothes for the rest of the week. It was only upon entering the parking garage she remembered her car wasn't here. Blakely had taken her to work.

She had just opened her phone and started looking for a car service app when the engine of a beat-up hatchback kicked over in the garage and startled her. Barbara held up her hand to shield her eyes from its lights as it idled to her and the window lowered.

"Can I offer you a ride?" Leonard asked.

"Kidnapping is a serious offense. Are you sure you want to commit it twice in seventy-two hours?"

"The first was a rescue, and I'm confident a jury of my peers would see it that way." Leonard pushed his glasses up from the bridge of his nose. "And this time I'm asking."

"You'd be surprised what All Century can make a jury think," she said and put her phone away. "I must be crazy, but yeah, I'll take a ride."

"You aren't crazy. Just like I'm not crazy for coming to talk to you again. There's something bigger at work, and we both know it."

Barbara circled the car and got inside. "You believe that? Do you think fate sent you, Leonard? If you really do, I'd be better off walking than riding with a lunatic."

"Not that. More like a big wheel turning, and we are along for the ride. I've felt that way since this all started. To be honest, I never wanted to be involved in anything like this for my entire life. Always been too afraid."

"That's a big surprise."

Leonard put the car in drive and rolled out of the garage.

"How'd you get in past the security booth?"

"You'll never believe it, but I made a fake pass exactly like the first one, and they sent me right through. I sort of knew they would, but part of me couldn't believe how lax things are here."

"We no longer do R&D at this site, and the angel isn't here anymore. Nobody worth a damn cares. We are just pushing paper over here, working in proxy for the news division."

"Pulse24 is the reason I came back to speak with you." Leonard took his gaze off the road to look directly at her, and Barbara had trouble meeting his eyes. "You guys are setting things up for a big fall. It's not the wars between nations Flueric is after, it's the wars in the streets he wants."

"I honestly don't know what his endgame is. He's upped the ante from what me or Blakely originally signed up for."

"You aren't comfortable with it anymore, are you?"

"Listen, I appreciate the ride, but we aren't bosom buddies, Leonard." She played with dirt on the floor mat with her toes. "You can drop me at the Hyatt or the Marriott down the road. Just take a right on Mill Plain Road."

Leonard made a turn in the correct direction but said, "No, I'm not taking that. You recognize what you're doing is wrong, and I'm here to tell you that it isn't too late for redemption."

"And how does a—what did Chelsea call me again?"

"A tramp."

Barbara pulled her shirt loose in the front and slouched in the seat. "How does a tramp find redemption?"

"I'm not sure. Not sure what a tramp really looks like or if you are one, either," Leonard laughed.

"It's someone who gets around, boy scout."

"I guess if you help us, you would make good on that and be a tramp."

Barbara looked at him. "Are you seriously just an honest-to-goodness nice person?"

"I think so. Rose once told me I was."

Leonard switched his turn signal on to turn into the hotel parking lot, and Barbara pointed ahead. "Keep going. I want to get a bite to eat." Leonard continued through a green traffic light as he was bid.

"I think she is right. I don't know much about all of you, but I'm a pretty good judge of character," Barbara said.

"They've been suspicious of you at All Century, haven't they?"

"Was that part of your plan when you spirited me away? Divide and conquer?" She pointed to a diner, and he turned in.

"We rarely conquer our adversaries over bacon and eggs."

"How'd you know I wanted breakfast?"

"Only a sadist goes to a diner at this hour for anything else."

"Not true. If we were drunk, we'd be eligible for greasy disgusting food."

"As mentioned, only a sadist."

"You don't drink?"

"Not often." Leonard blushed as he always did when made to feel childlike. "I do try some of Chelsea and Dodd's whiskey from time to time, but hangovers are the worst."

"That's refreshing," Barbara said and stepped out of the car to enter the diner. Leonard smiled and followed her up the ramp to enter the chromed building. The interior was the archetypal diner, and exactly what Barbara sought. "Sanctuary, Leonard. Sanctuary."

"Can't get us, we've got base. That sort of thing?"

"Kind of, except we are in plain sight and I'm not in danger. I just feel like I am."

"You experienced a traumatic event. That doesn't just get resolved overnight," Leonard said, turning to the old Greek woman behind the cash register. "Two, please."

"Follow," said the matron.

"I half expected her to be a Gorgon and turn you to stone."

"Now there's a stereotypical monster I hope we don't run into. Being forever petrified and trapped, unable to move beyond… that is a terrifying prospect."

"If there even *is* a beyond," Barbara said, hiding behind her menu.

Leonard chuckled. "If you are tormented by anything, that should be the one you get over quickly. David and Rose are definitive proof of an afterlife. Maybe not an *ever* after, but definitely an after. We also pal around with the angel of death."

"Well, *you* believe that, Leonard. I wasn't there," Barbara said, laying the menu down and motioning for coffees to be brought. "I was busy running logistics on the HOVAS program while you guys endured that saga."

"The existence of angels isn't enough for you?"

"Always thought they were really aliens, actually," Barbara said. "I never did get a chance to see them up close. The HOVAS, them I got to see. See and smell. Yuck."

"You're pulling my leg now."

Barbara shrugged and ordered a large breakfast platter after their coffees arrived. Leonard ordered a meager bagel with butter to nibble on.

"Why are you so fixated on Pulse24?" she asked.

Leonard's eyes perked open as he sipped his extra-sweetened coffee. "It's where all the attention is heading within All Century."

"How do you know that?"

"Communications through the servers have been referencing and directly connecting with that division three-hundred and eighty percent more now than when I first started to snoop on the company. More and more, other divisions are being poached and their manpower redirected to it—like yours, by the way—and the writing is on the wall from this end. Open your phone and it won't be three seconds before Pulse24 hits you with a news update or meme on some social media app."

"And Blakely thinks we are keeping tabs on you guys," Barbara laughed. "You're the one with the upper hand."

"Watching you watching me watching you, yes," Leonard said. "I've had some help from David. He's something of a tech phenom now."

"Oh, I see. And I just have to ask again, so please humor me, Mr. Handsome Geek, but what makes you think I won't just run back to All Century and Blakey to tell them all of this?"

"They won't care," Leonard said. Barbara noted he wasn't bluffing. "They believe they can't lose at this point and neither you, nor we, have any sway over that. Can't you tell by the way they are acting? You don't matter, and neither does our information."

"If you say so."

"I do. The sooner you learn that I'm right, the better," Leonard said as he tapped his mug with a spoon to force her to glance at him. "They've set the board of play and hit the button, Barbara. The pieces will fall where they may. There's no going back now."

"You're far too dramatic."

"And I think you're just in denial because you feel guilty for your hand in all this," Leonard said, earning a scowl from her. "It's not too late to help the good guys."

"Being the good guys is subjective. Every villain in history has considered themselves righteous or good in some way."

"Do you think Flueric thinks he's good?"

"No, but he is definitely self righteous. No questioning that," Barbara said. She began looking around the diner at other patrons.

"Does he keep tabs on you?"

"We can never tell, but he always seems to know what we are thinking during our meetings," Barbara said. "It keeps us in line."

Leonard made to reach for her hand, but the waiter brought out their food, and they lifted their arms to make room. Barbara immersed herself in the meal while Leonard pushed his bagel around the saucer plate and contemplated Barbara's role in his plan. He tore a piece of the paper menu and used a red crayon to write his number.

"We could use your help with Pulse24," Leonard said, sliding the paper toward her. "But we plan to defy Flueric one way or another, even if the news division is left untouched." He pushed his glasses up and sat back with his arms crossed. "Why don't you think about it tonight and get in touch with me tomorrow."

Leonard slid to the side of the booth as if to go.

"You're leaving?"

"The hotel is three buildings down, and there are well-lit sidewalks. You'll be safe."

Barbara stared at her plate for a few seconds and grabbed

Leonard's arm as he passed her side of the booth. "Don't leave. I know the rest of your crew are out of town, so to speak. Can you stay with me a bit longer?"

Leonard blinked down at her. "I wonder how you figured that out so quickly."

"The company uses surveillance on Chelsea's house. Satellites, infrared, and on and on, but all they know is that you're all gone. They don't seem to care that much at this point. Probably because you're right about them thinking they've already won."

"It sounds like *you* know a bit more than the rest."

She gestured for him to sit and sighed. "I do. I put a tracker in your duffel bag. They're in Denmark," Barbara said, and Leonard saw her eyes gloss over. "Please don't be mad. I didn't know as much about you after I woke up, and I did it out of impulse. It's not like I could just tell you after I left, and I got curious. I never told anyone else at the company where they are."

"It wouldn't matter much if they knew," Leonard said. "They'd never put together why they went to Denmark fast enough to do anything. The worst that could happen would be Flueric showing up, and he wouldn't bother. He sees us as flies."

"Even David, since he played perfectly into Flueric's plan."

"Exactly," Leonard sighed and relaxed into the red cushion of the booth. "You know, Rose almost died in a place like this."

"Yes, I learned that, though the intel we have about Lilith's children is sparse, we have pretty easy access to police records."

"Those monsters are mostly feral beasts now, anyway.

They were never part of what you guys are doing, but their release was a convenient phenomenon to use as an excuse to deploy the HOVAS on US soil without public backlash."

"It was the perfect test of how Pulse24 can spin the truth," Barbara said. "The fact is that we have a direct line to the hearts and minds of just under half the people on this planet. The other half see the truth, but they can't do a thing in the face of our people. It's a perfect plan for divisive politics."

"And you don't know what Flueric's endgame is in all of this?" Leonard asked.

"No, but I'm convinced whatever he aims to do will involve the death of millions of people." Leonard let his eyes drift to the window, and he watched the insects hover around a streetlight, drawn to it from the darkness of what to them must feel like an eternal night. She added, "I have more information for Pulse at my house, but I'm not going back."

Leonard brought his eyes back to the present. "I'll go with you."

"You aren't the one with superpowers."

"We don't need someone with superpowers, Barbara. We just need friends. I should know, I didn't have any until recently. It's made all the difference."

Ω

David produced the map he'd been given and double checked his location. He stood in front of a large building with medical response vehicles parked out front. The people coming and going largely wore face masks and carried with them aromatic bouquets of herbs and flowers, signifying to him that there was illness and death waiting inside.

Resonance of an energy emanated from the building, but it was thinned, a paradoxical occurrence and one David hadn't yet encountered. Certain the one he sought was inside, David mounted the stairs and entered. Nobody challenged him as he bypassed staff and continued walking the halls, letting his sense be his guide. India had been revelatory for him, as it was his first time visiting the country. The areas of poverty were as he'd expected them to be: packed with people, rampant with disease, yet filled with the upbeat optimism found only through faith. The more developed sections, far more numerous than he'd expected, were well laid and maintained. This building belonged to the latter, but nestled itself within the outskirts of a slum. Many inside received hospice care—the young and the old alike, for circumstance and luck are fickle with their gifts when people fall irreparably ill, and it never quite seems fair who the black finger of fate may land upon.

David entered the room where he felt the energy pulse. He was surprised to find that it came not from some object, but a man. Vajra sat up in a bed of white linens near a window open to the outside. His room didn't smell of death like so many of the others David had passed, but it was clear the man before him was ill. Though sunken deep into his skull, vibrant orange-yellow eyes set upon the boy as he settled in a meager armchair.

"I felt you," Vajra said. "The moment you laid foot on our soil, I felt you."

"Am I welcome?" David asked.

"Your type has never much cared if you are welcome, so come as you will."

"I'm not British," David said, assuming this was a reference to the imperialistic occupation India had endured.

"You're American. Same sheep with otherwise dyed wool."

"I'm a human. Any wool I had has been shaved."

"This may be an interesting conversation," Vajra said, closing his eyes. "You have my blessing."

David sat back and crossed his legs. "Do you know who I am?"

"Yes. Or at least, I know what you are."

"I'm not a member of the Host."

"Then I haven't the slightest idea, because you look like a duck." Vajra adjusted himself in his bed and grimaced. "You sound like a duck. But you don't fly like a duck?"

"That's about the gist of it, yeah," David said. "You know, I don't believe I've ever seen a god show signs of sickness."

"I am no god. My land is engulfed in the spoils of taint. The air is filth, the water is poison, and the food is riddled with toxins. It has made me grow ill."

David considered the other celestials he had met and wondered about their healthy states.

"It only affects us if we are in the world of the living," Vajra said, as though reading David's mind. "And rooted in the power of the cosmos, as I am."

"Ah, that makes sense. Why do you stay around, then?"

"You seem to misunderstand what I am, David. I am a tool. A symbol."

David looked over his taut skin and thin wisps of hair. "You look very alive to me."

"I am alive only as the tenets of belief allow."

"Your health problems may have more to do with that than the toxic land."

Vajra looked away from the window and to David. "You

may be wiser than I'd first thought. Tell me, is the Buddha about at this time?"

"I haven't seen him. Unless you're talking about the guy I was with. He goes by Yehuda."

"He is not the Buddha, but he is about as close as you may find otherwise," Vajra said. "Indra might be more called for. He is better when the people aren't behaving."

"I've come here for you, Vajra. Yehuda and Indra can't help now. There's a great evil at work turning the world against itself." David adjusted himself in the chair and saw Vajra glancing at his chest. "Is there something about me that bothers you?"

"Not you, but you have something inside that isn't natural to you. It churns and gathers power while you carry on here and there. I can hear it whispering to me about you like a child telling tales of his sibling."

David pulled his collar down and looked at his chest, half expecting to see it glowing like E.T.'s belly, but he was disappointed. His skin was as plain and bare as the day he awoke from his coma.

A nurse glided inside and gave David a sidelong glance as she attended to Vajra's needs. There was no beeping heart-rate monitor in the room nor IV drip leading to the avatar's wrist, just the fussing of dedicated caretakers and a calm environment for send-off.

"How long have you been here?" David asked.

The nurse replied, "He's been here longer than any other patient we have helped. Approximately seven months, and with little to no change in his condition."

"I've been sick for far longer."

"I see," David said. "What will you do with him?"

"He has been in luck," she said, motioning to the side of the room where she met David to whisper. "There are enough beds for the dying, but this is not often the case. Should more come, he will be ushered out as a man capable of caring for himself. I had hoped you were family, but clearly…" She motioned to David's white hands. "You may have to take him if you are around when he leaves."

"Let's hope this doesn't happen," David said. "I probably won't be staying very long. Why are you worried the beds will be full soon?"

"Wander the streets for an hour and return. If you do not stumble upon death in your travels, I will give you my day's pay."

David whistled through his teeth. "I get the point. Keep your pay. In fact…" He reached into his pocket and produced a billfold. Peeling a few from the top, he said, "Take this for your troubles." As she took the money and turned to leave, he tapped her shoulder. "And take the rest to put toward the needs of this place."

"You have too much trust, stranger."

"No. I know a woman who gently guides those to their glory wouldn't likely pick through the coffers of her hospital," David said.

She left the room as gracefully as she had entered, and David returned to Vajra's side.

"Didn't Yehuda teach you that you can't bribe your way to enlightenment?" he said.

"No, he taught me I can't rush my way to it, which is probably the same thing. It was my mother who taught me to help whenever and wherever I can. So I did," David said.

"The thing inside of you may whisper truths, after all," Vajra said, turning to his side and settling. "I need rest now."

With that, David saw the man fall into a deep sleep. In the distance, the sounds of thunder rolled through the sky to warn the people of nature's fury.

Ω

Leonard pulled into Barbara's wide driveway, careful to avoid the Belgium blocks lining either side, and left the car running.

"It's dark in there," she said. "I'm not sure I want to do this."

"Don't you have one of those voice-activated home assistants to turn on the lights?"

Barbara laughed. "No. When you work for a company that the routinely encroaches on the Fourteenth Amendment, you learn to keep the ears off inside of your own home. I'm actually surprised you didn't already know what tech I have."

"We aren't snooping all over your personal life, just the company as a whole." Leonard looked at the house and felt something ominous. "Did All Century send a crew to clean the house up?"

"Yes," Barbara said. "Blakely mentioned something to that effect. Things should be tip top in there."

"I wonder if there still aren't any ears in there now," Leonard said as he reached into the back seat for a square case.

"What's that?" Barbara asked as he undid the clasps.

"This is a little kit I made. It has an infrared scanner, which would tell us if anything with heat is inside."

"Not all the ghouls and goblins give off heat signatures," Barbara said, thinking of their drone deployments over Virginia. Many of the HOVAS fought adversaries that could not be seen on infrared.

"True, but the ones that came for you do, and I can't imagine there being another child of Lilith in the house if it was a random encounter. Their numbers have thinned quite a bit. It's not only guys like Detective Dodd that can massacre them for us anymore, either. With Lilith out of the picture, her children are true cryptids, and most die well enough from bullets."

Barbara seemed satisfied by this explanation and nearly asked about Lilith. Her concern about her home trumped her curiosity about the mother of demons. "And the other stuff?" she asked, leaning to peer into the box on Leonard's lap. Her closeness and posture sent a thrill through him that he wasn't expecting, and as though on cue, she looked up at him, realizing his shyness. "First time having a girl in Mom's car, Leonard?"

He ignored the question and looked into the box. "I have other stuff in here, but the thing you'll want to bring with you is this." He pulled a device from within that looked like a makeshift Geiger counter. "It sweeps for electronic listening devices and cameras."

"You think they bugged my house?" she asked, leaning back into her own seat.

"Doesn't matter what I think. It's your own peace of mind you are looking after."

She pondered this for a second while he scanned the house with the infrared reader. It was cool except for the boiler in the basement and a few other objects that ran a bit hotter than room temp. "Is that bug scanner easy to use?"

"Sure, you just hold the wand out and sweep it around like this." Leonard mimed the motion with the wand. "Then, if there's something to worry about, this meter will tick up.

You'll have to be careful of false readings, though, and they can happen around bundles of wires in the walls, but you can tell if you check this spot right here—"

"You're coming in and using that."

"Why? I just showed you that it's super easy to use."

"I'm no dummy, but I know I won't be as thorough with that thing as you can be, and now I won't get a lick of sleep tonight until I'm sure there isn't an egghead in All Century watching me."

Leonard sighed. "You were going to try to get me to come in anyway, weren't you? I thought you were going to bring me a file or something."

"You'll never know now, buddy," she said, flashing a smile and exiting the car.

Leonard keyed the ignition off and followed her out, holding the briefcase in front of him like some disenchanted bellhop. Barbara walked up the flagstone pavers to her front door and waited. "Chop chop, Alfred. Shouldn't leave a lady waiting."

They entered the house, and Barbara flipped on the lights. She motioned for him to follow as she illuminated the rest of the home. "How long do you think it will take to check the entire house?"

Leonard placed the case down on her kitchen counter with a grunt. "Maybe an hour, but I like to go slow. I've seen some crazy things on the internet. Drones as small as a housefly and so on. I'm sure All Century's R&D made some intricate things."

"We don't use the housefly. A girl I was seeing told me people will hunt those down far too much because, well, people hate houseflies."

"Oh, that actually makes a lot of sense."

"That I date girls too?"

"No, the housefly thing. I don't really care who people spend their time with, unless the person is mean to them or something."sg Barbara took a long look at Leonard, and he added, "I, uh, better get started. I'm getting tired."

"Good idea," she said. "I'm going to pour something. It's been a day, Leonard. A long, long day."

"While I sweep, can you check on where Chelsea, Rose, and Dodd are?" Leonard called back from the hall.

The sound of glasses tinging together in the kitchen carried through the hall. "Sure."

Leonard swept the wand of the device throughout the first floor and found nothing. The second floor yielded some interesting finds, but the device's electromagnetic detector remained well within levels below suspicious activity. He returned to the kitchen and found Barbara at her laptop with a glass of whiskey within close reach. She nodded to another she'd arranged next to her. "Drink up. You've earned it."

"One sec, I have to check here first," he said as he walked through the kitchen and wanded the appliances. Barbara watched him with keen interest and returned to her task on the laptop, only to glance whenever the device made a clicking sound. "It looks good in here, too."

"Okay, thank you. I didn't think they'd have much cause to bug me, but you can never tell with Flueric... I guess Blakely now, too."

Leonard sat and motioned for the laptop, and Barbara motioned to his whiskey. "It's a Manhattan. You said you've tried whiskey, and this is a good bottle. Let it take the edge off while I finish checking for the location of the tag."

Leonard lifted the glass and smelled the contents. He'd tried whiskey but didn't love the harsh taste, like Chelsea or Dodd. This had a sweet aroma that promised a lighter touch than he'd been expecting. He took a small sip and found he enjoyed it.

"See, they're tasty. I thought you'd enjoy the vermouth," Barbara said, spinning the laptop to face Leonard. "It looks like your friends are in the same spot in Denmark."

Leonard pulled the laptop close and explored the map. Barbara was telling the truth about trying to bug him, and despite the seemingly treacherous nature of such an act, her coming clean without first being outed made him feel better. "Do you mind if I do a quick sweep of your laptop to make sure there isn't any malware?"

"Why not?" Barbara said, topping her glass off to just above the ice cube.

Leonard produced a flash drive from his case and inserted it into her laptop then typed a few keys and sat back.

"That easy?" she said.

"That easy," he replied, taking more of the beverage. "The hard part is writing the code and setting up the executable functions. Once you get that out of the way, it's pretty smooth."

She nodded, stood, and opened the refrigerator and to retrieve more cherries to garnish her drink. Both looked to each other, bewildered, as Leonard's bug detector went haywire.

"What the hell is that?" Barbara asked, closing the refrigerator.

Leonard put his finger to his lips and grabbed up the detector. It guided him to the recessed lighting above the center island in Barbara's kitchen, and he pulled down the cover to reveal a small microphone ensconced within. He motioned for quiet again and joined her at the refrigerator, where he quickly dismantled the main board governing the appliance. Within, he found a small dongle with three wires soldered to the board and removed them, taking care to keep the board intact. He replaced it and said, "Okay, it's off, you can talk now."

"I get the idea of what just happened, but what the actual hell, Leonard?" she said. "Did they really set it to start recording after opening the fridge?"

"Looks that way. I would say they did it to preserve battery life, but both were wired directly into your home's electricity. I suggest we go through the house and turn everything on and sweep the rest."

They moved through her house and found four more listening devices and one camera set up in the vanity area of her bedroom that activated when the hot water in her master bath was turned on.

"They power off without motion or sound after a few minutes," Leonard said. "It's kind of genius."

"Yeah, thrilling technological advancements, bud," Barbara said.

The duo made their way through the house a second time and then throughout the yard to be sure there weren't any more bugs before returning to the kitchen.

"You going to work tomorrow?" he asked.

"I think I have to, even though they'll know I cleared these things out. I'm not sure how they'll play it, but what choice do I have?"

"We were careful enough to avoid being recorded tonight,

so they may just assume the equipment was installed poorly."

"Doubtful. The quality control these days comes with the unspoken threat of imminent death. I'm sure the team knows they handled things perfectly."

Leonard drained the now watered-down drink and looked at his watch. "I better get going."

"Not a chance. You're bunking here with me," she said.

He looked to the living room. "I had a feeling you'd say that. The cloud couch looks pretty comfortable. I could stay—"

Barbara cut him off by pushing him up against the cabinets to deliver a forceful kiss.

When they separated, he gave her a bewildered look. She reached up and gently removed his glasses before coming close to brush her lips against his neck, and Leonard sighed deeply. He started to push her away, ready to explain that they shouldn't be doing this or that she was acting out her intense emotions from her traumatic experience, but he quickly swallowed his words and pulled her back for a kiss of his own.

"Not bad, Leonard," she said, pulling his shirt up from his pants to reveal his toned midsection. "I knew it!" She smiled, cocking her head and replacing the glasses on his face. "Yeah, that's better."

Leonard had the presence of mind to place his whiskey on the counter as she pulled him to the stairs, and he wondered just how mad Chelsea was going to be at him when she found out.

Ω

Rose and Chelsea crept through the barn until they were satisfied that no evidence of the Nisse was present. As they exited the building, Rose triggered a motion-sensing floodlight and rushed to the shadows to conceal herself, but the jig was up. Lights sprang to life from within the home, and a few moments later, an older woman in a nightdress stepped outside with a heavy wooden cane.

Chelsea moved into the light with her arms out and palms up. "Miss, do you speak English?"

The woman stepped down the stairs and looked left and right before answering. "Enough of it."

"I'm sorry we are intruding on your property. The truth is, we are looking for something. Something special."

"Who is *we*?" the woman asked.

"I'm the rest of we," Rose said as she came forward. "We have two other friends looking on your neighbor's farm."

"Then they are Aksel's problem," she said, motioning her head in that direction. "That's his land. You ladies are my problem, yes?"

"I wouldn't say it like that," Chelsea said.

"You are here to steal the chickens?" she asked, hefting the cane and slapping it against her palm.

"No, but ma'am, would we tell you if we were?" Rose asked the woman, who raised her eyebrow at the notion. "Listen, it sounds strange, but we are here to find the Nisse."

The woman came forward a few more paces and thumped the cane down in the soil as she hissed. "We do not speak of them, and we do not seek them, stupid interlopers. They'll be your end."

"What is your name, ma'am?"

"I am Alberte," she said.

"What if I told you that I am a witch?"

"Rose, careful now," Chelsea said.

"No, it's true," Rose said. "I'm a witch who will curse you to the end of time if you don't help us."

Alberte balked. "Leave my property now, before I take this thumper to your empty head."

Rose kneeled and touched the ground, causing the grass to stir about Alberte's feet and vines to tendril up her cane and sprout thorns before flowering in a beautiful assortment of colors. "Alberte, we mean you no harm and do sincerely apologize for intruding, but I promise you that no hen will lay an egg on this farm and all your milk will be taken for gall for three generations if you don't tell us the best place to search out the Nisse."

Alberte stepped away from the cane with mouth agape. She looked to Rose and placed her hands out before her as if to block the girl's power. "They come at night when the moon is full. I've never seen one in all my years here, and this is where I was born and raised. It is where I'll die as well. I don't expect to see a single one before the day I leave this world, but I have seen sign of them. My husband once thought they made their home among the large rocks beneath Aksel's land in the great fields there."

She pointed out behind them, where Dodd and Lilith had headed.

Both Chelsea and Rose looked at one another, and Chelsea said, "Head inside, Alberte, and thank you for your help. Is there anything here you grow that can help you? The girl will ensure you have more than you've ever needed."

"Beets," Alberte said. "We sell the sugar for money."

"Very good," Chelsea said. "We will leave now."

Alberte retreated inside, and Rose suspected she would keep a watchful eye on them as they stepped through her fields toward Aksel's. At roughly the middle portion of the field, Rose kneeled again to feel the firm ground. All about them sprang mounds and leafy heads from a bounty of beets the likes of which Alberte had probably never seen. Chelsea imagined the woman bringing them to market in great barrels with a smarmy smile on her face, and it made her feel better for having scared the poor old woman.

"Can you really place curses on people now?" Chelsea said.

"I doubt it, but I can definitely still bluff better than Dodd ever could," Rose said with a smile.

"*Milk for gall*! You're too much, Rose."

Both looked up as sparks flew into the air over in Aksel's farm.

"Looks like they've turned something up," Rose said. "We'd better get over there before Dodd accidentally squishes one of them."

"He'd better not, or I'll squish him."

Alberte watched from behind a sliver of glass as the women receded into the moonlight. She considered calling for help or waking up her husband, but she knew they'd be of no use in the face of such fearsome women.

Ω

"Listen, we gotta go over there and check out around the barn. Time is ticking, and we want to find one of these squirrely little guys before the sun comes up," Dodd said, setting down a tractor he'd hefted to peer under.

Lilith nodded and went ahead of him. He was impressed with how vigorously she'd been searching over the last hour. It may have been that she was simply bored, or that she wanted something from the Nisse themselves, but Dodd thought she enjoyed feeling useful after having had her ordeal. It wasn't a simple thing to be stripped of who you were. He saw that when he looked into Ramirez's eyes in Virginia, and he remembered it after waking up outside of All Century finding that he'd been forever changed.

Dodd watched her go on ahead and continued to search the barn area. His instincts guided him to inspect around the building rather than enter it. Pavers sparkled in what remained of the fading moonlight, and he noted the farmer must have set them around the water pump he used to fill the troughs for his animals. The pavers themselves were in disrepair, with many having been displaced over time by water runoff or rising earth.

Lilith appeared beneath his left arm and pulled his sleeve while pointing with the other hand. Dodd looked around and noted the bowls laid around the building. The farmer had left tributes to the Nisse, hoping they'd get to work fixing his pavers. Lilith gestured harder with a look of frustration, and Dodd saw the pavers moved ever so slightly on the far side of their arrangement.

"I'll be damned, it worked," Dodd whispered.

Lilith shot him an intense glare with a meaning Dodd had been well familiar with prior to meeting the muted mother of demons: *Shut the hell up, idiot!*

Dodd motioned for her to circle around the barn and flush the Nisse toward the direction of the field, and Lilith understood his nonverbal cues well enough. She crouched and stepped softly, disappearing around the far side of the barn. Dodd smiled again and hoped she'd be half this fun after regaining her voice.

He remained stone still until Lilith emerged from the corner and stepped toward the pavers. The effect turned out exactly as predicted. Two small Nisse erupted from the pavers and zipped toward the fields far faster than Dodd would have expected. He sprang into motion and angled toward them. Had he been smaller, he may have grasped one at that exact moment, but the nearest spotted his shadow moving along the ground and instinctively leapt to the left in an impressive juke to ensure it didn't miss a stride. Dodd saw the expression of its compatriot as it looked back to see Dodd in close pursuit. He wagered they were not used to seeing a human move at this speed. Especially one the size of Dodd.

They put on more speed in response, and Dodd continued to sprint after them.

He hoped his limitless stamina might wear them down, but they leaped through the field and bounded between the rocks, letting Dodd practice the same movements he'd been enjoying earlier in the evening. From rock to rock they'd leap and circle then surge on, but neither of the Nisse ever left the other to split up, which made Dodd wonder if this was a particular strategy or if they were too afraid to strike out alone knowing there was at least one more human in pursuit.

Dodd kept his composure and enjoyed the game of cat and mouse, never allowing the Nisse to shake him from their trail for very long. Lilith appeared as though she was moving in slow motion as she made her way through the field toward them. She moved too slow, and he couldn't hope to use her to cut them off.

They didn't double back this time, and they clearly had a set destination in mind. He needed to get his hands on one and soon, or he might lose them for good.

One of the Nisse jumped atop a large boulder, and Dodd had enough time to see a small etching on the stone. The tiny member of the good folk quickly produced a hammer and rapped on it in specific places, producing an interesting assortment of hollow and full notes causing a trapdoor to open in the rocky outcrop beside them.

Dodd saw the opening in the ground and headed for it instead of chasing the Nisse, but he knew it would be a photo finish to beat them to the opening to what was no doubt their secret world beneath his own. The Nisse interwove between one another as they ran to sanctuary, but he didn't take the bait to reach for one, knowing it would cost him precious inches of ground should he miss.

"We mean you no harm," he said, continuing his chase, and one of the Nisse smiled at him, telling Dodd that they didn't much care what he meant for them. They weren't in the habit of finding out.

With a final leaping bound, Dodd launched himself through the air and surprised the small creatures once more by putting on an increase in speed they hadn't thought possible. Having chosen to dive, Dodd flew too far over the nearest Nisse and could not grab him, though he knocked the hat off of the fellow's head. The second disappeared within a small, cavernous hollow that had opened between two rocks, and Dodd expected the other to follow in an instant.

The little fellow uttered a mew of defeat from behind him, and Dodd turned to see his ankle had become ensnared by a tangle of dandelion flowers. Dodd approached quickly but ensured his movements were gentle while reaching to grasp the Nisse by his waist and lift him off the ground. The hollow shut to the night and appeared as a normal rock outcrop once more, but a keen ear would hear mournful cries from within.

Lilith approached, placed the green coned hat atop the Nisse's head, and gave his arm a little pat as she fought to catch her breath.

Chelsea and Rose arrived from the side. "You got him?"

"Only thanks to you. I used all my best moves, and these suckers still gave me the slip over and over."

"Don't feel bad, your gridiron glory days aren't all behind you, big guy," Rose said, appreciating Lilith's smile at Dodd's expense.

"Watching him move like that proves he's got plenty of good days ahead of him." Chelsea walked up behind him and smacked his ass. "And me, too."

"Mrs. Dolan!" Rose exclaimed.

Dodd laughed. "I always enjoy when she creeps you guys out."

"I wish that stood for police department association, Dodd," Rose said, turning her attention to the Nisse. "Oh my god, he's adorable."

The Nisse scowled at her from within Dodd's large hand.

"Do you think there's any chance we will get him to talk?" Chelsea asked as Lilith came closer to inspect it. She ducked a second later to dodge a missile of spit.

"Not looking too good, ladies," Dodd said, stretching his arms out to increase the distance between the Nisse and his face. The creature writhed in his hands as the first rays of sunlight pushed the night further across the horizon.

CHAPTER 7
VAJRA'S SPARK

Leviathan strained against Gungnir and the very bedrock itself. No manner of sea life dared approach, save those adrift at the whims of currents and wind. Fishermen had long since given up on approaching the area for fear of their catch being light at best and them losing their lives at worst. The area had become an aquatic wasteland where the seafloor itself bowed under the pressure of conflict, and a constant tremor marked the titanic struggle beneath the waves.

The spear held the great serpent firm despite her size, but its task weighed too heavily on it, even for a weapon forged in the heart of a dying star and wielded by gods. Gungnir, a symbol of ultimate power and unyielding resolve, was failing against a primordial force, a creature of chaos and ancient fury, driven by an insatiable hunger and a boundless rage that defied the very essence of existence.

In a cataclysmic upheaval, the ancient Leviathan tore itself free from the ocean floor, its monstrous form breaking the seabed with a destructive rumble felt miles away. The colossal creature's emergence displaced untold volumes of the sea, triggering a tsunami. The cosmic ripple surged in all directions; towering waves, born from the Leviathan's wrath, raced with unstoppable force, promising destruction—as did the beast herself. The nature of both was to swallow with wanton abandon. To devour truths, lies, hopes, and despair alike.

As the beast ascended, its scales gave off evanescent light, while her wake devoured islands in the Caribbean and reshaped the world's shores. Her rise signaled a shift that altered the fate of humanity forever, even those far removed from the perils of the sea. The land itself recoiled at the creature's emergence and sent the waves back with what spoils they had taken. Those who witnessed the event spoke of a darkness that blotted out the sun and a roar that shattered the sky, though no such cosmic event had been noted elsewhere.

Leviathan coursed through the Atlantic, a spectacle seen on televisions as nations worldwide watched footage of the serpent vector toward the northeastern coast of Brazil. Panic and dread spread across continents but none more than in the coastal city of Belem, where chaos erupted as the Leviathan's shadow fell over the city. Skyscrapers and ancient buildings alike crumbled under the crushing weight of her coils and were reduced to rubble in mere moments. Destruction was merely a byproduct of Leviathan's true goal, which became clear as she opened her mouth and devoured everything she coursed over. Her nature bid her only to consume and grow.

Onlookers like Keyana and Grace remained transfixed to the television, their hearts pounding as they witnessed the cataclysmic destruction. A thumbnail image of the beast's open maw remained fixed in the corner of their screens as they watched. The devastation was absolute; streets became rivers of debris, and the cries of the city's inhabitants were drowned out by the relentless roar of destruction. The serpent's eyes burned with a malevolent intelligence, and its every movement became a testament to its unstoppable might.

The world stood vigil in horror as the Leviathan continued her rampage, each moment a reminder of nature's terrifying power and the fragile existence of humanity. Governments and military forces scrambled to respond, but missiles and tanks did little else but aid in the city's destruction as it became evident that nothing could stand in the beast's way. Hours turned into days and the global community confronted an undeniable truth: the Leviathan was not merely a monster of legend, but an apocalyptic force that could tear through the very fabric of their reality.

Ω

"Something is wrong out there," Vajra said as he looked out the window at the trees swaying in a light morning breeze.

David pushed his chair away and stood. "I feel it too."

"Tell me something, David who isn't an angel but has angelic power. What would you choose to do with *my* power?"

"I don't intend to use you for anything but to help us open Eden."

"Eden doesn't operate under the laws I help govern. You're aware of this?" Vajra asked.

David shifted his stance and became restless in the diseased air. "I'm not privy to the entire plan. I just know I have to gather you and Gungnir and return to Rose."

"You seek all four governing laws of the universe. Nobody, mortal or otherwise, has ever wielded them together." Vajra took his eyes from the window and centered them on David. "There is good reason for this."

"I've never been interested in power. We aim to trap Leviathan," David said, showing signs of fatigue from the circuitous line of questioning.

"Surely by now you know of Ymir, who became the noble tree that holds the weight of creation."

"Yggdrasil, the tree that Odin hung from?"

"The same. It is also the tree of knowledge standing opposite the tree of life, for without one we have no cause for the other. I am but one large part of the grander whole, and without one of the laws which we represent, the fabric of reality falters and fades."

"I can't imagine Flueric would want to destroy reality."

"He may wish to control it, but instead destroy it in his hubris. It is for this reason I cannot allow you to harness my power."

David blinked, perplexed. "And what happens when you die?"

"I'm reborn as a new avatar of thunder and harnessed by another such as you."

"But not another who may already wield the power of the three others?"

"I may wield you, good Vajra who once aided the likes of Thor, Indra, Zeus, Raijin, Susanoo, and Marduk," Azazel said as he walked into the room followed by Iblis. "Then your worry about the boy having too much dominion over the avatars of creation is moot."

Vajra considered this and raised his hand. Metallic objects

within the room lifted and flew toward the angel, who bowed his head in concentration. All items ceased their momentum millimeters from Azazel's face.

"You understand the tenets of my power enough to wield considerable control over it already," Vajra said. "But I've never delivered myself to one so foreign to me without first learning his nature."

"Electromagnetism goes far beyond the generation of electric bolts from the sky," Azazel said. "It protects this planet from the fiery radiation of its host star as an invisible barrier and is what roots the building blocks of creation together to allow all compounds to form, leading to life. I understand you to the core of my being, Vajra. Come with me to help us save the very life your existence fosters."

Vajra looked to David. "Has a way with words, this one."

"Azazel doesn't wield the fiery sword of the Host, either, if balance is your concern. It was stripped from him when he fell," David said as Azazel walked through the floating metal and approached Vajra. "He's not the most patient at times, either."

"We go to the serpent now," Azazel said, hefting Vajra from the bed. "David, Iblis, grasp my arms."

They did as they were told, and Azazel rose from the floor and flew through the large ornate window in a flourish. David watched as Vajra shifted from his position as an old man being cradled to one who was younger. By the time they'd crossed the Indian ocean, Vajra brimmed with vitality and David's hair stood on end. The nearby cyclone ebbed in its fury, but this didn't concern the three men, nor did a hint of the remaining essence from Michael or Odin cause them to look away.

Their business rampaged in Brazil, and they kept their sights firmly planted to the south and to the west.

Ω

Rose and Lilith knocked on the door of the rocky entrance to the Nisse's home. "We have your friend out here, little guys. Open up so we can bring him in."

Chelsea and Dodd held their ears to the stones and could make out the faintest of frenzied speech from within.

"I think they're a little peeved," Dodd said.

"Of course they are, we have one of their children." Lilith kicked the rock with her bare foot and cursed. "Listen you little fiends, you will let us in or we will tear him—"

"Shhhhhh," Chelsea said, waving her off. "You'll only antagonize them."

"Great time for our ambassador to get her voice back." Dodd handed the Nisse to Chelsea and lumbered to the rocks to push against them. The ground rumbled, but he relented. "It's possible to break it, but I'm pretty sure it isn't just rock down there. I don't want to crumble what they've built." He retreated to where Chelsea stood and produced his pill bottle, looking at her while he gave it a little shake, then downed two.

"Right on schedule," Chelsea said. "How've you been feeling?"

"All's quiet on the northern front," Dodd said, tapping his head.

"I wish that was the case for the southern one," Rose said as she walked back to them from the entrance.

Dodd laughed, and Chelsea scowled along with Lilith. "Not really the time for fart jokes, you two."

"I disagree. They'll probably be laughing too and want to hang out with us."

All of them looked to the Nisse in Chelsea's hands and noted the ghost of a smirk on its face.

"Listen, we're friends. I know it looks bad because we captured you, but you're just a victim of circumstance in that regard. We have little time and need to speak to your leader," Chelsea said as she cradled the Nisse, whose expression had softened.

It looked around to the members of the party. "The sum veils its pieces."

"Oh my god, it's voice is even *more* adorable!" Rose rushed over to Chelsea, who shooed her away with her free hand.

"Are you saying they won't risk the community for just one of you?" Chelsea asked, but the Nisse ignored her.

"You," the Nisse said to Lilith while stroking his beard. "How did you know I am considered a child?"

Lilith threw her hair over her shoulder and stood with her hand on her hip. "Because I'm one of the few beings in this world who's older than the Nisse. I've been seeing yours scurrying for little caves since before humans held fire."

"It's a unique thing for a non-human to enter our home. Entirely different. Who are you?"

"I'm Lilitu—or Lilis, should you prefer—and your kind may know me as Lilljan, mother of goblins."

Rose whistled through her teeth as the Nisse's eyes grew wide. "That's genuine fear."

"No doubt," Dodd said. "What did you do, Lilith?"

"They've waged war on us since thousands of years ago, when she birthed her first brood of goblins," the Nisse said. "What do you want here, demon?"

"What is your name?" Lilith asked.

"I'm called Taavi."

"Taavi, I've come here to treat with your kind. You've no doubt seen my children are in disarray, yes?" Lilith said.

Taavi nodded with both hands grasping his beard. "More frantic and fearsome, like animals."

"There is a new enemy that threatens us both. We must speak to your leader and come to an agreement, or your kind and my children face annihilation."

Chelsea hummed to signal her understanding of Lilith's ploy, and a chill enthralled Rose as she picked up on the improvisation.

Taavi took a moment to think. "Take me to the door."

Chelsea carried him nearer to the rocks, where Taavi hollered at entrance. They all listened but heard no reply.

"Closer, so I may tap," Taavi said. Chelsea extended her arms and let him draw closer to the entrance, and he tapped a knock that reminded Dodd of the old shave and haircut style he and Ramirez had used on hotel doors to signal their entry. Five taps, a pause, then two more. Taavi's was far more sophisticated, with multiple rounds of varied taps and pauses. He delivered his diatribe to the rocks a second time and hung petulantly from Chelsea's hands while awaiting a response.

Just as Rose was about to suggest they try another method of entry, the rocks shuddered and an opening appeared.

"Now, how will we fit through?" Chelsea asked.

Two sets of hands flew from the opening and grasped Taavi's tiny legs, wrenching him from Chelsea's grip. "Oh, you little shit!" she cried and attempted to dive in, but the hole was already closing.

Dodd gently drew her back and grasped the sides of the

door to tear it open. This stirred the Nisse inside as they chattered and fled deeper within.

"On you go, ladies," Dodd said as he gestured for Rose to enter. She did and was followed by Lilith, Chelsea, and then Dodd.

Chelsea flicked on a flashlight and they crept down the tunnel, which led to a large cavernous opening. The Nisse had stirred what little silt and granular rock lined the floor of the tunnel they'd chosen, and the group followed on into more darkness.

"Why would they build tunnels large enough for us or bigger?" Dodd asked as he noted the height of the ceiling was beyond his reach.

"I can think of two reasons," Lilith said. "The Nisse weren't always so small. Recent times have seen them shrink smaller and smaller from the size they were when the Tower of Babel reached toward heaven, or before that, when the Celts hid from my children within the trees."

"And the other?" Chelsea asked.

"These tunnels weren't mined by the Nisse at all," Lilith said. "All manner of the good folk reside at this latitude and many burrowed deep to find succor. Not to mention how many of my children carved into rock for their homes."

"Look at you contributing," Dodd said and pinched Lilith's cheek. She lunged at his hand to bite and narrowly missed the mark. Rose could swear she saw a smile roll past her lips in a shadowy light.

"Trolls? You mean trolls?" Chelsea said.

Lilith nodded but kept further thoughts to herself.

"We'd better pray not to run into any of those down here."

"I'd imagine the Nisse have a good idea of where the trolls may dwell and avoid them at all costs."

"I'm imagining the Balrog from *Lord of the Rings. You shall not pass* and all that."

"Brendan, everything is a movie reference with you."

"I'll take that one for a book reference, thank you very much."

"Shhhhhhhhhh."

The tunnel emitted a faint light up ahead, and the group crouched as they approached the end.

"They'll have a trap waiting for us," Chelsea said.

"Maybe not," Lilith said. "They might be afraid of starting a war by attacking me."

"They are also likely confused as to why you are traveling with humans."

"So am I…"

"Well, I'll take the lead then," Dodd said, meaning to shield them with his bulk as they exited the tunnel.

What lay before them under the earth was a spacious cavern with earthen roots, but it had now been built up with more modern tinkering. Many foraged and collected items were in evidence and had been used to construct a cog-wheeled city where the Nisse made their home. Countless tunnels shot off in just as many directions, indicating just how far the Nisse may reach. Chelsea assumed they also led to other cities, though she couldn't imagine any were as large or impressive as the one before them. Using the illumination from vast crystals ensconced within the rock or hung with elaborate root structures, they could see far into the distance, and the limiting end of the city was hidden from their eyes.

"Now, no matter what they do, resist going all King Kong on them, Dodd," Rose said.

Dodd kept his hands out wide with palms back to show that they should stay behind him. "You're no fun at all."

The Nisse made themselves seen everywhere as some blew through wooden and metal horns to signal the entry of strangers. There was no direct evidence of an imminent attack, but Rose wondered at how ferocious the small folk might be in a fight. She looked to her right and saw Lilith smiling as they amassed.

"Why are you so giddy?" Chelsea asked.

Lilith said, "I have a plan. But I'm also happy to see them. They are a slice of the old world come back to grace this horrid present your lot have crafted."

"We've come in peace to speak to you," Dodd bellowed. "I mean you no harm."

A member of the Nisse stepped forward from the thousands hanging from windows and amassing in their streets and alleys. He bore a beard so long it would have dragged along the ground for feet behind him had he not arranged it into a braid and tied it around himself in an ornate structure. "We've heard why you come and who comes with you, peikko," he said. "We don't treat with those who break into our home uninvited."

"I'm guessing 'peikko' probably doesn't mean handsome," Dodd said.

"Likely not," Chelsea said.

Rose stepped forward. "We have an offering to you all. I know you love rice pudding, but growing rice is difficult under the ground. Take this for the freshest bowls of *risengrød* you've ever enjoyed."

Rose reached into her purse, produced handfuls of rice seeds, and cast them out in all directions with one well-practiced toss. The Nisse gasped at her gesture and many hid behind structures as though her movement signaled an imminent assault, but Rose continued to be deliberate in her movements as she bent down to touch the ground with her palms and cause the seeds to germinate and grow. The explosion of plants added a natural element to the outskirts of their city, and the Nisse's murmurs were those of delight before long.

Lilith asked, "What is your name, speaker?"

"Johtaja, Demon Mother," he said and looked to Rose. "Thank you for the gift. We will hear you out, human witch."

"Not very diplomatic, are they?" Chelsea said.

"Don't have to be if you spend your entire existence staying hidden," Dodd said.

"Taavi has no doubt told you of the common threat that brings me here," Lilith said.

"Kobolds, goblins, trolls?" Johtaja cried. "We have weathered any scourge you have thrown at us and will do the same with this!" The Nisse cheered behind him and their horns blasted once more, causing a ruckus throughout the city behind him.

"What brings us is more dire," Dodd bellowed. "What's worse, it comes from below your tiny little feet. You have ventured too low and awakened a Balrog!"

"What are you doing, fool?" Lilith hissed.

"We needed a big baddy. There's nothing bigger and badder than one of those."

"But how will we convince them it exists, you lout?"

"Let me worry about that. You keep them talking for a minute."

Johtaja stomped his feet for quiet amongst the Nisse. "No such creature exists unless she has borne it into the world."

"I have not," Lilith said. "It ravages my children even now, as we speak, and it will come to you soon unless we find a way to cage it."

"Your children are more savage than ever and dumber than a cave mouse," Johtaja said.

"It is the Balrog that makes them that way!" Lilith cried with her hands in the air. "Soon it will make you as feral as the goblins you decry before us now."

Rose felt heat from Dodd's direction and saw he was cooking something up. His bare foot stood on the rock floor, and he pushed his heat into the stone.

Rose took the cue. "Even now you can feel the Balrog's fire pulse through the floor of your cavern as it climbs to burn you and take your metal by the smelter of this city."

"Oooo, that was good," Chelsea said.

Rose smiled. "Thanks, I'm just really in the moment, you know…"

Lilith regained the floor. "It is only with your prized possession, what we have called the *Tinker*, that we can craft a cage strong enough to hold the Balrog and cast it back into the bowels of Manala. Will you take a stand with us, or will you let your city fall?"

The city grew alive with banter and scurrying as the Nisse felt the ground beneath them growing with heat.

"Quickly, to the työkalu," Johtaja cried and beckoned for his guard to retreat into the city.

"We will hold the beast at bay," Rose yelled.

"Nice touch there at the end," Chelsea said. "I'm really curious how you made it look like there's something coming out of the tunnel over there."

Rose and Dodd turned to look at an enormous set of golden eyes peering from an entrance hole hundreds of feet to their left.

"Uhhh, that's not us, Chelse," Dodd said.

"It's one of mine." Lilith stepped back where the cool breath of their escape tunnel kissed her neck.

Ω

Barbara woke to Leonard snoring gently beside her. She allowed the night's climax to wander through her thoughts as she often did when waking up next to a man in her bed. A smile lifted her lips, and she turned on her back and covered her eyes with her arm. *You're an idiot*, she thought, *but it didn't feel wrong. Still doesn't.*

Light invaded the room through her windows at an angle to belie the later hour, and she rolled to her side to check her phone. Blakely had called. A lot. She also saw a board meeting had been placed on her calendar for two days from now, and any pleasantness she felt from the night before fell away. Barbara had no wish to sit amongst the heavyweights of All Century on her best days, but especially not now if she was being seen as some kind of turncoat—or worse, as weak.

Leonard's fingers traced up her back, and she jumped.

"I didn't mean to scare you," he said.

Barbara rolled back toward him and enjoyed the view of his naked upper body uncovered by her white duvet. "Just a little jumpy," she said. "I've been hailed by work."

"That's expected," he said, continuing to trace her shoulders with his fingers. "What do you plan to do?"

She rested her head on the pillow and watched his eyes

strain to focus on her without his glasses. They were a hazel that benefited from the morning light. "I have to call Blakely soon, but I don't think I'm going into the office today."

"Might be a good idea if you did," Leonard said as he dropped his head on his pillow to match her. "Burrowing is usually associated with guilt."

"True, true," she said and ran her hands through her hair.

"Look away for a second," Barbara said, and Leonard obediently did so while collecting his glasses from the night table. She stood and walked to her bathroom door and stood behind it to don the silver robe kept there. When she turned, he was already wearing his pants and had gone to the window to inspect it.

"They painted over the claw marks, but they didn't bother to use spackling on it first. Seems like a rush job." He turned to see her looking at him. "Don't worry, I didn't peek at you."

"I know," she said, walking toward him. "That's not really your style, is it, Leonard?"

The surprise on his face was satisfying as she took his hand from the windowsill and kissed him. "What, did you think I was done with you?"

"Honestly, yes, a little. You know how high stress situations go."

She did and had fallen into the arms of partners from situations like that before, but this was different. She found Leonard to be genuinely interesting for reasons she couldn't quite place, at least not all of them. It didn't hurt that she also found him handsome and just innocent enough to be too hard to resist.

"You're not done with me either, are you?" Barbara asked, and Leonard did what he always did. He was honest.

"No, I'm not," he said, taking his hand from her hip. "But we have to talk about next steps. There are important actions being taken as we speak, and our goal is Pulse24."

"I know you well enough to know you aren't just here to use me, but I have to put more thought into Pulse24. That's the kind of espionage that *will* get a person killed."

"Not if you stay with us," he said.

She skirted around him and toward the phone. "There's no barrier Flueric can't vault over, and I think Abaddon might be more even more savage than his boss. Let me give Blakely a call and take their temperature."

"Okay," he said, grabbing his shirt. "I'll go start coffee."

Barbara watched him go and dialed Blakely's number. He answered as though he'd been staring at the phone, waiting for her call.

"Not a smart move, Barb."

"Good morning to you too."

"Why would you clear the surveillance devices from your house? It makes you look even more shady than before."

"Because it's my fucking house, Blakely, and I won't have some pimple-dicked tech asshole watching me change my clothes in my home. It's disgusting, not to mention illegal."

"You know as well as I do that you gave up any protection by the law when you signed on here."

"Yeah, yeah, I know."

"And why aren't you in yet?"

"Because I worked until almost ten o'clock last night, and I'm exhausted. And *you* know as well as I do that we don't have time cards at our level."

The line was silent for a time, and Blakely sighed. "Just

get in soon, because we need to hash out how to spin these protests now that the creature is loose and on a rampage. We have to generate news about All Century's plans to subdue it. There are some stories spinning already, but Species 0 is wrecking coastal cities in Brazil right now and people are terrified. Abaddon wants to make sure we don't lose the opportunity to capitalize on that fear."

"And what does Abaddon want to use it for? Are we going to invade Canada?"

Blakely grew quiet again for a moment and said, "Just get in. We can't talk about it on unsecured lines."

The call ended, and she took the time to take a quick shower and get dressed. She was halfway through pulling on a pair of pants when she thought "screw it" and put them aside. She went to her underwear drawer and smiled.

Leonard heard footsteps as Barbara descended the stairs and turned with mug raised. "Get it while its hot."

She stood halfway down the hallway in a slinky lace nightie and beckoned him toward her. "I intend to," she said as she turned back in the direction of the bedroom.

Leonard swallowed a last mouthful of coffee and stumbled over his own feet as he hurried to catch up.

Ω

Chelsea watched as the girl she'd known since a budding teen stepped forward to confront an enigmatic presence from the depths of the earth.

"What is it?" Rose asked as she reached into one of the many purses hanging from her waist.

Lilith remained behind Dodd. "He is Cherufe," she said

with the slightest of quavers in her voice. "The closest thing I can think of to what Dodd described as a Balrog."

"It's definitely your child?" Chelsea asked.

"Yes, one of my more formidable ones. Many a hero has found their end at its hand, and even the demigods were quite careful in approaching him. I remember birthing Cherufe. Had it been more wieldy and obedient, I'd have made it a child of great status. It never met that station, though. It cares for only its solitude and the consumption of flesh. Luck was with humanity, because he must stay near great heat."

"Oh shit," Dodd said. "Did I call this thing?"

"Might be the case, big fella," Rose said. "Which is another reason we can't let it melt this city."

"Your plants will do nothing but provide fuel for it to burn, Rose," Lilith said. "Cherufe is made of molten magma and especially hardened gemstones and crystals. He has no doubt absorbed much diamond in his time under the earth and from tributes given by those who wished to save their lives."

The Nisse continued their frantic preparation at fortifying the side of the city facing the approaching Cherufe. Their building speed was as admirable as the legends would lead one to believe.

"Do you really think they can use the Tinker to create a cage for it?" Dodd asked as he replaced his foot into his shoe and took up a place next to Rose.

"Not unless they can mold one out of a material the core of the earth couldn't melt," Lilith said. "I won't have any sway over him either. As Rose saw in the woods at the cabin, my children will not head my calls any longer. This one was never very good at heading them even when I was at my apex, anyway."

Rose turned to the Nisse and shouted, "Do you have a lot of diamond?"

The few that gave her their attention appeared confused.

"Timantti," Lilith said.

Johtaja emerged from the crowd and addressed them. "We won't appease the beast with offerings. That will give it cause to return for more and more until we are barren."

"Not wise to forgo an assured victory today for hopes of a better outcome tomorrow," Chelsea said.

"That's my wise gal," Dodd said. Rose looked at him and could tell he was gauging how much power he might use without losing himself to the ifrit within.

"What about enough to use the Tinker to create a cage of diamond?" Rose asked.

"Not nearly enough for the size of that thing," Johtaja pointed to Cherufe as it came close to emerging from the tunnel. A radiant orange glow preceded the monster, and the acrid smell of sulfur invaded their nostrils.

Rose threw her seeds at the entrance to the tunnel and placed her hands on the ground while yelling to Johtaja, "If you have enough for a spear, we have a plan to use it."

Johtaja considered her words with a faithless posture until he observed Rose's seeds sprout into yellow pine trees to block the entrance to the Nisse city. "We will try," he said and turned behind him to call for a company of Nisse pulling ropes to halt. The Tinker rested on a well-constructed platform behind, and it appeared tiny and unremarkable to the humans as they glanced toward it.

"Not much of a machine," Dodd said.

"It is no machination, but the means to repair and build all forms of them," Johtaja scolded as he climbed the platform and received bags upon bags of gemstones and ore. A group of Nisse arrived with similar beards to their leader and hats with gold bands tied about the tops to cause them to droop. They climbed to surround Johtaja. The group reached into the Tinker, turned to the piles of gems and ore with various tools and machines, and were quick to get to their work.

"They're melting down that ore with those tiny furnaces and speckling it with diamonds," Dodd said. "Not a bad idea if the metal they are using can hold up."

"Is that metal from the stars?" Chelsea called. The Nisse merely waved her off. "I think they are using meteorites. The metal will already have been very well-tempered from the heat produced when entering our atmosphere."

"They'd better hurry," Rose said. "The yellow pines are the best thing I could think of to resist fire, but they won't stand up to lava for very long. Especially without their roots being in water." As if on cue, the trees Rose had sped to growth began to shudder and move. She looked back to the Nisse and appreciated their speedy work. They might very well complete the spear in time for them to use it. "Dodd, can you hurl that thing into Cherufe's face?"

Before he could answer, Lilith said, "That won't work. He will just form a new one from his core."

"Well, how do we kill it?" Chelsea asked.

"Immersion in icy waters would be best," Lilith said.

"You're joking, right?"

Lilith read the expression on Chelsea's face and understood. "Oh, we can't kill Cherufe with what we have here. We need to grab that bag from those little pests and flee the way we came. It's the only way to achieve what we came here for."

"They'll grab the Tinker and flee into the bowels of

Denmark if we take one errant step toward it right now," Dodd said. "They're under siege, but they're still crafty, and that's their most prized possession. Mark my words, that would be a mistake."

"And we won't be abandoning them," Rose said. "You should think of another way."

Lilith considered her odds of fleeing and knew they were favorable. It wasn't likely that Baba Yaga would chase her once she'd emerged and fled, and she knew herself well enough to know she could find a man to keep her in hiding for as long as she needed. With nobody being privy to her inner thoughts, she was left to be the only one surprised as she stepped forward instead of backward. "You can bury the spear deep into its chest, where the majority of its essence surrounds the spoils it has consumed."

"Aim for the heart, you mean," Dodd said.

"If you want to consider that its heart, then yes, but it won't kill it, just wound it enough to make it retreat to the deeper depths and regain itself."

"How long do you think it will be doing that?" Rose asked.

"Hundreds of years, if you land a devastating blow."

"I'm satisfied with that," Rose said. "The Nisse will have plenty of time to plan and prepare."

"Johtaja, is the spear complete?" Chelsea asked.

"Nearly," he called back. To Chelsea's surprise, they'd constructed a hastily made ballista upon the platform as well.

"Crafty indeed," she said. "Dodd, it looks like you're off the hook for throwing that thing at it."

"I'll move up there to distract it while they aim," he said.

Rose patted him on the shoulder and pulled her hand back

from the heat. "Be careful, galoot. I'll do what I can to help give you help from above."

"Love you too," Dodd said and leaped ahead toward the tunnel as the trees disintegrated into flames.

"Even he won't hold Cherufe back for very long," Lilith said.

"We have to circle around and grab the Tinker once the fighting breaks out," Chelsea said. "Will you come?"

Lilith nodded and walked with Chelsea as Rose established a series of trees and vines to grow from the edges of the cavern. It was hard to say what she planned to do with them, but Chelsea trusted her ingenuity and ability to coordinate with Dodd.

Yellow pine bark splintered and flew inward, and the Cherufe reached inside. Molten rock rolled inside of the cavern, and the Nisse chattered and scrambled at the sight of their enemy. Dodd hefted a boulder of considerable size and held it out before him as a makeshift shield. The heat didn't concern him. He wasn't certain, but he assumed he could handle any form of terrestrial fire. The cosmic furnaces of the angels were another matter, but this was no angel. Cherufe's head entered the cavern, and it fixed its eyes on Dodd and then the city beyond him. Chelsea looked up at it as she and Lilith circled to behind the Nisse battlements. She could feel its gluttonous aura.

"How could you have created that thing?"

"Imagine someone doing less in my circumstance, Chelsea Dolan, and I'll commend you your creativity."

Chelsea considered why Rose had allowed herself to forgive Lilith, despite the unimaginable pain she had suffered at her behest. Shame is a fruit-bearing tree. It was true that people committed unspeakable atrocities when wronged or after being backed into a corner, but Lilith's actions were still difficult to overlook. Chelsea focused on the matter at hand. "Follow me," she said, and they sidled closer to where the Tinker lay nestled behind the ballista.

Rose continued to throw seeds and grow bramble thickets in front of the Nisse battlements, hoping to shield them from any incoming shrapnel they might produce by firing the spear. The contorted branches and leaves could do little else in the face of such intense heat.

Dodd hurtled over to the right as the Cherufe's hand swept along where he had stood, and he crouched down to avoid falling droplets of liquid-hot magma. He reached down and hefted a boulder to his shoulder with his free hand and spun in place to build momentum. It lofted as a shot-put toss at the thing's malformed head.

The boulder splashed home, knocking magma from Cherufe's shoulders, but just as Lilith had said, the head bubbled back into place within seconds.

Cherufe smiled down at Dodd and spit liquid fire upon him before pulling itself completely through the tunnel entrance. At its full height, the monster filled the cavern to its ceiling and melted stalactites into itself.

The stone shield Dodd held had weathered the onslaught at the cost of itself. He cast it into Cherufe's chest and took three heaping leaps backward and away from Rose and the Nisse, hoping to draw it toward him. The creature gave him little notice and stepped toward the Nisse, making Dodd change his plan.

"Hey, little fellas!" he called. "Get that spear ready and fire it as soon as I'm clear."

"Dodd, open up its chest," Chelsea called from behind the Nisse, drawing unwanted attention and the sidelong glance Lilith was famous for.

Knowing better than to ask for clarification, Dodd grasped a vine from the rooftop and a stalagmite from the ground. He ran in an arc and swung out and around toward Cherufe.

As a kid, he had watched Ron Ely play Tarzan on TV more times than he could count. Not a day would go by where he didn't wish there were vines hanging from his ceiling so he could swing through the house like the famous character. Rose saw the smile on the big man's face as he swung around and she called, "Go, Dodd!" across the cavern. Even Chelsea smiled at her partner's actions—what she would consider *antics*—as he acted to save the day.

Cherufe didn't see Dodd until the man was nearly in front of it and had little time to act. Dodd launched his boulder into its chest and grabbed an adjacent vine to swing away, but his momentum wasn't in his favor. Cherufe lifted his arm to grasp him and engulf the once-ordinary detective in a fiery grip that would have proven once and for all how the man would handle such heat.

The Nisse loosed their ballista bolt and it flew in an arc at Cherufe, leaving glints of gem in its wake. Dodd's attack had moved the molten rock core of the monster enough to allow for the spear to hit dead center in its chest and, as Lilith had said it might, dislodge a core of amalgamated diamonds and gems from within.

The monster fell in on itself as Dodd smashed into the ground with force enough to shatter the floor. He had no hope of gathering the core of Cherufe, but he did grasp the spear and sprint back toward the city. Rose saw the monster collect itself as it slinked toward the tunnel from whence it came, and the Nisse erupted in cheers.

What remained of Cherufe retreated into the tunnel, to slough itself deep within the earth and gather strength as the planet's pressure allowed for it to seethe and grow over centuries to come. One among them knew its mind well enough to predict that one day it would return, but she didn't much care if the Nisse would be ready.

The victorious uproar was short-lived, however, as much of the molten magma that had made up the monster rolled downhill and toward the city.

Chelsea and Lilith watched as Johtaja directed the Nisse to dig a trench in front of their fortifications and allow the magma to form a mottled moat around the city instead of engulfing it in fire. With their pride deeply rooted in their skill, the mystical creatures stole the show through their supernatural engineering.

The unlikely pair made use of the distraction and climbed onto the platform. The Tinker lay before them—an empty burlap sack with a large rope drawstring. Chelsea lifted it and shrugged at Lilith as they climbed down and walked toward Rose.

Dodd limped back, holding the spear and smiling. "You see the rope-swinging thing I did?" he asked. Rose smiled and slapped him on the back, and he had time to watch her eyes grow wide before she ducked behind him. A rock slammed his head, rattling his mind along with his teeth. "Gah, that smarts. What gives, little dudes?"

"They grabbed the Tinker," Rose said.

Chelsea and Lilith had broken into a run and bypassed them to the tunnel ahead.

"Cheese it!" Dodd cried as more projectiles came their way, though without the Tinker, the Nisse could craft nothing powerful enough to knock Dodd off his feet. He covered Rose as they ran to the tunnel with an army of Nisse at their heels.

The trek to the surface proved perilous for Chelsea, whose eyes were far past their prime. "Reach into the bag," Lilith said.

Chelsea did as she was commanded and produced a high-lumen flashlight, which she promptly switched on. "I had a feeling that's what it did."

"What's that?" Chelsea asked.

"It gives you the tool you need for the job you're doing," Lilith said. "Right now, you needed light to see. Poof, there it is."

Chelsea threw the Tinker over her shoulder and rushed on, hoping to have more time to explore its abilities if they made it out of the cave alive. A rumble shook the surrounding tunnel. Dodd had used his fire to illuminate the way for Rose as she set down seeds and grew barriers behind them, but many Nisse found their way through and pursued.

"Guys, we need it to save the world," Dodd yelled. "We will bring it back when we are done."

More rocks pinged off his forehead and he cursed. Chelsea thought she could hear Rose laughing as they made up ground on Lilith.

Soon, the light of day graced them, and they were in an open sprint across the field with hundreds of Nisse filing out of the ground behind. Dodd had done everything he could to avoid harming any, but masses of tiny warriors nipped at their heels, and he didn't like the idea of what it might look like if the party became overwhelmed by a screeching horde of primeval gnomes.

As he came to terms with the idea of using force on the Nisse, Baba Yaga's hut erupted from the trees and sprinted on chicken legs toward them through the field.

Chelsea found the sight at first odd, then unnerving as it came upon them in a way she would have thought a tyrannosaurus might have during the late Cretaceous period. She peeked behind to see the Nisse less than twenty feet away.

The mouth of Baba Yaga's house of brown opened, and the door flung open as it lowered to the ground and scooped them up along with a generous portion of the field itself before slamming shut and taking flight.

"Your backs'll hurt fiercely in the morning, but it's a mite better than being stoned to death by the likes of them," Baba Yaga said. "Their memories are longer than their beards. You'll want to take care if you ever choose to return to these lands."

"What did you do to them to make them so angry, anyway?" Rose asked.

Baba Yaga laughed as she stirred her cooking pot. "A trio of them thought it wise to use sharp tongues on me. Two, I made into chocolate for their insolence. The other I held captive and starved until he had withered to naught. On a bright sunny day, he found his chains unlocked and two bars of chocolate laid before him. A perfect meal to be had before sending him home to live a long life knowing what he'd done."

Chelsea and Lilith exchanged looks as they thought of the meal they'd shared not long ago and stood to help tidy the mess they'd made by crashing into the house.

Rose, unfazed, studied the Tinker, the innocuous bag that would help them bind the other three avatars together.

Ω

Azazel swung low and sliced through the clouds as they neared the vile serpent. Gripping the powerful angel's arm, David's keen eyes observed the wanton destruction the monster had caused.

"If she wants everything we have, why does she destroy it?"

Iblis looked to the young man with sad eyes. "Leviathan is no mere rampaging beast. She doesn't just *want* humanity. She craves it. The result of her being unchecked is exactly what you see before you, but are you truly seeing? Pay attention, there's more than mere destruction occurring before us."

David looked to Azazel, whose attention was wholly set on Vajra. The two didn't speak, but they appeared entranced with one another in communication David didn't understand. He moved his attention below to the writhing coils of the primordial snake and saw what Iblis spoke of. She coursed through the ruins of the city and devoured all she'd crumbled.

"She is consuming it?" David asked. "Is her goal to grow?"

"The beast grows, this is true, but that is not her goal," Iblis said. "She has a void within her. One that leaves her with the perpetual feeling of bareness. She will do anything to fill that void."

"I can't imagine why the creator would make such a dangerous thing."

"It begins with hope, despair, dreams, pain, happiness, rage—all aspects of life and emotion that we hold dear.

Leviathan is want. Envy is her loveliest scale. The ouroboros you met caged in a mountain beneath the veil belonged to a universe of chaos. Left unchecked, she will devour and grow until she has consumed the very light of creation."

"I can't wrap my head around why Flueric would unleash her if what he wants is control of our world," David said.

Iblis motioned below. "Look about you and consider what Flueric truly wants."

David shook his head and firmed his resolve to face the monster ahead.

"Keep her busy," Azazel said. "I need more time with Vajra before I can act. Don't go for the spear until I give you the signal. She's far too powerful for that now."

With those words, Azazel threw David and Iblis at Leviathan. "Remember, distract her, and above all else, do not allow yourself to be devoured. If she takes you in, she will grow and all is lost."

David, cutting through the wind, landed boldly on the body of Leviathan rather than on the nearby ground with Iblis. She continued to coil her body round, and he leaped from section to section, awaiting her discovery of him. The scales beneath his feet had grown considerably, and if he had to guess, David would assume she was at least ten times the size of the mountain she'd erupted from in Valhalla.

You!

The word so powerfully delivered compressed the very air around him and caused a shock. She hadn't merely said it, but delivered the notion through sheer force, and David knew Leviathan craved him more than anything.

"I guess that's why I'm supposed to distract her," he said.

From within her coils emerged the colossal head of the

snake, and her eyes leaked an emerald essence. David had thought her hatred of him fueled her advance, but one look into her eyes proved him wrong. It was a *need* that drew her to him.

"Run, you fool!" Iblis cried as Leviathan's open mouth cascaded toward David. He leaped away and felt his speed was with him again. For the first time since Flueric had disrupted his being, he moved without thought and with natural fluidity.

"I don't know what you did, Yehuda, but thank you," David said.

"Find the spear, David," Iblis called from somewhere beyond the writhing beast.

Leviathan crashed into herself as David leaped out of harm's way, and she tore into her own body before launching her scaled neck to follow David. Her speed took him by surprise. He should have guessed, but the mind tells you something so large could never move at such a rate.

Iblis aided him and countered her by bathing her face in a torrent of fire from below. The distraction gave David enough time to skip free of imminent danger with the lessons of the exchange at his disposal for the future.

Leviathan paused and regarded Iblis. "What makes the great king of the jinn bow to Adam's sons?"

"I bow to none," Iblis said and became lost in a vortex of flame that scattered into many, making his location hard to discern. "I choose my allegiances. They are not ordered upon me."

David found his resolve inspiring, though the meaning of their exchange was beyond his ability to grasp. Above, he saw Azazel consorting with Vajra. He hoped Azazel would complete whatever ritual he was conducting soon.

The flaming vortexes encircled Leviathan and bewitched her as she snapped her jaws shut on one, and then another. Iblis distracted her, and David meant to use the opportunity to see if he regained more than just his ability to defy the laws of physics with his speed. He leaped again atop the monster and place his hands on her neck below her head. Conjuring the swift feeling of a raging fire, he unleashed his power in a brilliant flash. His torrent of flame felt more like the charged particles of energy Azazel had used to defeat him rather than mere columns of super-heated fire.

The ground shook as Leviathan's severed head fell to the earth, and David stood perplexed as the light left her eyes.

"Guys, I think Stella just got her groove back," he said, gesturing down to Iblis, who'd appeared as his trick attack was dispelled.

Iblis waved David off from below. "Run! It won't be so simple!"

"I mean, I didn't believe it would be, but the proof is in the pudding—" David said as he leaped to Gungnir, where it protruded from a wound encircled by green scales.

The spear felt warm in his grip, and he pulled it free with more ease than he would have guessed. David felt Leviathan's body spasm beneath his feet, and his instincts took hold just in time for him to avoid an opening salvo of bites from two smaller heads within the serpent's coils.

He looked to Iblis in time to watch as a third struck out and clamped down on the jinn's leg and arm. She was merciless in savaging him to the ground, and Iblis bathed her face in flame to little avail. Despite being smaller in size to the original, the newly budded heads were by no means small. Iblis was lucky to have avoided being consumed outright.

David attempted to get to his floundering friend, but the other heads continued in merciless pursuit of him.

This is just like the hydra. So why didn't the fire stop the heads from growing back?

David found the guiding lessons from mythology to be frequently less and less helpful in dealing with the beasts of legend and remembered his mother explaining that the stories had changed, passed down, changed again, and so on and so on. Some aspects were likely completely different now from what they once conveyed. It could also be that Leviathan was immune to such trickery. The hydra monster from myth could have been an offshoot, much like the Beelzebub Rose had faced so long ago.

Careful to ensure he did not decapitate another head, David engulfed himself in flame to cloak his movements and dropped within the coils to further confuse the beast. Gungnir had become heavy in his hands and hindered him as he made his way on and around the crashing body until he saw a route to Iblis.

Without forethought, he leaped away from the body to where the third head thrashed and leaped from the ground to the neck, where he felt less exposed. Conjuring all his speed, David dashed forward, aiming to wrench Iblis free at the cost of his limbs and deal with the injuries later. But just as he came within grasping range, the other two heads converged on Iblis.

The jinn never uttered a last word before he was lost within the avatar of envy.

"No!" David cried. He reached into his chest to produce the weapon he had earned during their first encounter together to put an end to her once and for all.

YES…

He felt her lust for the item and knew within his bones it was the wrong move. Not wishing to make the same mistake again, he leaped free to consider his options. The heads had no intention of allowing him the luxury of a plan and cascaded toward him with increased speed. *Consuming Iblis strengthened her.* The realization of this filled David with despair, and he assumed his defeat was imminent.

Flueric's move upon the board had been enough to win the day. They were done.

"Fly, David," Azazel said. His lack of urgency struck David as odd, but he leaped with renewed vigor, trusting in the angel.

A column of lavender lightning fell upon Leviathan's core, and she screamed. The shock wave that ensued propelled David further away, allowing Azazel to increase his onslaught.

David watched as he channeled the power of Vajra onto Leviathan with venom of his own leaking from his eyes. The angel relished in the pain he caused the monster. Iblis had been his confidant and friend for longer than David could fathom existing. He watched Azazel's movements and saw his jaw set firmly to hold back the grief to come.

Vajra had given itself over to Azazel. This development was to their benefit, but David wondered at the conditions it took to convince the avatar of electromagnetism to do so. He knew harboring his own was what had caused Vajra to reject joining him. It was possible that Azazel's lack of one, combined with his proclivity for understanding science, tipped the scales in that debate.

Leviathan writhed at the sudden influx of power, and for the first time since landing, David felt they had a chance to subdue the beast.

Azazel flew to her head, enshrouded in a vortex of lightning and cloud. The heads lashed in all directions and at the cloud, and David saw he was using his strikes as a means of misdirection, once again delivering a masterclass in celestial combat. Two more columns of lightning formed from the thunderheads above and struck down the main body and all three heads in a devastating show of force, and Azazel manifested to land near David.

"How did you convince Vajra that you were worthy?"

"It asked me of my resolve and continued in a line of the same question over and over. I realized it didn't want to hear an answer, but to see one. This is why I stood idly by as Iblis was consumed. Vajra knew then that I would allow my dearest friend to perish in service to my cause, and this was enough."

"A hefty cost. I'm so sorry we had to pay it."

"Yours will be heavier still, David." Azazel turned to the boy who'd once tried to destroy him. "To you, I am many things. One, and seemingly most important to you, is a father. I am not your father, David, though I have enjoyed the role. You once told me of Kharon's words to you. You were more than you know and more than you seem. This sentiment still holds true. Continue your course. Answers await on the other side."

Azazel lifted his arm and gestured to the single golden vambrace upon it. "This is Vajra. Now in this form, it cannot easily become personified again. At least not for some time." Lifting his hand, Azazel made a slash and cut himself at the elbow, catching his imbued arm as it fell. "Take this to your party and open the gates of Eden. You must enter. She will follow you now that she has your scent. It is you she seeks to consume over all else."

David tried to understand what had occurred and stumbled upon what Azazel planned to do. "No, don't—"

A fiery wing cast David through the air and away from the rising serpent. "Go north," Azazel said and flew toward the heads cascading at them.

David had learned many lessons from those he'd met since falling into the river as little more than one of eight billion souls searching for meaning in their barefaced reality. Many had come from the teachings of this angel who he'd thought was responsible for his birth. In that time, he'd delivered his unending trust to the one the Greeks had called Prometheus.

In one motion, David turned and fled across the ground as the sounds of cacophonous battle ensued behind him.

Even without Vajra, Azazel's might would contain Leviathan for a time, David knew. The sound of fluttering descended from above, and two ravens of the deepest black descended in a spiral to him. One, with a mouthful of red feathers, gently collected David in its talons, while the other lifted Gungnir from his hands. The relief of the weight was immediate, and for the first time since meeting Odin in Valhalla, David recognized his need for rest.

He closed his eyes and relaxed in the grip of the raven as tears rolled down his cheeks. He didn't bother to wipe them away. His heat evaporated them before they could fall.

PART THREE

BOUNDLESS

CHAPTER 8

ALL FOR ONE

Stephen Cappodak arranged his purple duffel bag on one of two queen beds within his seventeenth-floor hotel room. He settled in the easy chair the good people who'd designed his suite had seen fit to place within it and stared at the bag.

The trip had been easy to organize, since he had been scheduled to be in Phoenix through the previous week for a Kid Scouts of America conference. Though he'd never had children of his own, Stephen—or Den Master Steve, as the kids called him—had made a lifelong commitment to the scouts. He credited his time in the woods with den mates to his love of the outdoors, which was the backdrop to many cherished memories with his father and uncle, both of whom he'd buried within the last few years.

The scouts gave Stephen the bedrock foundation to go from a merited condor level member into university and then the marines soon after. Special forces schools came and went, and before he'd earned his title of Den Master, he had become Lieutenant Cappodak, with several tours of duty behind him and an honorable discharge into retirement reserve. A family man without a family and a pillar of his community, Stephen had little cause for complaint or discomfort given the fruits of his labors. A twenty-five-hundred square foot home on an acre of land all his own being the pinnacle trophy he'd earned.

He leaned forward in his chair and slipped the zipper down the length of his bag to reach in and unload its contents. He hefted three soft sacks that he placed to the side. Gently, and over a long period of time, Stephen removed magazines and boxes of ammunition to undertake the laborious process of pressing the .223 caliber rounds into each magazine until the clips sat filled. Stephen had grown to prefer this caliber over the NATO-issued 5.56 millimeter rounds he'd used in the service. In fact, choosing the M4 from his secret, very illegal, stockpile of weapons showed his nostalgic nature as the military had retired the M4 for the newer M27 model that, by the accounts of many, was the far superior long gun. But Stephen appreciated how the M4 felt and reacted within his grasp, and his muscle memory with this weapon always proved itself when he compared targets side by side.

Once the supplies were accounted for and inventoried, a process which he'd undertaken many times since planning this event, Stephen opened a camping stove to warm up his bag of dehydrated pasta and steak. Plans didn't call for him to begin until thirty-six hours from now, but he didn't like the idea of leaving the room with his cache present, and he never minded camping meals. In many ways, it was comfort food to the man who'd spent a good portion of his life eating below an open sky.

With the food warming over his propane-fueled flame,

Stephen walked to the window and opened the curtains. Below lay an open courtyard where tents had been strewn for a makeshift music festival, which had turned into the ideal location for a planned protest scheduled for the next day. The angles of approach felt comfortable at this height, and Stephen was easy with satisfaction at his planning. From the window, Abaddon's face smiled back at the man who'd grown far too blind to notice.

He turned and opened his phone to make a video call to his wife at home, who thought the scouts' convention ended in a few days. Stephen enjoyed seeing her face and hearing her voice. Feeling her warmth had likely already occurred for the last time. His plans had made this an unfortunate fact.

Ω

On the peninsula of Sinai under a cloudless sky, before the birth of David or Rose or the pervading silence of the creator, Flueric sat perched on a granitic outcrop. His chosen seat rested atop a tall mound of rocks too meager to be called by the name of a mountain. Petals from a coarse bush rained to the ground as he reached over to pluck branches and gently pull them, enjoying their oily sheen between his fingertips.

Looking up at the sky, he closed his eyes and breached the void-ridden expanse between himself and his old seat in the heavens with a cry that reverberated amongst the members of the host. After a time, he stood and milled about amongst the rocks and slid his feet through the dust, performing a solo tango as he waited.

It didn't take long before a presence filled him.

"It's been a long time since you've given me an audience, Father," Flueric said. "Not since the times of scripture."

He felt the intentions and meaning of the creator flow through him and smiled. "Well, yes, I did call for you, but this isn't the first time I've done so since we made a small wager near this very spot. A bet, I'll add, you cheated me on to win."

There was silence within him, and Flueric feared he'd lost his audience. "I'm here to stake another bet with you. Today, here and now, once and for all, and one without your twirling interference. If you win, I'll go back to the pit for a thousand years and we can let your favorite creations go on without my influence for that time. But, *if I win*"—Flueric's forked tongue lashed out and swept his lips of dust—"*I take it all.*"

The eternal presence remained within and around Flueric, and he took this for a good sign. "If you truly believe in their potential, you should be certain of the outcome."

Flueric cocked his head and walked over to the bush. "It was one just like this that gave Moses the ability to hear your word, wasn't it? He was an excellent specimen, but I tainted him too, didn't I? Ended up just like me after all of his service. Disgraced and stripped of divine love, and for what—showing pride in his achievements? It's pettiness that makes you worry about some shining above others. We can't be equal, Father, that's simply not the way of the creation you molded."

A wind blew over the hill and covered Flueric's suit in dust. He patted it away. "Petty, I see," he said. "But if you don't like my assertions, take my wager and silence me. That's what you want, anyway, isn't it? For me to leave them from my meddling to walk their path alone. That intention is why the watchers were cast down to their earthen prisons and my flock boils in the flames below Tartarus."

Silence came, and this time, it kept its residence. Flueric waited on the mountain. Days and nights passed without meaning or merit to the light bearer, who had more than enough time and patience beyond what those of the Host might imagine. He'd waited this long for his chance, hadn't he?

On another cloudless day in another season and years beyond, the creator returned to Flueric on the mountain and found him kicking the dirt with his coat cast over his shoulder. "See, it's been nearly a decade, and they've been doing quite well while I've stayed here. Imagine what a thousand years could do for them!"

He stood and donned his jacket. "My conditions are simple. You must carve yourself out of the divine seat and take up residence down here, like me. Join their ranks, but not as their creator or their *God*. No, you come as a fellow struggler. I will do as I've always done and continue to show you why they are weak and worthless in the shadow of me and my kin."

The presence remained.

"If they stay loyal, you win, and I'm banished. But if they tear themselves apart—*and they will, Father*—then I receive dominion over this existence in lieu of the sons and daughters of Eve and Adam. No more postulations about free will and virtue, but a definitive truth about your failure in creating them. Do we have a deal?"

The presence of the creator rolled around Flueric, and he felt the significant weight of the cosmic power from which everything he'd known had come. Flickers of light emerged from the stone and the bushes upon which insects found rest as they burst into flames. Flueric smiled and danced amongst the fires for a time before departing the sacred spot and returning to his toils amongst humanity to prepare for when the Seraphim's songs would silence, and he would begin his time as the lord of all creation.

Ω

Baba Yaga's home landed astride Chelsea's, and it strutted about the yard before stopping to scratch beneath its wing. Within, Dodd and Chelsea milled together by the door, and Lilith and Rose continued to play with the Tinker. Lilith reached into the bag and produced a wood planer to shave down an uneven floorboard. When she finished, the tool returned to the bag, and Rose reached in to find a needle and golden thread to sew shut a tear in her pants she'd earned while underground at the Nisse city.

"Tut tut, little chickens, it's time to leave my house to its rest," Baba Yaga said as they reached ground level and the door swung open.

The party disembarked and stretched in the open air before entering Chelsea's home to rest and replenish themselves with some of her more trusted cuisine. Dodd held the door as they entered and was surprised to see Baba Yaga and Princess were coming with them.

"Aren't there eyes of newt and legs of frog to gather or something?" he asked, earning a toadish frown from Princess and a crooked smile from the crone.

"Don't worry yourself, Princess," Baba Yaga said. "You've not misbehaved enough to earn yourself a place in my pot. Not yet."

The toad croaked a whine and hopped inside the temperate home. Chelsea wasn't too fond of seeing her scratching her ears on the corners of walls, but kept it to herself.

"David's returning," Rose said. "He will be here soon."

"You don't look so happy considering the love of your life will be here today," Dodd said.

"Things have progressed, I can feel, but he has suffered a great loss."

"Damn. I'd prefer it if we could stop hemorrhaging for just awhile. It feels like every step forward is followed by two steps backward."

Baba Yaga arranged herself in the kitchen and opened cabinets to inspect their contents, giving off a slight *hmmmm* every now and again. "This is a war we're in. One should expect loss, and much of it."

Chelsea did a passable job of pretending not to care that one of the prototypical witches was giving her kitchen a cursory inspection. "I wish more than anything that you two didn't have to endure the hardships you've had, but she's right." Lilith rose and left the room in a swift motion. "There comes a time when we leave childhood behind, and that goes hand in hand with collecting scars."

"Well said." Baba Yaga sidled up to Dodd and peered at his face. "You've a drinker's nose, you do."

"You're quite fetching yourself…"

"Where's the spirits in this house? I've a mind to take a nip on a night like tonight."

"Doesn't alcohol not work on you?" Chelsea asked.

"It settles in the stomachs of the likes of me and Rose just fine," Baba Yaga said. "Doubly good for the one who ran to the loo. Just as good for me as you."

"She's already rhyming and she's stone cold sober," Dodd said. "I don't think this is a good idea."

Chelsea walked into the dining room and gestured for the witch to follow. Dodd and Rose listened with skewed grins as bottles clinked and Baba Yaga inquired to their contents.

"Ever seen her drink before? I don't want her to get hammered and start turning people into"—Dodd looked to Princess—"you know."

"I've only ever seen her take mushroom tea, and that is an experience in and of itself," Rose said. "You wouldn't worry about her getting loose with her spells as long as nobody crosses her. At the end of the day, she is the boogeyman, after all." She stood and collected Chelsea's crystal glasses from the cupboard, counting out five. "David won't want any, but I bet he wishes he could have a drink right about now."

"Any clue what happened?" Dodd asked.

"Not the specifics, just his overall feeling of loss," Rose said.

Dodd got up and turned the local radio on to one of Pulse24's AM stations to listen to the news.

"…and other coastal cities have seen complete and utter destruction. Drone footage has captured the moment when All Century's special units descended on Species 0, or what many on social media have dubbed the Kaiju, and subdued it."

"Are there any indications on whether or not the creature will strike again in Brazil?"

"Great question. It appears nothing is strictly off the table. The Russian government made claims they would use nuclear torpedoes on Species 0 if it enters waters near their country, but the United States has remained silent on what they have planned, and with the success we saw from the agents of All Century, such drastic

measures may be unnecessary. For now, it has gone back into the sea and appears to be on a northward heading…"

Dodd switched the radio off. "That was David, no doubt."

"David and others. Based on what the radio said. Pulse24 is spinning things to look like All Century is positioned to save the world. Why?"

"Because it gives them credibility, and without that, they can't morph the minds of half the population into listening to their lies. If they can't do *that*, then there's no way to divide us," Dodd said.

"I guess wisdom does really come with age," Rose said.

"And a very regal look." Dodd brushed his hair back. "The procedure they did on me didn't just heal me but took ten years of wrinkles off this face."

"I'll bet Mrs. Dolan loves that."

Chelsea and Baba Yaga reentered the kitchen. "Not as much as you might think, but it does feel interesting being the older woman with her boy toy."

"Interesting, you say?" Dodd wrapped her in a hug and pulled her into his lap, where she pretended at protest before settling bottles of whiskey and tequila on the table. Baba Yaga hopped onto a chair and placed another down. Gin.

Lilith returned to the surprise of Rose, who arranged glasses between them, collected ice, and poured draughts based on preferences she knew. "What will you have?" she asked Lilith.

"Anything will do. I don't have much experience with the luxuries of humanity."

Rose decided on tequila for Lilith and even garnished the beverage with a wedge of lime. They sat in collective silence, sipping and resting until they heard Chelsea's car pull into the driveway.

"Leonard's home," Dodd said.

Chelsea placed her glass down with a clink of ice. "Oh good, I wonder what he's been up to."

Leonard entered with his telltale crouch and flipped on the kitchen light to reveal his friends and nightmares having a drink together. "Oh, ahhh, hi."

A chorus of hellos greeted him, and he saw Rose smiling at his discomfort. Baba Yaga merely waggled her eyebrows at the man.

"I've brought a guest back. Well, a guest we already had actually. She's, ummm, well…"

Barbara entered the kitchen. "He's trying to tell you that I'm back."

"Well, this is a surprise," Dodd said. "You've been busy, Leonard." The grown man blushed like a teenager.

Rose stood and collected two more glasses, placed them on the table, and said, "Sit and let me know what to pour you."

"Gin for me," Barbara said. "Do you have any tonic?"

"I'll check," Rose said.

Leonard left the room and returned with a wine spritzer.

"Why am I not surprised?" Barbara said. Lilith sized up the woman while Leonard and Barbara took the chance to return her glare.

"Barbara, this is Lilith and Baba Yaga," Rose said as she returned with a bottle of tonic and poured some into her glass.

"A Baba what?" Barbara asked. Rose, Chelsea, Dodd, and Leonard all hissed and motioned for Barbara to be careful.

Baba Yaga raised her head and looked directly at the woman. "You smell like sex and idiocy."

"Holy shit," Rose said, spitting out her drink. Everyone laughed except Lilith and Leonard, for reasons respective to each.

"Well, other than that, what have you two been up to, Leonard?" Chelsea asked. "Anything helpful?"

"Actually, yeah," Leonard said. "Barbara is going to help us infiltrate Pulse24."

"And why would we do that?" Dodd asked.

"Because we have to do something about the fact that they control the narrative and have poisoned the minds of both good and bad people alike," Rose said. "That it, Barbara?"

"Yes… something like that," she said, taking a seat at the counter away from the group.

"She was also made into something of a pariah by All Century. They had her house bugged."

"Is that what they did?" Chelsea said with a sardonic hint. "Must be part of their training protocol, eh, Barb?" Chelsea reached into her pocket and flicked the tracker to Barbara.

"Listen, when I planted that, I didn't know what I know now."

"Don't worry about it," Rose said. "What matters is we are here and we are talking. The entire group."

"The full monty."

"All the village people."

Baba Yaga grinned. "The congregation."

"Good one," Dodd said.

Within a few moments, the sounds of wings beating from a distance grew louder within the yard. "Curses," Baba Yaga said and rushed out the door to see to her house, which was now positioned back with its wings splayed in a defensive stance. The sound of a hard thud was followed by a conversation, and the group watched as a single black raven walked by the door.

David entered the home. "Hi, guys," he said and placed Azazel's arm on the table, followed by Odin's spear, Gungnir.

Chelsea groaned at the sight of the limb on her breakfast table and quickly made off to gather paper towels to place it on.

"You don't see that every day," Dodd said. "Whose arm is that?"

"Azazel's," David said as he walked to Rose, and she scooped him into a deep embrace.

Lilith gasped and stared at the table. "To think he could have been felled."

"He sacrificed himself for the greater good," David said. "Iblis went ahead and did it first."

Dodd stood and walked to David, placing his hand on the boy's back. "I'm so sorry, son."

Chelsea came and joined Rose in her hug. "Baby, it's going to be okay."

"There's a chance for that now, that's why they died," David said as they let go of each other. "But Leviathan ate them—well, at least, she ate Iblis, and she got a lot stronger just from that. If she has Azazel too…"

"You never had hope to kill her," Lilith said. "She's an essence. Something vile given form. That can't be struck down with fire or swords."

"Speaking of vile," David said, looking Lilith up and down. "I hope you've been behaving."

"She has," Rose said.

Dodd sat back down and poured himself more whiskey. "She's doing fine."

Baba Yaga reentered the house. "I've a mind to turn whoever caused that commotion into slime! Who comes crashing through the air without cause or concern like that?"

"Odin's ravens, Baba Yaga," David said, turning to her. "But I'll take responsibility for any harm they caused your home."

Baba Yaga paused and looked at David. "Rose, you've caught yourself something special here, haven't you."

"I told you we shouldn't let her drink," Dodd said.

Rose laughed and watched as David extended a small bow to her mentor. "A pleasure to meet you."

"Good manners take second to looks, but they never hurt, dear boy," said the witch as she approached David and touched portions of his body with her palms. "And looks ye have."

"Can we stop molesting my son now?" Chelsea asked.

"Just buttering him up because I need a lock of his hair," Baba Yaga said. "One can create wondrous divinations with the locks of a celestial."

"Sure, if that'll make us square for the commotion outside," David said.

"It'll do that and more." Baba Yaga returned to her seat and inspected Azazel's arm. "And what've we here?"

"The second of the four rivers. Now, with the one inside of me, we have three of them."

"You have one inside of you already?" Dodd asked.

Baba Yaga sniffed at David. "He does. The very same that Pendragon held at my neck all those years ago."

"Vajra wouldn't let me wield it because I already have the one she's talking about from Valhalla. That makes three."

"Four, actually," Chelsea said, producing the Tinker from a cabinet in the corner. "We have all four."

Baba Yaga's eyes glowed.

Vajra, Tinker, Caladfwlch, and Gungnir.

Leonard said, "Electromagnetism, the strong nuclear force, the weak nuclear force, and gravity."

"Lenny, honey, I think I'm in a bit over my head here," Barbara said.

Despite certain members of the group protesting, with Chelsea leading the cause, they decided to fill Barbara in on the details.

"You mean to tell me that you're breaking into Eden?" Barbara said.

"*We're* breaking into Eden, darling," Chelsea said. "You're in this now and to the end, whatever it may look like."

"You can't tell me it's hard to believe when there's a snake the length of Puerto Rico rushing toward us as we speak," David said.

"It's that huge now?" Dodd whistled through his teeth. "We'd better hope Eden has a large door."

"It does," Lilith said. "It just also happens to have a great lock on it."

"What's the plan for tomorrow?" Leonard said.

"I'm coming with you and Barbara to Pulse24," David said. "I have a pretty good idea how to help with that narrative control problem. The rest of you need to figure out where we are opening the door to Eden. Lilith, you said any large body of water will do?"

"Yes, I believe so," she said.

David looked to Baba Yaga and Rose, who nodded in unison.

"Let's lead that big bitch up the river to the Rip," David said. "This all started on the Hudson. Let it end there, too."

"The Rip?" Barbara asked.

"The Rip Van Winkle Bridge upstate," Dodd said. "It connects the towns of Hudson and Catskill." He looked to David. "Not a bad spot. It has lower traffic and a much smaller population than around here. We can prepare whatever we need to on the bridge."

"You still have the problem of manifesting the door, even if you have the location and keys to open it," Lilith said.

"I think these will help," David said, producing the red feathers from his pocket. "Michael's feathers."

"You claimed these?" Baba Yaga asked.

"Odin did," David said.

Baba Yaga's cackle cleaved through the relaxed mood. "If anyone could and survive to tell the tale, it's him. And what of him now?"

"Muninn left a while ago to fill him in on the goings on," David said. "Huginn is right outside in case we need to travel fast."

"I'm not flying to Manhattan on a filthy bird," Barbara said. "I don't care whose it is."

Miss, I belong to none but myself, and I'd wager I am far cleaner than you.

The group looked about and shared another laugh. Even Barbara, whose shocked surprise worked with the gin to lower her guard.

Dodd walked to the door and stepped out. "There's a huge black bird out here that sounds like James Earl Jones," he said.

"It's nice to meet you," Huginn said.

"Nice to meetcha, too. Thanks for giving the kid a lift." Dodd walked back in and took his seat. "Barbara, you might have to take an L on this one. Huginn there is going to move a lot faster than a car, and you'll need to get out of there and head north pretty fast when you're done in the city."

Leonard consoled her. "Why don't you tell them how we can get inside."

"I hadn't considered landing from above, but the original plan was to use my security access and walk right in. If we can do that, the rest is easy. There's a server room on the twelfth floor below the major television studio, and we can hack it there or do whatever."

"I'll need to be brought right to the studio," David said. "I can manipulate the servers remotely."

"There's been near-constant violence and protests outside the building for a while now, so we may have to be crafty getting into the lobby, but once we are inside, it's a straight shot to those floors. I have the elevator codes."

"Baba Yaga, can you make us some pots of gas that will put people to sleep?" David asked.

"I can cook up something to that effect," she said. "Rose, do you remember the ingredients?"

"Yes," she said. "I'll gather the recipe."

"Good," David said. "I'd like to avoid killing people if at all possible. If Barbara is any indication, there are good ones working within All Century who deserve a chance to change their minds."

"Thank you," she said, and Leonard took up her hand.

The party broke up soon after. Leonard and Barbara retired to his room, while Lilith arranged herself in the living room, which she preferred over sharing the same bed as Baba Yaga—who was known to be gassy in her sleep. Dodd and Chelsea took the master bedroom, and Baba Yaga retreated to her hut, which remained fixated on Huginn, who stood sentry outside. David and Rose crept up the stairs to his room, which felt like the last remaining slice of the life they'd had before all this began.

She carefully disrobed him, relieved to find he had no grievous wounds hidden beneath. Her clothes fell to the floor, and they entered the shower together to wash away their worries until the sun rose to bring them back.

CHAPTER 9

PULSE24

The protests in front of the All Century's sleek, glass-walled office building had devolved into utter chaos. A sea of diverse faces, each person driven by a shared purpose, made up the crowd, and their voices blended in a chorus of chants and slogans. Hand-painted signs bobbed above many, their messages bold and clear: *Justice Now*, *Equality for All*, *No More Corruption*. Others lined the street opposite them with their own messages boldly displayed: *Born ONE Way*, *Go Home*, *Keep Them Out*.

On the steps of the office building, a line of security personnel stood firm, their expressions stern but watchful. A stark contrast to the passionate crowd before them. The building's reflective surface mirrored the bustling scene, distorting it slightly, and David could see the fruits of Flueric's labors in the rage flying between protesters and counter-protesters.

"Abaddon's at work down here," David said. "I can feel him sliding around the crowd."

"We'd better get inside before he notices us," Barbara said.

The streets around the building filled with the blaring horns of impatient drivers. The sound blended into the cacophony of the protest. Leonard, Barbara, and David navigated sidewalks packed with onlookers, some sympathetic, others curious or indifferent, almost all recording videos of the scene. News vans lined the curb, a haven for reporters standing by ready to broadcast updates.

David paused as they passed through a group making up part of the counter-protest. One member who'd been chanting and hefting a sign reading *Blood and Soil* paused as he noticed a hooded young man staring at him. A flash of recognition crossed his face.

"David?" he asked. "David Dolan…"

"Mr. Eryn. It's been a while." David stepped closer to the man. "I'm glad you remember me."

"One of the best US History students I've ever had. How could I forget?" Eryn said. "Here to exercise your First Amendment rights like I taught you?"

"Yes, something like that," David said.

"We have to keep moving," Barbara said to David, earning a glance from Eryn.

David's eyes never left those of his once teacher. "Can I ask you, why are you so angry?"

Eryn's expression changed at the idea that David might be challenging his convictions. "My son didn't die in Afghanistan for us to open the borders and allow everyone in. Our country was built on American pride, kid. You should try to have some."

David remembered how Mr. Eryn helped students after school if they fell behind, despite the school's policy of not providing pay for extra tutoring. His work in the VA, where he helped bring families to veterans who didn't have any of their own to enjoy the holidays. His time in the food pantry, helping supply needy families with holiday meals.

"I see, thanks," David said and placed his hand on Eryn's shoulder. "I hope I can help you soon. You're a good man, after all."

Eryn's righteous repose lifted, and he opened his mouth to say something, but David had already begun moving away behind Leonard and Barbara. They crossed the street and made their way through the group of protesters who split themselves in half as they chanted toward the building or the counter-protest. The band stopped at a small alcove of space just before the stairs.

"Who was that guy?" Barbara asked.

David pulled his hood up, and Leonard could feel the heat building within him. "He's why we are here."

Leonard nodded and said, "The plan is to walk right up to security and have Barbara flash her badge. There shouldn't be much trouble getting in. From there, it's straight to the elevators, right?" Leonard looked to Barbara, who nodded and fidgeted with her coat.

"Having second thoughts?" David asked.

"No. My time with Leonard and hearing your story made it clear I have a penance to make, so it's not that."

"What is it?" Leonard asked.

Barbara looked into the crowd. "I keep seeing Abaddon's face out there."

"He may know we are here, but it won't matter," David said. "He doesn't have what it takes to stop me alone."

"See, we have an ace in the hole," Leonard said. "Don't be worried."

Barbara steeled herself and looked up the stairs. "Come on, let's go," she said and mounted them with her shoulders back and chin held high. Protesters hurled insults and small objects at them when they became aware they were walking into the building and, as such, assumed to be in the employ of All Century. The security team stopped them with raised palms, looked at Barbara's badge, scanned it, and said, "Welcome, Ms. Cole. You'll have to sign your guests in at the security desk." Barbara simply nodded and gestured for Leonard and David to follow. A scant few security officers looked after David as he walked by, and Leonard wondered if it was the hood on his head or the intense aura about him.

Once inside, Barbara ignored the security desk and walked confidently to the metal detectors, which the three bypassed with ease, and approached the elevator bank. Leonard pushed the "up" button and looked around.

"Don't seem nervous," Barbara said in a low tone. "Behave like you belong here and always have. That's the trick."

Leonard nodded and observed David's easy posture despite the clear fact that the boy was in deep concentration. A center set of elevator doors slid open with the telltale ding nearly every citizen of New York subconsciously knows, and the three entered. The doors closed and Barbara punched in her code. The elevator didn't move.

"They've dropped your clearance but left your badge active," David said.

"I get why they might have stripped me of clearance—things have been a little dicey between me and Blakely lately—but why would they keep my badge current?" Barbara asked.

"They wanted us to get in," Leonard said.

The elevator shuddered and hummed to life.

"Don't worry, it's called us to the thirteenth floor," David said. "That's where we were going anyway."

"It's going to be an ambush, David," Barbara said.

"Yes," David said. "You two had better stand aside from the doors."

Leonard and Barbara retreated to respective sides and exchanged terrified looks despite their powerful escort, and the elevator surged upward before coming to a smooth stop. David stood in the center until the doors slid open to reveal a dimly lit hallway lined with shadows. Flashlights clicked on to showcase a security team with rifles aimed at the elevator.

David walked out with his hands in the front pocket of his hoodie and his head bowed. He moved at a deliberate pace, which caused the security to stir, but not fire. "So this is the welcome wagon, then…"

"You had to know we wouldn't just let you saunter in here to destroy our sounding horn," Abaddon said.

Leonard heard Barbara gasp as she peaked from behind cover on her side of the elevator, and he risked a glimpse as well. Her reaction wasn't without merit, he noted. The entire security force wore the face of the acting CEO of All Century.

"Stay put," David said, and the elevator doors slid shut.

"What a neat trick, but it won't work," Abaddon said. "You may have become the world's most apt hacker, but that confidence has given you blind spots."

Leonard and Barbara heard the sounds of tense cables snapping from above as the elevator shifted, and he leaped to her side, grabbing her in his arms and bracing them both with the brass handrail. She screamed as the elevator fell free and cascaded downward.

"A fitting end to a turncoat, I'd say, but far too quick," Abaddon said from a different security officer. "I like to peel their flesh away in layers. Like an onion."

David listened intently as he accessed the computerized brakes and locked them on to bring the elevator to an abrupt stop before he stepped forward toward the security detail and took his hands from his pockets. Within each were four glass vials nestled between his fingers that glinted in the flashlights.

"Oh, you think you're going to solve this problem without getting blood on your hands?" Abaddon said. "Some crazy purple knock-out gas isn't going to cut it."

"You underestimate my chemists," David said with the ghost of a smile, and for the second time since emerging, Abaddon's own grins wavered.

The security forces opened fire on David, who threw the vials amongst the numerous men and women without ever leaving his place. Sparks flew as bullets bounced off of the elevator doors behind David and slowed in tempo as the guards fell to the floor. David replaced his hands inside of his hoodie to walk forward and through them.

One officer had covered his mouth and held his breath, and David crouched before him. "Flueric should have stayed. You're nothing compared to him."

Abaddon's eyes flashed, and he pulled in a single breath to utter, "You'll live long enough to watch them all die." With that declaration, the body lost consciousness, and Abaddon was left staring at his own reflection in the mirror.

David stood and moved into the studio. "We'll see."

Ω

"Jesus Christ," Barbara panted and gripped the bar to step away from Leonard.

"That wasn't my favorite three seconds either, but it's over now."

Barbara tried the buttons out of instinct and then looked at Leonard.

"They cut the cables from above," he said. "We have to climb up and out. Or maybe…" Leonard approached the doors and inspected the seam between them. He took off his belt and used the buckle to wedge a space large enough for his fingers and tried to pull them apart, but they stopped after a few inches. Barbara came over and grasped the right side, leaving Leonard to the left and they threw their weight in opposite directions to satisfy the resistance. Leonard put his foot in front of the door to ensure they wouldn't slide closed again and looked at the elevator shaft in front of them. There was a gap of nearly a foot between them and the wall. Below were the doors of another floor somewhere between thirteen and the ground.

"Hold this?" Leonard asked, and Barbara positioned her legs on one side and leaned over with her arms to the other to keep both doors open at once. Leonard crouched and crawled beneath her to examine the outer door, and Barbara looked down at him with cocked eyebrows.

"Not exactly a position I expected to be in at this point in our relationship," she said.

Leonard, satisfied with his inspection, rolled to his side to grasp the belt and looked up at her. "Yeah, I've never been trapped in an elevator, either—" He looked past her smooth legs to see her blushed smile. "Oh," he said, and turned to his stomach once more.

Barbara laughed to herself, and Leonard quickly worked the buckle into the new set of doors, which he expected to be just as stubborn, before sliding them apart easily and watching as they remained open. "Perfect," he said as he slid backward and replaced his belt. He stepped up behind Barbara and against her to replace her feet with his and held the doors of the elevator car. "You go first. Slide backward through the gap and drop down to the floor."

Barbara hesitated and then removed herself so Leonard could increase his purchase as she awkwardly bent in her pencil skirt. "This isn't going to work," she said. She grasped the slit on the side, tore it up to her middle thigh, and kneeled again, freer to move. She oriented herself on her hands and knees, facing away from the door, and slid backward. "I'd better not get cut in half by this thing if it falls again."

"At least you'll die before it crashes into the ground."

"Comforting, Leonard," she said and continued her awkward scoot until her bottom half hung outside of the elevator car.

"Don't forget to push yourself back at the last second. It's small, but there's still a gap big enough for us to fall through if we aren't careful."

"Wish you'd mentioned that before I passed the point of no return," Barbara said and let herself slide further before gravity overcame her upper body strength and she pushed herself at the last moment. The fall was short but long enough to knock the wind out of her as she crashed onto the tile floor six feet below.

"Hello, Barb," Blakely said, and she grunted as two officers wrapped her head in a black sack and dragged her away.

The male voice and sounds of a scuffle reached Leonard

in the elevator car, and he crouched to come through the door but was slowed by having to keep the interior doors open. He sat, slid his legs through the gap, and pushed himself through. Scraping his back against the floor, he landed on his feet before crashing to the ground. He looked up and saw Barbara being dragged away, then focused on Blakely, who stood over him.

"Barlowe? Leonard Barlowe." Blakely called down the hall to Barbara, "Really, Barb, this guy?"

"I haven't known Barbara long, but since meeting her, the *real* her, I've wondered if you had a secret crush," Leonard said as he stood.

Blakely approached Leonard and delivered a knee to his stomach, causing him to crumple to the floor once more. "I could slide you right over there and shove your worthless body into that shaft like dirty laundry through a chute. I'd watch what I say if I were you."

Leonard straightened and sat up. "You're not a pawn, but hardly a queen either. No, you're a knight on the chessboard, and we both know a knight has to follow certain rules. You can't just get rid of me before letting your boss have a look." Blakely squared his stance, and Leonard went on, "Because if the knight doesn't follow his little L-shaped pattern, doesn't stay in his lane, then he's going to get spanked by the next piece up on the totem pole."

Blakely kicked Leonard in the chin, and the man crumpled to the ground, pulling rhythmic gasps of air his unconscious brain forced into his lungs. "I hope you feel that right up until Abaddon licks your flesh straight off your bones."

Ω

David relaxed into the anchor's chair and didn't speak immediately. Those who hid in offices and the control room of the studio would remember that he spoke to the camera with vulnerability and strength. But at the onset, he gathered his thoughts in the weight of the moment.

"Hey, everyone out there, you're probably wondering why a kid with bullet holes all over his clothes is suddenly sitting in the anchor chair during the evening news cycle. The reason for that will become pretty clear to you in a little while, but for now, I need you to clear your minds and just listen. That means not worrying about taking out the garbage, or paying bills, or multitasking."

David's body shimmered with heat as he pulsed his will to circle the globe.

"What I'm about to say is important, and the stakes are higher than any one of you is aware of. By now, all of you can clearly see that things aren't normal. What's happened over the last few years is unprecedented to us, but I'm not just here to talk about that, and this isn't some canned protest. I'm not going to cover the studio in tomato sauce and then get arrested to raise awareness of something. I'm speaking of the enslavement and eventual annihilation of humanity. And if that comes to pass, we will have few others to blame except ourselves, because we are serving our existence up on a silver platter. We've been fed lies, spoon-fed a narrative that keeps us divided, scared, and chasing after false promises. It's time to wake up and see through the smoke and mirrors."

David's voice left its easy pitch and carried a mix of frustration and determination. He raised his head for the first time since he began his speech, and the world saw his eyes reflecting a deep sense of urgency.

"Look around. We live in a time where we are more connected than ever before, yet somehow, we become more divided by the day. That's not by accident. It's by design. A design that benefits those who thrive on our fear and our distrust of one other. In order for that design to work, we have to allow ourselves to be distilled beneath our humanity until we are nothing more than numbers.

"But we're not just consumers or statistics. We're human beings with dreams, aspirations, the capacity for empathy, and artful creation that can catch the breath right out of our chests. We've let ourselves be manipulated into thinking that success is measured by what we own and how much power we have over others, or that the paltry differences between us amount to reasons enough to wish death and suffering on our brothers and sisters. And we are all brothers and sisters. A unique creation divided and evolved from a common ancestor. No matter where you place your belief or faith, that is the common truth."

David's voice rose as he filled with conviction.

"Enough is enough. We can't keep letting fear dictate our choices. We can't keep buying into the idea that our differences are more important than our common humanity. There are forces at work against us who've wound us up and set us on a collision course with none other than each other. We've become frenzied and powerless to see the truth that lies right in front of us or, at least, to accept it."

David gestured to the camera to draw the mechanized device in closer, but to the people, it appeared as if he gestured at them, and many leaned toward their screens as they watched or bent closer to their radios as they listened.

"It's time to reclaim our power, our unity, and our

compassion. The forces that seek to divide us—they thrive on our insecurities, our doubts, our willingness to buy into their narratives. *We* have the power to change this narrative. We have the power to build a future where justice, equality, and respect for each other is the guide our actions rely on and once again the judge for our malfeasance. But it starts with us, right here, right now."

David paused and gave the camera a smile while he increased his concentration into tethers that reached out from him to people all over the world, until not a single soul was deaf to his message.

"Many of you are probably wondering just who the hell I am right about now. The answer isn't very simple, but at my core, I'm just like you. A person who grew up a few miles north of where this studio sits, in a town just off the Hudson River. I went to school, dated girls, even got locked down by one for the long haul—"

Somewhere between Beacon and Hudson, New York, Rose smiled.

"—I played sports, rooted for the Yankees and cursed the Red Sox, went to college and managed to actually mold myself into someone who could contribute to society. That all ended the day of the Newburgh-Beacon Bridge collapse. The second the forces that work to divide you decided it was time to come out of the shadows and destroy me. They saw fit to snuff me out because they knew I could someday realize my potential and get through to you like I am today. But that doesn't mean we've won. Sure, the monsters have been beaten back and the giant snake—Species 0 I suppose—has left Brazil, but she's coming this way to devour me. Don't worry, I'm not scared for myself. I'm scared for *us*. Because if she succeeds in devouring me, the Leviathan will be unstoppable. She'll continue to consume and consume until there's nothing left of us or who we once were. And the worst part is, you'll let her.

"By now, some of you watching me on a screen might have noticed that my lips haven't been moving. Try muting your devices for a second." David paused for a beat before he continued. "Are you wondering how I can reach into your minds and be heard? It's because I'm one of you and one of *them*. But I've learned along the way that, in reality, we're not so different from the beings from beyond our world. And that's not all I've learned.

"There's been no shortage of guides to help me along the way, and my struggles over the last few years have revealed many truths. One of the most important lessons I've fallen upon is that *I* cannot accomplish much on my own. Despite this power I've just proven to you, *I* am just a blip on the cosmic radar. Insignificant if standing alone. And I didn't come here before you all to pretend otherwise or have you deify me as some pinnacle of leadership. I'm just a kid at the end of the day. What I came here to do is ensure that you know *you* are important. That *you* have what it takes to stop the bloodshed and remove the harnesses we've been yoked with.

"What wisdom I've managed to gather has shown me an important fact. Fact. That's a word I don't use lightly in an existence riddled with possibilities, but I'm using it now because I believe the same thing that those who have worked so hard to divide us know is true. There are few things in existence more powerful than the concept of *we*. Humanity was molded from the source to give thought to creation.

We'd be foolish to believe we are the only ones, but that doesn't change the miracle we experience every day when the lights turn on and our first thought emerges from the murky cloud of our minds.

"If we are so special, how have we been allowed to fall into this spot of danger? The story beats on a weathered drum that our ancestors were far more familiar with than we are. The chips have always been stacked against us, because what the ultimate source of creation decided to do was allow for its art, *us*, to think for itself. Angels, demons, gods of myth—they're all real and they all have their own motivations and limitations just like we do.

"One of those creations became aware that it shined brighter than all the rest. Instead of choosing to use that gift for the greater good and advancement of the universe, he sought to usurp more power and change creation as he saw fit. This bright angel walks before you today and goes by the name Flueric. The very same Flueric who just stepped down as the CEO of All Century."

Somewhere in the same building, Abaddon watched through the window as protesters lowered their signs and took pause to listen to David's message. The demon could not leap within most of them any longer. For the first time since coming into being in this reality, Abaddon felt fear.

"Why is he choosing to dismantle us? Well, I don't know outright. But I have a guess. I think it's because *we* are loved. Doted upon by what created us, and by many of its other creations as well. I think that tells us just how special we really are. Humanity may be some sort of divine experiment where life and consciousness were molded together not from the cosmic power of the stars but from the fertile soil of what the stars created. A new stage of sentient life. Science has a term for this. It's called evolution. None of the entities from the veiled world evolve in the way we do. It's as if we are sped up on an infinite scale compared to what came before us. Yes, we die, but I've seen the after. There's purpose to our struggles, and I hope you truly believe me in my telling you that. I think it will give many of you some peace, and peace quashes anger. But death isn't the end that matters most when it comes to our short little lives, and it shouldn't be feared. In fact, I've met the angel of death. He's actually a really nice guy."

Freja gave Samael a pat on the shoulder where they waited together for the final act to begin.

"What matters is what we experience in our journey to the end, and what we take with us to the beyond. From the warriors of Valhalla making meaning of their demises born of conflict, to the souls of people in a formless purgatory who undergo a timeless cleansing before they move on in their existence, our experiences matter. For what purpose, I'm not yet sure. I'm still young, like I keep saying, but I aim to find out one day, and when I do, I promise to deliver that treasured secret to humanity. Because we deserve to know, and at the end of the day, despite this power I've been imbued with, I am human too. Burdened by the same things as each of you: doubt, fear, hope, and even love. All things that make our light special as the void cascades and turns around us.

"But I have a luxury you did not, at least not until you heard my words today. I've peeked beneath the veil and left that experience with one truth that rises above all others. *We*, if united, can never be defeated. Not even in the face of physical annihilation."

Ω

Outside of All Century's Pulse24 media headquarters, sounds of conflict had drifted away. The people, some with looks of bewilderment and awe on their faces, listened to David Dolan's message. The security officer's hands left the butts of their batons and cans of mace as the fervor fell from a fever pitch.

In Keyana's childhood home, the woman known as Lady Perez to neighborhood children sat transfixed by her television screen. She was one of the many who'd heeded David's request to mute her set, and she believed she was watching a miracle transpire as David's silky words flowed through her mind. She felt a peace in those moments that no prescription could ever hope to deliver.

Keyana herself sat at her desk in Manhattan and listened to David while looking at the woman security had been dragging. She sat on the floor and struggled with the black hood over her head while the officers shared looks of bewilderment. Keyana began to question whether putting her morals aside for a comfortable apartment and future was ever going to be a sustainable choice.

Just outside of Puri, India, the nurses comforted one another at the first sign of hope and change they'd experienced since the recent start of a war with both China and Pakistan. They paused in their frantic preparation of rooms and beds for the soldiers who would be brought in at any moment and let their tears fall free. David's voice was familiar to one nurse in particular, and she smiled. "Indra," she whispered, and the other nurses began to laugh and cheer in agreement. Nearby, the man called Yehuda stepped softly down the beach as he listened before wading into the sea, never again to emerge.

A small door opened in Kansas and out peered Grace, who'd been lost in unbridled fear since her experience outside of All Century's west coast headquarters. She had seen the face of evil and felt its breath upon her neck, but hope bloomed in the form of David's voice. There *were* two sides to this conflict, after all. Things might be saved, she dared to hope.

Stephen Cappodak's sight became blurred as he stared down the scope of his M4 rifle at the people below. He wiped the lens clear and aimed down the barrel once again to begin his task when David's voice filled his mind. More resistant than most, Stephen tried to shake the presence free and continue on his course, but he was unable. With his eyes clear, Stephen saw the faces of the people below him and recognized them as something else besides entities of otherness that so allowed them to be slaughtered. A woman walked through his field of vision holding a small child, and he shifted his aim to a man who had been sitting on the lawn reading a book. It was a copy of an American classic that featured another gentleman who was handy with a rifle. Two other men stood holding hands, transfixed by the message, and Stephen let out a breath he hadn't known he was holding. He moved his finger from the trigger. He folded his tripod and began the process of dismantling the gun and packing his belongings. It was nice, he thought, that he'd be able to see his wife again.

Somewhere in the innocuous space between the veiled world and the one of the living, Kharon, wearing the visage of Sir Patrick Stewart, pushed his ferry across the river of lamentation. He looked up from the woman he had been comforting and toward the far dock they'd recently departed that was becoming obscured by the murk.

He uttered, "Or more than you knew, David. Or more than you knew."

Ω

Barbara shook her arms free from the flimsy grasp of security officers and pulled the bag from her head. She scanned the room and recognized her surroundings. A small office space on the fifth floor used by data entry professionals and the like. Many looked at her with blank faces, their attention elsewhere as David's voice flowed through their once-busy minds.

She settled on her knees between the men and saw Blakely pulling Leonard across the floor in their direction. Luck struck a chord in this stanza of her song, and her onetime counterpart didn't turn to peer behind him as he worked.

One officer shook his head from side to side as if to free himself from David's voice, while the other looked off into space with an expression of bewilderment. Barbara didn't know why, but she stayed free of David's beguilement, though she heard his voice as everyone else. She realized now that the boy didn't mean to hack the servers of Pulse24 to spread his message at all. He aimed to transmit his will directly and use the broadcast equipment to magnify his ability. This was his plan to dismantle All Century's misinformation machine in one motion. A clever trick, Barbara thought.

The guard who continued to look around on the ceiling for some speaker turned his body, revealing the taser on his leg, and Barbara slipped it out in one swift motion. She recognized the device as a pistol grip handheld model that packed a punch, and not one that shoots out the cords. At her level, she saw a prime target and placed the taser on the guard's crotch before letting thirty-thousand volts race through the man. He barely emitted a whimper before crumpling to the floor, and the other guard lagged in his response, allowing Barbara to hit him with the taser in the calf and then again in the chest once he'd fallen.

She rose to her feet and made sure everyone else remained preoccupied before crouching and walking toward Blakely, who muttered and cursed as he pulled Leonard through the main floor toward a corner office. Barbara switched directions and entered the office first.

"Yeah, yeah, if you say so kid," Blakely said in response to David's words in his mind. Barbara could see an LCD screen in the room's corner and David's image on it. Despite sitting stone still, the young man appeared to leap off the screen. Bullet holes all over his hooded sweatshirt made her worry after him before she remembered he was more than human. It was easy to forget given his young features, which lent him endearment as he spoke.

"Drop him," Barbara said, brandishing the taser at Blakely as he turned to see her.

"Ever the resourceful Barb," Blakely said, letting Leonard slump to the floor. "What's the plan now?"

Barbara recalled Blakely using that turn of phrase often when they were evading pitfalls and mitigating disasters within the company. A touch of nostalgia hit her, and she wondered if Blakely felt as sad as she about them being on opposite teams.

"The plan is you let us walk right out of here and look the other way while we do it."

"That gets me shredded by Abaddon, and I'm not interested in looking like a burnt pulled-pork sandwich just because you decided to lose faith."

Barbara's expression softened. "You're the one without faith."

Meeting Leonard and his merry band of cohorts had done quite the opposite for her, she knew. Faith was something she had lacked, and that missing piece had led to her continued involvement with the company that would ultimately shatter the world order and stymie any chance for peace to be sown. She found that camaraderie through endeavoring for something she actually believed in to be something far more worthwhile than living in denial-clad luxury. "Join us, Blakely, and leave. Your side is the wrong one and you know it. Abaddon is literally a demon. Can't you see that?"

"I do, yeah. Just like you and I saw Flueric for what he really was long before you left." Blakely took a step toward her. "We both agreed at that point that there was no coming back from where we were going, and we tacitly signed on for seeing things through. I can't leave now."

Barbara held out the taser as he drew closer. "Then I'll have to use this."

"Give it a try." Blakely smiled. "I don't think you can."

Barbara pulled the trigger, making the taser click and snap, but Blakely continued forward, closing the distance between them by another two feet. An obscured figure moved outside of the frosted glass panes lining the office, and Barbara thought one of the security guards may have gotten back up.

Blakely seized his moment while her attention was off him and dashed toward her, grabbing the arm that held the taser. She pulled the trigger and bent her wrist to hit his arm, but he manipulated his body away just enough to avoid the current.

Blakely shouldered her into the corner and got his other hand on the taser. Barbara felt his strength and knew she was seconds away from losing her only advantage.

She raised her knee to catch him in the groin, but Blakely was turned sideways and took the brunt of the blow in his hip, rendering it ineffective. He twisted her wrist, and Barbara felt the rubber band snap of her tendons stretching far beyond their design protocols. She let go of the device, and Blakely stepped back with it in hand, pulling the trigger for effect.

"Now that that's out of the way, let's take a trip to the top floor," he said.

"Fuck you." Barbara squared herself and rubbed her wrist.

"Alright, I guess we do it the hard way for you and the easy way for me." Blakely walked toward Barbara until a wet thump sound issued, and he stopped. She watched his eyes cloud over, and Blakely collapsed onto the floor as blood spread in a growing pool.

"Oh god, I didn't kill him, did I?" the young lady asked.

She held a crystal award for outstanding performance in the previous fiscal year, issued to one Keyana Perez. Blood ran through the etchings of her name and dripped from one of the sharp edges of the ornate desk piece.

"No, but you shouldn't care if you did," Barbara said. "He's not worth saving." She walked over to Leonard and rubbed his chest and neck to try to rouse him. "Thank you, Keyana. That was very brave."

"I heard what you said about faith and lying to ourselves. You're right. I couldn't keep ignoring what we are doing.

What's going on everywhere," she said, looking behind her into the office.

Leonard moaned, and Barbara got him seated. It didn't look like Blakely had broken his jaw, but his two-thousand-dollar wood-soled dress shoes left a massive welt. "Lucky for you, he didn't break your glasses, stud," she said. "Don't you know better than to rush in and try to save the damsel in distress? That trope never seems to work out anymore."

"Not in our story," Leonard mumbled and rubbed his cheek.

Barbara looked at Keyana and saw the girl was scared. David continued his speech, which may have helped to over-sensitize the poor girl. "Do you have some place to go?"

Keyana nodded. "My mom's place. I'm worried about her and don't want to be alone. But I need to take the train."

"The trains won't be running right now, you'll have to walk most of it, but here..." Barbara handed her a wad of bills. "Take a rideshare or cab if you can find one. That's at least eight hundred dollars. They won't be able to say no to that."

She took the bills in a tentative grasp and looked outside again to make sure nobody was coming for them.

"Go now. Get clear of the building and leave All Century behind you. They're going up in flames now, anyway." Barbara pointed to her head. "My friend is making sure of that—or the other outcome."

"What's that?"

"That Flueric wins, and All Century takes over the world. If that happens, it won't matter what you decide. We're all dead anyway. You can make your choice when you see where the chips fall."

"The people will hear him, but not everyone will choose to follow what he's saying," Keyana said and pointed to Blakely. "He didn't."

"David is going to tell them where we will make our last stand," Leonard said. "I'm guessing we will have an audience from news coverage on the scene."

"That's not a wise decision," Barbara said. "What if they try to interfere?"

"Let the chips fall where they may, like you said. David believes in humanity, and he's betting they'll stand with us."

Keyana said "faith" one last time and skirted toward the door. She smiled at them. "I hope you feel better. Good luck." And with that, she vanished toward the stairwell.

Barbara helped Leonard to his feet, and they walked in the same direction. Both banged up. Both feeling as if they might win.

Ω

"—It's time to wake up to the truth of who we are and what we're capable of. Let's reject the voices that profit from our division. Let's stand together, not as adversaries but as allies in the fight for a better world."

David paused to feel the feedback of the people he was reaching.

"Because if we don't, I can assure you of one thing. We will be dismantled into parts and systematically annihilated. Enemies of All Century will go first, then the neutral parties who thought staying out of things would keep them safe. After that, Flueric will carve through his faithful and let the remaining cohort begin to devour itself before Leviathan ultimately devours everything. Sound familiar, history buffs? I thought it might. Consider who gives tyrants their playbook when you assign your allegiance today and don't be afraid to stand up to what's wrong even if you're unsure if you're right.

"Charlie Chaplin was a man known for his great work despite not needing to utter a single word, but in a great movie he shocked the world when he said this: *The hate of men will pass, and dictators die, and the power they took from the people will return to the people. And so long as men die, liberty will never perish.* The problem with our situation is that when a dictator dies, up rises another—and another, and another. With each, the liberty the people receive whittles down until we ultimately revolt in a bloody massacre only to install yet another dictator. It's true that tyrants die, but *evil* doesn't. And I can assure you the evil *we* face will be ever present in our world unless we divine the courage to stand up, stand together, and push back.

"So, I ask today for you to stand together with me as I go off to face unmentionable horrors. Not by taking up arms and joining my crusade, but by changing your hearts to stop ignoring the nagging feeling inside of you that screams not to hate but to love one another. In these next small moments, return home, console your family, your loves, and find solace in them and yourselves. The moments that follow will give you a chance to lend a hand to whomever might need it and forget our petty differences in the face of the greater good.

"It is difficult for me to say goodbye right now, unsure of whether you will choose to stand with humanity or be beguiled by the side that saps at your virtue, but I can leave because I have faith. Not in some higher power or superhero, but in you. Every one of you. Because I believe we exist to push back the dark."

David stood from the chair and removed his hood to show himself to the cameras so at least the people at home could see him fully and take his measure. He smiled, turned, and leaped through the exterior wall of the building to cascade down the thirteen stories to the ground below.

Ω

Leonard and Barbara progressed down the stairwell and had reached the midway when they heard David's sign off.

"What a kid."

"Part of me wishes he and Rose got to stay that way for longer," Leonard said. "It feels wrong that they are on the front lines, tackling a problem that isn't their doing."

"You could make that claim for most people born after 1990."

The lights in the stairwell dimmed and then shut off within the column of concrete. It filled with quietude as both Barbara and Leonard held their breath. "Barbara," Abaddon called from above. "Oh, Barbara. You've been a very naughty girl. Come on back up here so we can *have a little chat.*" His voice took on a guttural quality that rolled horrid images through Barb's imagination.

Leonard looked up the stairwell and saw a figure crawling down the interior banisters toward them. "Go. Fast." He ushered Barb ahead of him and followed, taking care to mask the sounds of his footfalls as best he could.

"Do you think I don't know where you are? I can hear the blood rushing through your veins as your hearts quicken." Abaddon crashed into the stairs and sounded as though he

239

was making his way down them on all fours. "I was going to make you employee of the month! Imagine that. This is how you repay the company for all it's done for you?"

Barbara focused on her feet to keep from tangling. She stepped ever more quickly, thankful for all the mornings she put in on her stair climber. A door whirred past as she carouseled around the banister, and it read "four" in bold font.

"Almost to the bottom," Leonard said. "We can make it."

"Once you get there, take the far door into the lobby. It'll take us out to the protest."

"*Barbara… don't give me the cold shoulder!*" Abaddon sounded as if he was a few floors above them, and the two gave up the pretense of stealth for speed. Risk mitigation was no longer on the table. Barbara grabbed Leonard's hand and leaped, dropping two to three steps in a bound before the pair hurtled around each turn to continue down.

"Is it a push or a pull door?" he asked.

"What?" Barbara said.

"The door, does it push into the lobby or do we have to pull it?"

"It pulls into the stairwell," she said.

Leonard put on a burst of speed as they reached the ground floor to get in front of Barbara. He grasped the door first and flung it open for her. She escaped into the lobby, and Abaddon rounded the corner but paused on the stairs.

"*So, you're the little interloper who's been eating my porridge… Would you care to sleep in my bed?*"

The depictions of Abaddon were well known in his field, but Leonard wasn't prepared to face them in person. The demon, often portrayed in a neutral light like Samael, bore four locust wings on a back carpeted in algae-green fur. Its face was bare and cracked, with scars and crevices around an abnormally large hooked nose and surrounded by a coarse russet mane.

Leonard made the first move and pulled himself around the door and toward the lobby, narrowly being missed by Abaddon as he leaped past and slashed at the area Leonard had just occupied. Barbara, halfway across the lobby, gestured frantically toward the doors and Leonard made a mad sprint to meet her.

Three security officers at the desk appeared confused, but they snapped to attention when they saw people running. "Hey, wait a minute," one cried as Abaddon crashed through the door behind them. "What in the holy hell is that?"

"He's getting bigger," Leonard yelled as he and Barbara paused for the automatic door to slide open.

"We're out," Barbara said as the two cascaded from the doors and onto the steps with a crash of glass issuing out behind them. They fell upon the unforgiving stone stairs and tumbled down amongst the protesters. Leonard rolled to his side and tried to help Barbara to her feet, but she faltered at the knees and fell back. He turned, resolved to face Abaddon.

The demon had lost size since leaping through the glass entry to pursue them, and Leonard noted a hint of something in its once-frenzied expression.

Doubt?

Leonard glanced around and saw the protesters from either side were no longer facing one another and the building, but had all turned to look at him, Barbara, and the beast. Many showed a lack of surprise one might expect when confronting such a circumstance—the last months of Lilith's children rampaging and the entry of Leviathan had largely disillusioned them.

They watched as Leonard placed himself between the monster and Barbara in an act of selflessness and virtue.

They watched as Abaddon descended upon the man with a flurry of frenzied swipes, and how Leonard used his legs to lock the shrinking beast far enough away to save himself from the worst of the slashes.

They moved toward the imperiled couple as Leonard's glasses were knocked away and blood from his scalp dripped to the stone. One woman helped Barbara to her feet and tried to pull her clear, but Barbara freed herself and attempted to attack Abaddon, only to be knocked through the air into three other onlookers who broke her fall.

A man named Bill Eryn was the first to reach Leonard and confront Abaddon head on, using his sign to smash the beast about its head. Another member from the counter-protest attempted to pull Eryn away, but he was quickly subdued by the influx of more and more who had heard David's message and taken it to heart.

Abaddon itself, left with few to none in which to leap and manipulate, was put on the defensive against its aggressors, who were not content with simply warding it off as one might a bear.

They had taken its measure and with minds clear of distraction descended upon Abaddon, pulling tufts of mane with their hands, biting at its tough pelt, and scratching at its eyes.

Leonard sat up and felt the flow of warm blood drip into his eyes and wiped them clear to search for Barbara. He felt the soft cotton of a bandanna being pressed on his wound and tied around his head as do-gooders consoled him. They asked if he was feeling up to standing. Barbara limped to him and kneeled at his side as they watched their aides rush into the fray to stake their claim on Abaddon's body.

The beast howled.

A pile of people who'd been crowding the demon fell inward, and it looked to Leonard at first as if Abaddon had been spirited away back to the furnace of whatever hell he enjoyed before Flueric bore him into this world. That notion became dispelled as an explosion of locusts erupted from the pile of people and flew in all directions.

"Down!" Barbara yelled and covered Leonard with her body as the locusts enshrouded the crowd and flew up and beyond the confines of the city to spread throughout the world beyond. Leonard risked opening his eyes and peeking between fingers at the scene of people swatting away the pestilent cloud.

A tornado of fire rose from near the entrance of the building to meet a falling David. He landed in a flash of brilliant light that cascaded through the sky above the crowd in a blinding moment. Leonard's vision cleared in time to see husks of locusts fall to the surrounding ground, but further inspection showed the cloud dispersing in all directions beyond them.

David walked through the people to gasps. The crowd remained transfixed on him and the remnants of fire as they danced about his shoulders.

"Did you mean it, what you said?" a woman asked as she helped another to her feet. "About us being able to stop this?"

"Yes," David said. "But it won't be a free ride. If you can remain resolute against them, they'll be powerless over you, and I'll be free to stand against them on even terms." He turned to the sky and whistled before walking to Leonard and Barbara. "Abaddon played his trump card. Those locusts will devour every living plant on this planet, and it won't take long, either."

"Will he be done after?" Barbara asked.

Leonard put his arm around her and held her close. "He can't hurt us anymore. They saw to that."

David looked to them and uttered two simple words that proved more important to the crowd than most he had streamed directly into their minds. "Thank you."

Huginn descended from the clouds and took up Leonard and Barbara. David leaped upon the Raven's back, a seat of distinction rarely allowed by Odin's messengers.

They flew north to the bridge that would cover the gap between two worlds.

Ω

As David and company flew north, the great serpent cascaded toward the Hudson–Raritan Estuary, giving onlookers a glimpse of approaching waves. Their vantage showed a wake driven by some unseen terror befitting a summer blockbuster. As her heads left the sea and entered the brackish waters of the estuary, witnesses filmed her progress. A nearby young man took a selfie with the action in the background and captured a glimpse of a mysterious figure walking upon the waters toward the Leviathan. When he turned to see with his own eyes, the person had vanished, as though a specter, though many others would post the scene from different vantages as the night drew on. Hashtags emerged online and excited people postulated whatever it was might be some savior come to help David. Others believed he was the bringer of dark tidings.

Amaranth and viridian light leaked from the monster, who'd grown vastly larger from her ill-gotten meals since leaving Brazil. She traveled with the fervor of one who hungers for more power and thirsts for endless sorrow—coursing through the waves to devour the boy who'd galvanized the people and quash their hope once and for all.

CHAPTER 10
ONE FOR ALL

Dodd hummed as the group neared the center of the Rip Van Winkle Bridge, surrounded by the deep wooded beauty of New York.

"Brendan, I swear if you keep humming that song…" Chelsea said.

Dodd smiled. "But Chelse, *they say in heaven, love comes first.*"

"I will scream, I'm not kidding."

"*We'll make heaven a place on earth,*" Rose sang, and Chelsea made good on her promise.

"Keep that racket down. This is no time for games." Lilith covered her ears.

"You'd scream too if you had to deal with these two all the time," Chelsea said.

Baba Yaga, silent for most of their trip within her flying house of brown, piped up. "We are not alone here. I cannot tell exactly where, but celestial power courses around us."

"I feel it, too," Dodd said. "Another perk of having been imbued with some."

"You're a gallant and just man," the witch said. "I've grown to like you. So take heed when I tell ye to be mindful of how you use that power and to whom you choose to use it upon. None of the Host will shudder at your might. They're boiling over with what you've got just a smattering of."

"Aw, Dodd, she likes you," Rose said.

"I do well with the older crowd," Dodd said. "Any word from your boyfriend?"

The group had received David's message just as every other soul on Earth—and many immortals besides. They knew he'd set into motion the events of their last conflict, which made Lilith wonder why they were just so calm and free while she felt the weight of the moment upon her like a miniature Atlas.

"They're coming. It looks like something big went down, but I feel optimism from David," Rose said.

The group began arranging their three items on the ground when the sunset skies above became blackened by passing locusts. They descended upon the green leaves sprouting from everywhere around the bridge but gave the party a wide birth, either out of reverence to Baba Yaga or fear of Dodd's fire.

"I'm wondering if this might be that big thing that went down," Dodd said.

"Definitely a top contender," Chelsea said, producing the red feathers David had entrusted to her and placing them on the ground in front of Vajra, the Tinker, and Gungnir. "Does anyone have the slightest fucking clue how to do this?"

"Nope."

"Nah."

"No."

"Not I."

"Well, I guess we can just play canasta while we wait, then," Chelsea said, throwing her hands up.

A news van pulled up on the western side of the bridge beyond the now-defunct toll plaza, followed by another and another.

"Well, that's not ideal," Dodd said, walking toward them to ward them away.

"Leave them be," Lilith said. "David called them to purpose, and those who wish to see deserve to."

"Hmm, very succinct," Chelsea said. "I agree with her, Brendan. Let's leave it be."

Another van pulled up on the eastern side of the bridge, close enough to Baba Yaga's house to cause it to fly into the barren trees beyond. The witch wrinkled her nose at the situation but didn't bother further. Rose took notice of how locked in she was and was thankful to have her at their side. Though she had a storied history of being a hateful and wrathful entity that stalked the woods, in reality, she was a well-learned woman with thousands of years of wisdom to bear. It was only those who mistreated and used edged words who earned her ire, mostly, because we all have bad days.

The sky grew loud with the sound of wings, and both Rose and Dodd crouched in anticipation of some unannounced attack, but none came. Huginn swooped close to drop Leonard and Barbara in gentle heaps upon the ground, and David leaped off his winged chariot to land beside them. Baba Yaga approached and produced a fruit from the folds of her clothes and held it out to the large raven, who scooped it from her hands with wide eyes and devoured it. Huginn nodded and flew off.

"He has business to attend," Baba Yaga said. "It seems we are not the only ones mobilizing."

David nodded and looked around. "Abaddon's tantrum is going to starve the world."

"Will they really eat everything?" Chelsea asked.

"Not a single grape will be left the world over before the sun rises on tomorrow," Baba Yaga said.

"We'll have to worry about that if we see tomorrow," Dodd said. "Tonight's got enough danger to make the odds of that a little shaky."

"We have a leg up now," Leonard said as he approached with Barbara.

"Leonard." Rose gestured to the keys to Eden. "How do we activate these? Even Lilith doesn't know because angels opened the door when she entered the garden."

"I have no direct context. Maybe one person needs to hold all of them and the door will simply appear, or it could be more intricate than that. Maybe a ritual. There are some references to Eden that exist in the—"

He stopped speaking as David picked up the feathers and handed them to Dodd. "You should be the one with these, I think."

He walked to the items and felt the power emanating from each one. In a similar fashion to how he reached his consciousness to deliver his will to the world, he reached out to the avatars. Every one received him, but barred him from their gifts. "I don't think I'll be able to hold all of these. Not even sure anyone or anything ever has." David reached into his chest for the first time in front of his group and pulled forth the sword he'd taken from Leviathan's lair.

The blade had taken on a more refined quality since last

he'd brandished it, with the size and length having been halved and the hilt established where there had been none. David found himself unable to lay the weapon down and appraised it. "It's talking to me for the first time."

"You said the Leviathan told you it takes different forms for whoever holds it. Maybe you have changed your goal since you first took it within you," Rose said.

"I have," David said. "It's not a massive dragon slayer to ward off the world serpent anymore. It's a symbol now, and it also wants us to be victorious." David gestured to the three remaining rivers. "Leonard, take up Tinker. Rose, hold Vajra—it should allow you to."

Lilith approached Dodd and held out her palm, and he placed one of Michael's feathers inside of it. "You aren't ready to be canonized or anything, but I'm happy I got to learn about who you are and what you've been through."

Lilith opened her mouth and closed it again. Having spent the majority of her existence living outside the confines of understanding, she felt vindication in the recognition of a valorous person.

"Mom, can you lift the spear?"

"I don't think I want to."

"That's exactly why you should be the one to do it."

Chelsea knelt down and made ready to lift the heavy weight of the six-foot piece of metal decorated in beatific runes, but it came from the ground with little more effort than hefting a broom handle.

David nodded in satisfaction as he surveyed them. "Baba Yaga, I believe you're the next piece of this puzzle."

"Aye, it appears the Caladfwlch guides you true," she said and approached the group while throwing back her hood. "The seam makes itself easy to see with you all oriented so."

Baba Yaga used no tincture or spell circle to aid her ritual. It called for intense concentration while also demanding looseness of thought, making her task a difficult divination. She placed her hands on the bridge in a manner not so different than Rose's way of conjuring the growth of living things.

Leonard and Chelsea both noted the witch didn't seed the ground prior to calling forth great columns of wood into a large frame, within which reality shimmered and danced.

The feathers glowed in Dodd and Lilith's hands, revealing the image of a gated door from the portal. It was David's sword that reached out to it first in a glow of particulates that emanated to reach their opposites that crept from the door. Vajra came next, closely followed by Tinker and Gungnir, each superimposing their own contributions in a transference of natural force and technical attributes.

The four rivers met upon the door to Eden, and the feathers erupted in flame before the spectacle raised in fervor to a fever pitch, casting winds in all directions. Onlookers at home would see the items coalesce into a single beam, but the mics weren't close enough to catch Dodd calling out to not cross the streams or David's laughter at his quip.

The door breached open by simply disintegrating into the cosmos that had conjured it, and the band looked inside to see heEden staring back.

David took two steps toward the door before his eyes widened. He turned to scoop his mother and Rose in both arms and leaped away. Dodd collected Barbara and Leonard and cleared away from the door the second before a torrent of red flames emerged. The wood frame showed what may have happened to the party should they have been a few seconds late. It didn't simply burst into flames—it disintegrated under the heat.

From the garden stepped Raphael, Michael, and another angel they had not yet met. All three brandished their fiery swords at David, who ushered Rose and Chelsea away to the east end of the bridge.

Dodd approached from the west side behind them, and the third angel turned to face him as he licked his lips. "So you're the one who stole my brother's fire—"

Ω

Baba Yaga credited her long tenure on Earth to being cleverer than most of the bigger fish in the pond. That thoughtful nature bore itself a certain instinct she had grown very proud of. The same instinct that had caused her to walk to the side of the gate of Eden and near the northern side of the bridge before the door opened. The torrent of flame that Michael expelled preceded the entry of three angels guarding Eden.

Raphael, whose task it was to man the gates, Michael, and a troublesome third. Raguel had brushed up against Baba Yaga in the past, and she'd measured him as far more radical than the other archangels in the Host. Nearly equal to Michael in power and rather ambitious to boot, not so unlike another bright angel who'd come before him.

Raguel wasted little time in pursuing Dodd, who led the angel away from the humans he'd saved from certain death, and Baba Yaga hunkered down and whistled for her house to fly along the edge of the bridge. She leaped upon its roof and clamored down the chimney, which was no simple task with the hearth alight.

"Mind your hind legs, Princess, the time for redeeming comes nigh."

Princess croaked and leaped to the door with a satchel upon her back filled with reserve stores for Baba Yaga. The witch wished the stories of flying brooms were true as her knees creaked, and she took up the ladle upon her cauldron to fill three flasks with a clear liquid. With great care, she placed them in the folds of her cloak and met Princess at the front of her little house of brown, which circled the bridge. She watched as Michael and Raphael stalked toward David, who held his sword out to them. Raguel engaged Dodd in a pitiful game of cat and mouse.

"House of brown, set me down."

The house did as it was bid and skipped to the end of the bridge to skulk in the growing shadows as Baba Yaga and Princess crept along the side of the bridge, quiet as mice.

Ω

"Mind your manners, thief, and bring yourself here for redemption," Raguel said.

Dodd angled away from the angel and backed under the trusses of the cantilever bridge. "I told you, I didn't steal anything. I was taken hostage and your friend's power was forced into me. For Pete's sake, Azazel was helping us until the Leviathan ate him! We don't have any beef with you guys."

"I'm not so new a spark to be taken in by the beguiling of a human and jinn," Raguel said and leaped forward with speed Dodd had expected but could not counter.

The former detective leaped into the steel beams of the

bridge and crawled about within it to buy time. He could tell by Raguel's eyes that his flames would be orange like their own sun, a small contrast to Raphael's golden color, but more similar than the crimson fire of Michael's.

"That massive monster is coming up here right now to take a heaping bite out of David's ass, Mr. Avenging Angel. I think you'd better stop this nonsense and talk to your boss about a plan to deal with that."

"I intend to. Right after I peel you apart like a date."

Dodd had roped the angel away from Leonard and Barbara, who were both gone from sight, and switched his tactics. He held the beam behind him with his hands and flexed his legs while building fire beneath his feet to explode toward Raguel and land a crippling blow on the angel.

Raguel's movements were fluid enough for Dodd to see them, but too fast for him to interpret exactly how the angel slid to the side. He countered Dodd's momentum with a quick blow to the man's midsection and then caught him by the neck to hold him.

"Foolish, but more admirable than fleeing," Raguel said. He raised his hand and unleashed a torrent of orange flame into Dodd that flung him hundreds of feet back toward David, where he rolled to a stop in front of the door to Eden.

The angel took his time walking back to the detective to deliver the finishing blow and hurry him to his end.

Ω

David felt the weight of his sword and doubted his ability to harness its power without utterly destroying the bridge beneath their feet. Had he suspected Michael may leap out and begin a fight, he'd have chosen a different place to open the portal—though their plan had worked, and that was half the battle.

"Drop to your knees, mortal, and hand me thine blade. I'll bring you to justice more quickly that way."

"No dice, big guy," David said and pointed to Raphael. "I've got bigger fish to fry than you and golden boy over here. Why don't you stand around and do nothing like you did when you watched a demon burn my innocent girlfriend alive."

"It's not our design to interfere unless explicitly ordered."

"And the circumstance of your boss going silent caused you to sit back, completely impotent, while your greatest enemy expertly consumes the world. If I didn't know better, I'd think you want Flueric to win and humanity to perish."

"Oh dear," Raphael said. Michael's eyes exuded his red aura in tendrils of flame, and he aimed his sword point at David.

"You take liberties in your assumptions of me, *human*. I do as I am bid and none else."

Michael stepped forward, and Raphael turned away to look after where Chelsea and Rose had been hiding. The women had vanished, and the angel took flight to find them. He didn't notice the tiny spores that had seeded the air as he flew through them and circled the bridge.

"We do not use pseudonyms for the adversary of which you speak. If Lucifer is to show himself here, I will expel him to the pits once more."

"He is coming as we speak. Can't you feel him?"

"Enough time for talk. You've committed the highest of treasons by attempting to regain the garden from which all your ilk have been expelled. My orders are explicit in this circumstance. You and all here must be purged."

"That's where the discussion portion of our little meeting ends, then, because nobody threatens my mother and Rose."

David stepped forward, and Michael unfurled his wings to float into the sky before descending upon him. David braced himself and riposted the blow in a maneuver that would make Mukhulai proud. He used the angel's momentum to partially pass before attempting a straight kick at his armored breastplate.

Michael's eyes widened in recognition of David's prowess, and he turned his chest to make the blow a glancing one. Despite the skill of his defensive move, David's attack sent him reeling, and he regained his balance in time to see Caladfwlch arc toward him. Michael raised his sword to deflect the blow, but David rained a flurry upon the fiery blade. He had no intention of letting Michael regain his composure.

Nearby, orange flame poured off the side of the bridge, and David glanced to his side to see Dodd rolling clear of the torrent. His own powers would only help him so much against the titan he faced.

A moment of distraction was all Michael needed to score the concrete with his fingers and fling the brittle substance at David. The rock never reached its target as David's own heat disintegrated it before it could hit home, but Michael placed an orb of flame in the air with his left hand and moved in the opposite direction as it lofted fire at David. The move gave the angel all the space he needed to find his feet and gain distance.

David took the moment to feel the heft of his sword, and he found it held him as much as he held it. He was tired.

The act of connecting with the world had been a double-edged play. It weakened Flueric's hold on the masses, but at the cost of David's own personal stores of power. Azazel had told him that if he burned too brightly, he risked consuming himself, but David still held the hubris of youth. The notion that he had limits or would face physical consequences for his decisions still eluded him. He sent his thanks to the sword for its part in this and stood tall before the general of the host.

"Can we try to discuss this again?" David asked. "I am not interested in fighting you or defying the Host, but I won't let the world be devoured either."

Michael smiled and raised his palm to David. "You speak as though you have the high ground, boy."

A torrent of fire enveloped David.

Ω

Chelsea had been clever enough to hide behind the portal. She found from this side there was no view of the garden, but a shimmering version of the scene on the bridge. It hid just enough for her to be spared the intricate details of the battle, but she remained anxious anyway. Despite this, and her nature, she listened to Rose's request for her to stay put no matter what. She even beckoned for Leonard and Barbara to join her from nearby, and the two made their way as she waited.

The scene was chaos all about them, and many of the news vans had fled, save one or two who would rather die than miss the story of all time. Chelsea saw Baba Yaga's house of brown skip off into the barren trees and hunker down and wondered at the location of the witch while she scanned the area for Rose, who'd also vanished soon after creeping away.

The woman who'd born the weight of much responsibility since becoming pregnant with David felt her heart flutter in her chest. She paused to take note of her stress response. She wasn't Dodd, after all, and had nothing else besides her wits and own mortal body to guard her soul.

A golden light grew brighter from above, and Raphael came circling around the top of the bridge. Chelsea thought he would fly on by, but her luck ran dry when the angel turned his head and caught sight of her. She was stricken by the sheer beauty of him before her terror reminded her that he meant to burn her to a crisp.

Raphael pulled himself into a hover some fifty feet above. "Don't be frightened. I take no delight in this task, and I'll ensure you feel no discomfort as I send you to the next world."

"Is that really called for?" Chelsea asked.

"Oh yes. This affront is on par with the original sin. Very taboo," Raphael said. "No entry to paradise until such a time as the creator deems your kind ready."

Chelsea stood.

"Please don't flee. It will make you fearful if I must pursue."

"I'm not running," Chelsea said and stared at Raphael, who was taken aback but raised his sword to begin his ugly work.

He paused and looked at his hand more closely and with a scrutiny that confused Chelsea. His inspection carried beyond and down his arms before Chelsea made out what the angel was seeing. Mushrooms had bloomed from his body and exploded in growth.

"Oh dear," he said as they consumed his face.

"Run, Chelsea," Leonard said as he leaped from his hiding place near the side of the bridge.

He, Barbara, and Chelsea rounded the portal, where they stopped cold, not more than three feet from Raguel.

Ω

Dodd raised himself to his hands and knees and shook his head clear of the tantalizing promises whispered by his enemy within. He knew unleashing too much power from the ifrit would cause him to lose control, and he doubted doing so would subdue Raguel. The angel had barely showcased his strength, and he toyed with the man.

Raguel walked past Dodd to block him from jumping into Eden. "It's time for you to die."

Dodd stood and prepared to rush off the side of the bridge to draw the angel away and buy time just as the rest of the band, headed by Chelsea, appeared from the far side of the portal and nearly collided with his foe.

Rose cast seeds at his feet and channeled a briar patch of thorned branches to envelop the angel. Leonard pulled Chelsea and Barbara through the portal in the brief instant Rose's distraction afforded them, and Raguel tore through the cage to catch where Rose had been. He was surprised to find not the petite girl standing before him, but a comically large toad with a backpack. "I grow tired of these games, mortals."

"Mortal games *are* tiresome, I can agree," Baba Yaga said.

"And now it becomes clear. The crone appears."

Lilith emerged from the darkness holding one of Baba Yaga's flasks and threw it at Raguel's feet. A mist rose from the ground in tendrilous wisps that touched the angel, staining him in gray. She picked up Princess and fled toward Eden, and Raguel moved to incinerate her. He paused at the moment the flames should have fired from his palm and balked. "What did you do, impudent witch?"

"Impudent—says the one who can't give rise to his power," Baba Yaga cackled.

"You're thinking of 'impotent,'" Dodd said, and Raguel howled as Lilith disappeared into Eden.

He turned his rage toward Baba Yaga, delivering a blow to knock her into the cantilevers. Dodd dove for Vajra on the ground and lifted it. The object vibrated in his hands, making it hard for him to hold, and he pressed his mind toward it.

I know you're worried about the darkness inside of me. But look into my heart, Vajra. Am I not worthy?

The object settled and Dodd flicked his eyes to Raguel, who'd turned back to the garden, trying to decide if he should kill Dodd or pursue the humans.

Vajra changed form into the shape of a gold-plated pistol with onyx sheeting. Dodd hefted the sidearm, pointed it at Raguel, and fired.

Ω

Rose approached the bundle of rags under the dented cantilever and turned Baba Yaga to face her.

"You didn't have to do that," Rose said.

"Aye, and ought one good deed be enough to dispel a plenty of mal actions. I shan't expect recompense in kind."

"You didn't do it for any reward. You did it to save me."

Baba Yaga showed her crooked smile. "You are the future, lassie. I'm the past."

"Rest now," Rose said. "I can patch you up if we can get to your house."

"I'm done as a duck cooked over a hot stove," she said. "But worry not. It's for the young to fear death and the aged to welcome it. You carry on and ensure my promise to Princess is kept. The girl's debt has been paid."

Baba Yaga looked to somewhere far away and fell limp within Rose's arms. The girl placed her down on the cold road and turned back toward the battle behind her. Dodd fired bolts of lightning at Raguel, who did his best to dodge. The mystic item had chosen an excellent form for the detective to use. Dodd always had been a crack shot.

Rose didn't know how long Baba Yaga's concoction would last on the angel and knew it had been conjured from the hair she'd borrowed from David. If the girl's experience with the witch's work was any guide, they had minutes at best.

She wiped a tear from her cheek, reached into a pocket to gather a handful of seeds, and threw them into the air where the wind dispersed them widely. These seeds were from a very special shelf in Baba Yaga's house—one she was not to use errantly. When she called upon the seeds to grow, she felt a hateful heat in her belly. One born as much from the rage she felt at her mentors passing as from the plants themselves.

These predatory stalks resembled perverse carnivorous vines with malicious mouths at their ends. In their native fields, beneath the veil, these plants wrought Demeter's wrath upon those who might encroach into an area sacred to the goddess. Here, they were tasked with bringing pain to Rose's enemies.

The first stalks to grow over thirty feet latched onto Raphael, who still struggled to burn off the ever-growing fungus upon him. The plants slammed him to the ground and drove their spiked teeth into the flesh of the angel, causing him to cry out in pain.

Raguel took a bolt of lightning to his shoulder and cursed Dodd as his leg was caught up by one of Rose's vines. They climbed the angel's leg and viciously chomped, allowing Dodd the ability to land multiple shots on his face and chest. Rose felt satisfaction hearing Raguel's pain, despite knowing they should fight for the same cause. He just wasn't very nice.

Raguel's breastplate disintegrated to show a scar on his perfect chest, and his eyes erupted in flame. The angel drew his sword.

Ω

"Rose, get in the garden, now!" Dodd cried.

She ran forward despite Dodd's warning and picked up the Tinker, then dove for cover.

Raguel unleashed a torrent of fire at the detective, who instinctively returned a salvo of his own, but held down the trigger causing the pistol to emit a constant stream of electromagnetic power. The same power that protects the earth from solar flares shielded them from Raguel's power, and the angel cursed him in a language Dodd didn't believe had existed on Earth for centuries.

The retired cop circled to place his back to David and Michael and force the angel to face away from Rose. She whistled, and Baba Yaga's house rustled in the trees before taking flight, scooping the girl inside and flying through the door to Eden.

"We had planned to make your deaths quick," Raguel said. "It isn't in our nature to be wrathful, but to deliver the judgment of our creator. Why couldn't you just die and keep this clean?"

Dodd felt movement from behind him and heard David's voice, "On your toes, old man!" David flew past and connected a kick to Raguel's side to throw the angel off balance, but received a blow from Raphael, now freed.

Michael landed beside his brothers, and they looked at the door.

"They have reentered Eden. We've failed."

"We haven't failed," Michael said. "This is merely going to plan. Did you forget what waits beyond that door?"

Raguel smiled. "Right."

David and Dodd looked to one another and moved to the door, only to be stopped by three blasts of flame.

"Looks like we have to find a way out of this before we can get in there," Dodd said.

"I don't think we can match them," David said. "At least not without the intent to destroy."

Gungnir rose from the ground in front of the angels, and Raphael uttered, "Ahhhh," as the spear flicked through the sky and into the hand of Odin, as he floated down from the clouds with Freja and Samael.

"And another of my brethren betrays me," Michael balked. "Have you not learned from the lessons of the watchers?"

"I've made a choice to fight for them." Samael pointed to David and Dodd. "But I have no wish to destroy you." The angel's black wings extended wide, and David and Dodd felt the gravity of his power for the first time since meeting him. Michael stood firm, but both Raphael and Raguel exchanged glances.

"Lucifer draws close," Samael said. "And I'm not one for idle hands in the face of a crisis. Freja, send them."

Freja nodded and emitted a cry that sent the clouds above into a vortex. From within flew her Valkyrie, clad in beatific armor and with weapons held at the ready. They cascaded down and through the portal without giving notice to the scene upon the bridge.

Raphael gave chase without word or warning and disappeared into Eden.

Odin approached Michael. "You have a choice to make, and it must be made soon. There are no divine orders raining down upon you from the notes of a Seraph's song. You have been handed free will, Michael. How will you use it?"

The angel pointed the tip of his sword at Odin, who stood boldly before him.

A roar raked through the air from the south.

"What will it be?" Samael asked.

"With me, Raguel," Michael said and assumed defensive posture before the door to Eden.

"Full disclosure," David said. "We aim to let her in."

"Absolutely not," Michael said. "If we stand together, we do so to smite the beast down here."

"She's older than all of us," Samael said. "I'm not entirely sure we can destroy her. But we can trap her within Eden."

"Of all the decrees we have received, our most urgent was to never allow to be breached the sanctity of the garden. Within lies the tree, of which you know well, Odin, for from it you hanged and suffered. If Yggdrasil is destroyed, there will be nothing to tether reality together, and all will fall."

"I know," Samael said. "But we don't intend to let her devour the tree."

"All she knows is hunger and want," Raguel said.

"They make a pretty compelling argument," Dodd said. "What's the plan for when she is in there?"

Odin shrugged his shoulders and faced the south, where the forward-racing wave grew visible and Leviathan's light emerged into the night.

"We cage what can't be killed."

Ω

Rose dropped from the house onto soft grass and looked around as the house found a cozy perch. Barbara and Lilith sat nearby, looking to the sky, and Rose followed their gaze to see battalions of angels floating above. Their number was ludicrous, and it dawned upon the girl why biblical numbers always seemed so high. Whether it be angels or demons, they were indeed legion. The Host plodded down from on high.

"What the hell are we supposed to do about *that*?" Chelsea asked.

"Probably die," Barbara said.

"Leonard, honey, can you shake her or something. I think she may be having a breakdown."

Barbara sat staring in wonder at the garden around them. The door behind showed a world of gray. A wasteland. What surrounded them within were the archetypal designs of the creation for which each and every human passively yearned.

Barbara sat entranced by the flora and fauna of Eden and cared little about all else. A euphoria gripped each to some degree, but Barbara appeared to be the only one battling shock and wonder simultaneously. Leonard stood dond gave Barbara a rattle to bring her eyes to his.

"We should find cover over there," Leonard said, and the group worked their way toward a grove surrounded by fruit-bearing bushes that were frequented by various animals. A stag of an even larger stature than the one that Rose had resurrected bent its head low to chomp upon the leaves and shake its rack through the air as it did.

The more Chelsea observed, the more she wished she were struck as stupid as Barbara had been. Along the way, with everything she'd been through, that open door to wonder that existed within Barb had closed further within Chelsea. It hurt her more to understand that she hadn't noticed at all.

"Why aren't they descending on us faster?" Lilith asked, pointing to the oncoming angels.

Rose laughed. "If I've learned anything about them, it's that they don't do well without direct and explicit orders. I wouldn't let it lull you into a false sense of security, though."

"By no means," Lilith said. "They will obliterate us."

The group reached cover and hunkered down. Princess croaked and hopped to the stag, which kneeled and sniffed her pack before standing tall and walking further into the bushes. Rose looked at the pack the toad had on and opened it. Within, there were more flasks that Baba Yaga had prepared to dull the angel's flames. She didn't bother opening them. This tonic would do little to help them here in the garden against so many.

Rose felt no wind and saw no clouds above. There was no reason to believe this place ever experienced a change in the weather, and the light they enjoyed didn't flow from a singular point, but from some ethereal source she didn't care to identify. She placed her hands down and found her power held no sway over the life here, yet the great tree hummed to her from far away.

"It won't work. This place is more like Leviathan than it is your world," Lilith said. "Everything in the garden lives forever and sees no decay. Your power is the sway over the cycle of existence, not growth."

"Where does the water flow from?" Leonard asked.

"There's a fount nearby that flows down into the garden and to the trees beyond."

"There's more than one tree?"

"No, if the tree you speak of is Yggdrasil. Other unique trees *are* rooted here. Each with its own mysteries. The tree from which Adam and Eve sampled their fruit is an example. Yggdrasil will be the only noble tree nearby. It's just beyond the way here." Lilith pointed beyond them. "Had we looked up in the opposite direction of the angels, its trunk and canopy would have been clear to you, rising into the cosmos where the light of this place cannot follow."

The angels had closed the distance between them and halted in the air nearby. A small party formed and made for the ground to pursue them into their cover.

"We have nothing. Not even Dodd is here to try and buy us time," Chelsea said.

"There won't be a need for him," Rose said. "Listen."

Chelsea strained her ears to hear, and in the distance, the sound of a horn issued—faintly, as if muffled by a cover. A moment later, the first of the Valkyrie flew through the door and engaged the small party of angels with merciless blows, forcing them to beat a hasty retreat.

"There's not enough of them," Barbara said.

The Valkyrie flew to meet the Host of angels, who descended to meet the armor-clad warriors of the Fólkvangr. Their conflict frenzied the serene sky.

Rose smiled. "There are more than enough of them."

Ω

Leviathan coursed through the river, carving out new channels in its soft bed. Her intention could be felt by all on the bridge.

"David, flee into the garden," Odin said. "Now."

Raguel moved to block him as Freja raised her mace and wagged her finger.

"Let him pass," Michael said. "By now, you should feel what approaches. The serpent has supped upon one of our brethren."

From the base of the bridge, where the iron supports met the rocky shore, rose a faint, eerie glow. It started as a pinprick of light, barely noticeable amidst the shadows as a low hum vibrated through the metal and stone. The glow intensified, coalescing into a swirling vortex of crimson and violet.

A figure birthed from the supernatural maelstrom.

Dodd could make out the outline of a tall man as he emerged, his form shrouded in a fleeting cloak of darkness as the vortex subsided. His skin was pale, almost translucent, and his eyes glowed with an unsettling red hue. Horns gnarled through his trilby hat, which hid from where they protruded.

Flueric had arrived. Dressed in smart clothes, but somehow different in that the coals of his being charred and frayed the fabric as it consistently reformed around him.

He stepped forward, his boots crunching on shredded asphalt, and the air around him crackled with energy. He surveyed his surroundings with a cold, calculating gaze, taking in the bridge's towering structure and the river's dark expanse.

"Ah, the Rip Van Winkle," he mused, his voice a deep,

resonant whisper that echoed from the very depths of the earth. "How quaint. And yet, how appropriate."

With a wave of his hand, the remaining traces of the vortex dissipated, leaving only the lingering scent of sulfur in the air. Flueric stretched his arms, relishing the freedom of his corporeal form. He glanced up at the bridge with a malevolent grin. "It appears I am not the sole member of the choir to arrive," he murmured. "How delightful."

He raised his hand, and with a flick of his wrist, summoned a swirling orb of amaranthine flame. The fiery sphere hovered above his palm, casting flickering shadows across his face. "Let the games begin," he declared, and with a sudden burst of energy, he hurled the orb into the night, its light vanishing into the portal.

Leviathan made for the door, but Flueric held his hand to hold the beast. "Not yet."

"That was a part of Azazel, wasn't it?" David squared himself to Flueric.

"I'd like to think of it as power borrowed from me," Flueric said. "This is my inheritance, after all."

"What is?"

"Everything."

"You're due nothing, traitor," Michael said.

Flueric laughed and nodded. "What a merry band of thieves we have here."

"Thieves?" Raguel asked.

"*You've* stolen my seat, haven't you," Flueric said and gestured his hat toward Michael.

"We've had no bearer of light since you fell to darkness. Whatever glory you had fell with you, brother. Mine is of my own making."

"So on-brand for you," Flueric said. "Your claim to fame has always been that bright and shiny sword you have there. What do you think, Michael, will it be so shiny if you use it on me?"

Michael and Raguel leaped into the air and crashed into Flueric, who cast them back. "The lunks of this charade dive in while the wise stand back because they know they pale in comparison."

"I'd keep my hubris in check," Odin said. "If I were you."

"Oh, were you *me*," Flueric said. "What if you were really *you,* All-Father?"

Odin's eye flashed from red to blue, and he pointed the spear at Flueric, forming a ball of increased gravity. Freja dashed ahead with her chain aglow as she harnessed all of her power to land a single blow. Flueric raised his hand to catch her mace, and she saw his multiple forms acting in unison as they had during his battle with David. Odin smiled and lagged Flueric's efforts with Gungnir as Freja's attack smashed home, sending him through the first layer of bridge.

The group looked to the hole, and Odin motioned for David to head to Eden. The boy hesitated, unsure of the correct course of action before deferring to the wisdom of his elder and disappearing through the door.

"Michael, you could learn a thing or two from them," Flueric said, climbing back to the surface. "That's how you coordinate a proper attack."

Samael said, "Move." And Flueric laughed as he pointed to Leviathan coiled and poised behind them. She snarled at the onlookers and bypassed them to cascade after David.

Flueric leaped atop the serpent's body to enter Eden.

"Enough!" Michael cried, unleashing a torrent of flame

upon the serpent and fallen angel alike. The pressure of his blast emanated enough force to cause Raguel to cover himself with a wing. When the torrent subsided, Flueric lay on the bridge and Leviathan continued through the door unfazed.

"I want to show you something," Flueric said as he stood. Michael had maintained his aggressive posture, and both Odin and Raguel moved to attack, but Flueric no longer stood at the hole.

The angel became confused when he felt Flueric's hand on his shoulder. "Never take your eye off the prize, old friend."

Michael remained in place and was paradoxically torn into innumerable versions of his reality. Within each, Flueric ended his existence differently. Many were so alike that the only dissimilar aspect might be a stray spark or beam of light. But within each, Michael found his end.

Odin attempted to save him in some and had been further injured in others, but was never dead, and Michael glimpsed a hidden truth on the rare occasion when the ancient god's helmet had been knocked away.

Raguel was absent from these macabre plays, indicating he had been the first to meet his end. The reality of each scenario on its own was not horrid to observe, but feeling himself obliterated into nothingness infinitely and all at once was unbearable.

In their reality, Odin, Freja, and Raguel watched as Michael, the indomitable and magnificent Michael, fell to his knees.

"There wasn't a single version where you live. Don't bother with the idea of winning. You've never even escaped," Flueric said.

"Do you ever tire of playing with your food?" Samael asked.

"Is my food telling me it wants to play?"

"I'll handle this from here. You two"—Samael pointed to Freja and Odin—"go to the tree. It's time to end this."

Raguel looked from Michael to Flueric, unsure of what to do.

"Follow us, or stay and die," Odin said as he brushed past the angel and entered Eden with Freja in tow. The general of the Fólkvangr held a tiny bundle in her arms, and if you listened well enough, you would hear the whine of a little brown house from inside Eden.

Raguel scooped Michael and leaped through the door.

"I hadn't expected this from you," Flueric said. "The great and dark Samael has always flown so far below the radar it was hard to pinpoint what side you were even on."

"I'm not on a side," Samael said. "Never felt the urgent need to choose one. Each action warrants its own consideration, and I choose in the moment. In this moment, I choose to humble you."

"You were before I fell, and it was a surprise to see you at all afterward. With such an important charge, no less. Deliverer of the dead. Come to the winning side, and I'll give you your just due."

"Been doing much winning, lately, have you?" Samael asked, strolling about the bridge to watch the last segment of Leviathan enter Eden. "You may want to review your record."

"Cute," Flueric said. "You remain here with me. Does this mean you're done playing in the sandbox?"

Samael sidestepped the question. "I came into being when you collapsed under your own weight. A simple progression of evolution is all I am—the birth of death. What was once permanent now made temporary. For what purpose, I'm not really sure, but it does make the morsels of time humans spend in their reality all the more precious." Samael sat on the railing of the bridge and curled his wings behind as he took off his glasses. "And in those morsels of time, they've toiled and created magnificent things. Things I doubt you've given more than a cursory glance." He unbuttoned his shirt sleeves and rolled them to his elbows. "Have you stood in the shadow of the Palace of Parliament building in Romania, or marveled at the Derawar Fort in Pakistan? Perhaps you've been to the Sistine Chapel to reflect on Michelangelo's enduring faith despite your incessant meddling?"

"I'm more keen on hearing war drums beating and seeing towers fall."

"Yes, and all by just the seeds of greed you plant to set the discord in motion. We've reviewed your playbook. Very simple."

"If it ain't broke, don't fix it," Flueric said, producing his weapon. "Care to see some things you've never imagined? Don't worry, I'll give you as much time as you need."

"If I had to guess, I'd surmise that pitchfork is made from a very resonant material. Perhaps even the exact material from the great tree beyond the door there." Samael pointed to Eden. "Perchance, did you happen upon the branch felled at the end of Odin's hanging?"

Flueric smiled. "Why is it that they made the only smart angel their garbage man?"

"Ferrying souls to the river is not akin to delivering garbage. It is transporting the very fruit of creation. And I am not half as clever as the blue-winged angel who outwitted you, light bearer."

"The one who was dead and gone, leaving a glimmer of himself for Odin? Oh no, that's right, you use terms like 'destroyed' or 'annihilated' to sum up the destruction of an angel. Quite taboo, that. I wonder why the creator broke its silence in that moment but refused to step in further."

"Probably because the creator didn't destroy Uriel, you fool," Samael said.

"Then who did? I can't take credit for that little ditty."

Samael stood from his seat and flexed his wings. "You'll have to persevere beyond me to find out."

"And what makes you think you can withstand feeling a thousand deaths?" Flueric asked, spinning his pitchfork.

Samael rolled his shoulders and flashed a smile. "Because I am the very nature of singularity."

Ω

Rose heard the commotion increase when Leviathan entered Eden. The Valkyrie, having been harried by Hosts of angels, found a moment of calm as the defenders of Eden descended upon the greater threat to their charge. The serpent had grown in scale in their reality, but it appeared small amidst the infinite scale of the garden, the very nature of which exuded infinity's purpose.

"We should stay wide of that scuffle there," Dodd said. "The tree is this way."

"Won't Leviathan head to the tree?" Chelsea asked.

"Seems a safe bet," Leonard said. "But my guess is she will go for David. She has a soft spot for him."

David crashed through the brush and came to a sliding stop in front of the group. "Leviathan's coming."

"We know," the group said in unison.

"Oh, good," David said. "Run."

Freja and Odin pulled up beside the fleeing group. "The angels will slow her down, but it would be best for your band to move off to the side there and take refuge near the river. Your part in all this is done for now."

"Will we make it in time?" Barbara asked through gasping breaths.

"I'm unsure," Freja said. "If I had my chariot, I'd gladly lend it."

Dodd plucked Chelsea up and put her on his shoulders. He and Barbara picked up the pace.

Freja reached out to Rose. "Take her."

Rose collected Baba Yaga's body and marveled at how light her burden had become. "I'll take good care of her."

Freja nodded and gestured for Odin and David to vector off toward the tree. "She's coming with us," David said.

"It may not be wise to keep any mortal within the radius of that monster," Odin said.

"The angels won't take you into consideration, either, Rose," Freja said. "It seems a poor plan."

"My safety isn't our goal," Rose said. "And besides, it's long past due for David and I to stand together."

Odin and Freja exchanged a look of common understanding that eluded the rest of the group.

Chelsea and Dodd embraced Rose.

"I love you," they said.

Before long, Dodd stopped under a lotus near a tributary to the larger river beyond them. "This is probably about as safe as it gets."

Chelsea sighed and grasped Leonard and Dodd's hands,

and they basked in the glow of what has been called the world tree. It stretched to the cosmos beyond the limits of Eden's skies. The trunk rose and twisted from roots that submerged into the soil, only to jut out again in various spots throughout the garden, giving it both a regal and haunted look. It was impossible for Chelsea to assume the scale of the tree, as the garden itself provided no barrier limit for comparison.

"It's the most breathtaking thing I've ever seen," Chelsea said.

"I thought I was the most breathtaking thing you'd ever seen," Dodd chided.

Leonard let loose a laugh, which caused the entire group to turn to him. "We've reached the outer limits of Nirvana. Even amidst this chaos and with the weight of the moment upon me, I can't shake how wonderful I feel."

"This is what that bastard stole from us," Chelsea said.

Barbara sighed. "We have a long legacy of falling for deceitful promises. It's time to start making up for some of those. Especially if this is the prize at the end of the road."

The group watched on as corsairs of angels harried Leviathan. Raphael and Raguel struck at her with their divine weapons. All to little more avail than to distract the serpent as she coursed toward David and the tree.

Ω

Flueric flicked the end of his fork and emitted a note that rattled through the bridge, the air, the soil, and on down to the infinitesimally small building blocks of matter humans work so hard to glimpse. Samael felt the wave drive through him and he fell back a step, causing Flueric to smile. He then pivoted off of his hind foot and lunged ahead to swipe the fallen angel with his obsidian wing. Flueric flew into the steel of the bridge, causing it to bend and mold around him. Samael watched with a cocked head as he struggled to free himself.

"You're not the only one who likes to use deception."

"Don't get ahead of yourself," Flueric said. "I was merely extending you a courtesy by throttling the technique." He grasped the fork in both hands and plunged it into the pavement, causing a cacophony to radiate about them.

Samael had chosen wisely in clearing the battlefield before provoking Flueric to this point. The surrounding wildlife experienced such a severe fragmentation of their understanding of time and reality that some suffered brain hemorrhages, while others could not rationalize living in their four-dimensional reality ever again. They'd lay stupefied until the earth took them back. The effects on the humans would have proven similar, if not worse. Flueric's trump card was as insidious as it was deadly, which is why the former CEO of All Century stood stupefied as Samael walked toward him during the barrage.

"How are you doing that?" Flueric raged.

"I'm not beholden to the whiles of time. It's that simple."

"You should still be seeing what is happening to you in all the other realities you exist within!"

"Take a long look yourself and see if you can figure it out."

Flueric realized Samael's confidence had distracted him from surveying the very thing that had felled Michael—Flueric's own dominance. He looked within the fork's vibrating ends and saw those same eventualities where the other versions of himself were battling Samael. Only the outcomes were looking much less one sided.

"You have used that fork carved from the world tree and made contact with all versions of yourself in every reality. A handsome achievement to be sure, and one I am admirable of. I'd wondered if, given the devil's insane amounts of pride, some found you to be insufferable and refused to join, but it looks like not. Perhaps this unity is a byproduct of your great strength and skills of wit, though I'll likely never know." Samael neared the fork and reached his hand toward it, causing Flueric's eyes to burst into white flame. "But did you see, yet, what you stand against in those worlds?"

Flueric's face morphed into a demonic visage more akin to how he was known by the people who fear him most, and his wings emerged as those of a leathery gargoyle with the barest remnants of stark white feathers clinging to the ends.

He stared into the fork and watched as his other selves were tossed and tussled by Samael, but the dark angel of death continued to look back at this Flueric through the fork, as if to ensure he paid attention before delivering further blows upon the doppelgangers. Flueric looked into Samael's eyes on the bridge and saw the same expression, and it dawned on him. "It's the same one. They're all you."

"Bravo," Samael said as he grasped the fork and stymied its resonance with great effort.

"How can it be that you are in all realities simultaneously?"

"I was not born to conjure the materials that form life, as the other members of the Host. I was born to devour that light for a singular purpose. All made things find their way to me. I am ever present in any reality you know of. Every thought that has ever been conjured will cascade through me to its ultimate place of rest at the creator's pool of consciousness, and all tidings and deeds are forever within my memory. Most fear me until they know the warmth of my embrace, and there is nothing in this existence to rival my eventuality, for all things end. Even you. I am not like you, and yet I am. I am not like them, and yet I am. I am death."

Flueric stepped back as Samael crushed the fork in his grip, causing a flash of light and rupture of sound. The effort taxed the angel, and the devil leaped at opportunity, as was his known trait.

Flueric dropped to the ground and crawled on all fours to swipe at Samael's legs, but he rose into the air before the blow could land. Flueric smiled and unleashed a powerful blast of white radiant light at his adversary who floated helpless to outmaneuver it. The barrage was immense, as Flueric knew Samael to be his match, and his hopes lay in causing great harm through this attack. It was with a whimper that he realized Samael hadn't bothered to avoid the blast, not out of lack of ability, but out of lack of interest.

"I've told you, I am the great devourer. Not that serpent that wants for little more than to feel whole. She craves and gnaws, but I eat. No amount of light you can emit will fill the vastness of the void that dwells within me." Flueric ceased his attack, and Samael absorbed the remaining light and dropped to the bridge. He produced a book from within his chest and held it out. "This is a tome of the pain and sorrow that has occurred since your fall. It is quite literally all-encompassing and bears the weight of your deeds." Samael hefted the book, and the bridge shook. "If I was to stop using my strength to help hold it up, it would cascade down through the earth until it met the center."

"Stop blabbering and fight," Flueric said as his clothes tore and his body grew larger with skin toughened by scale. "Even if you manage to defeat me, I will still win. The world is barren, fool. The people will fight one another just to lap at the pools of blood to survive."

"You made your wager against humanity long ago." Samael lifted the book and floated to meet Flueric's now-considerable height. "It is in this moment that I make mine on the side of them. We will meet in a thousand years and see who is the victor." The book connected with Flueric's head, sending him rocketing through the atmosphere and on to space.

Onlookers would observe little more than a fleeting flash of light.

Ω

DAVID.

Leviathan's voice vibrated through the serene garden.

"Best be moving along quickly now," Freja said.

David scooped Rose in his arms, and she marveled at the tree as he leaped through groves and small forests. "I think I can hear it."

David looked down at her. "That actually makes a lot of sense. What's it saying?"

"I can't really understand, but it's whispering to me," Rose said, smiling up at the tree.

David heard a crash from behind and turned to see Leviathan making a direct line toward them. He frowned. "I'm going to have to drop you off at the base of the tree and lead Bertha there away."

"Okay," Rose said. "But don't go far. I think the tree wants to help."

David looked at her and opened his mouth to say something, but shut it again. He elected to give her a lasting kiss instead.

The two slid to a stop at the base of the tree, and David set Rose down. He turned to leave, and she grabbed his hand. When he turned back, she kissed him again, longer, and with all the love she had. They embraced once more and he said, "I love you."

"We'll be together soon," Rose said.

With that, David dashed off to keep Leviathan from crashing into Rose and the tree. The Host of angels had scattered about and did little to stymie her progress. She was minutes away when Odin and Freja caught him.

"You've grown fast again," Odin said, and David could swear he saw admiration in the eyes of the lord of Valhalla.

"Be sure to tell Mukhulai for me," David said. "Jubei, too. They both swore by speed and decisiveness."

"I cannot," Odin said. "The hordes of Valhalla have dwindled, David."

"The Fólkvangr as well, and most of the creatures from Helheim," Freja said. "They've joined together."

Odin's hands moved to his helm. "All felled by finding valor without seeking it. By living justly and giving their lives for another, just as you did that night on the river. The warriors and dismayed creatures found their purpose once again in helping you fend off Flueric's horde."

The helm lifted from Odin's head, and David once again beheld the face of his teacher. Before him, with one glowing red eye, stood Uriel.

"I only found out just before you did," Freja said.

David stepped forward and embraced his friend. "I should have known from when we first met in Valhalla. It was something you said back then."

"We all exist to push back the darkness."

"Yes, that's what Uriel said when he died."

"But I didn't die," Odin said.

"And how does the real Odin feel about you masquerading as him?"

"He *is* the real Odin," Freja said. "You recall the similarities between them by now, I'm sure."

"Well, yeah, but how can an angel be a god?"

"Many gods are named as other gods. It takes a cursory glance at the histories to find that out, as I'm sure you know. I simply became known as Wuotan during my exploits. Though I never sired children as the stories tell, I did hang from the tree." Odin pointed to Yggdrasil, the world tree. The tree of knowledge. "And I did see what could become of this moment, but nothing is ever certain, David. And we needed—"

"Us," David said. "You needed me and Rose."

"Our part in your story has come to a close, my friend. But you may take solace in knowing we will not remain strangers. In the end, everything returns to the source, and nothing is ever forgotten."

"It's time," Freja said as she gestured to the approaching cataclysm. "Luck be with you, David. And hurry to Rose— you'll not win this without her." David nodded and cast his eyes down. "Don't worry. She's stronger than you know."

"I know how strong she is." David smiled. "She's the only reason I'm still standing."

Freja and Uriel departed, and David waited for the great serpent to come upon him. As he stood, he could see Lilith lifting Raphael from the ground and shouldering his burden. Aside and miles away were his mother and friends, and above hovered the Host of neutered angels. All with little choice but to watch.

David stood firm when Leviathan approached and pulled up before him. They stared into one another's eyes, and hers flicked to the sword he held out to his side. "I'll have back what is mine."

"You won't. If it were that simple, and you'd be satisfied, I'd gladly let you choke on this sword. But it isn't a sword, is it? Not really. It's the flavordyamics gifted to those that came after you were made. Fission, fusion, those words don't matter to you, but they were the precursors to our existence. This sword is simply a symbol, and once you have it, you'll hunger for more. You're envious of the Host just like Flueric was envious of humanity. It's what made hell his prison, and why you belong in the abyss. And that's just where we will send you."

"We? You stand alone, mortal." Leviathan heaved air at David that blew away trees and boulders and scoured the ground him of grass. "All others have failed. As will you."

He lifted the sword in answer, and Leviathan lunged at him. David remained still for so long that the onlookers became worried he intended to let the great beast devour him, but at the last instant, he moved with such speed none were certain if he teleported or resorted to trickery. In reality, he'd found his calm, his muscles relaxed until the moment of absolute need, just as his teachers had instructed.

Leviathan barked out a mouthful of Eden's soil as her eyes

rolled to find her adversary. David stood atop her head with the sword and drove it down between her scales, releasing a cascade of green light that knocked him free of her.

She writhed upon the ground at the pain he'd driven into her, and he left the sword encased in its living sheath because he did not need it. In truth, he was becoming aware he never did. It was just a symbol of strength, after all, and he traveled to where his true strength stood beside the tree.

"Take me up there," Rose said, and David lifted her from the foot of the grave she'd made for her mentor.

She remained fixated upon the tree as it lifted mysteries away from her mind, and the truth of her and David coalesced from the fog that cloaks mortal minds. She dug her nails into his shoulders at the bliss of understanding. And they traversed beyond infinite realms and worlds all balancing their own strifes and eternal charms. The great snake pursued them and coiled around the Yggdrasil, bypassing spoils she'd have lusted for if not for the ever-alluring prize of devouring David.

"Stop here," Rose said, and David leaped atop a branch bearing no leaves or fruit, as many of the others did. Rose settled her hands upon the tree and closed her eyes. "Lend me your strength."

David wrapped her in his arms, pouring himself into her, and she sighed as the branch bore a small black fruit and sprouted leaves the color of the void. The fruit swelled with her intentions as Leviathan lunged for them, only to be ensnared by the invisible draw of this poisoned world of solitude. Her eyes widened at the feel of helplessness as she became enveloped by the growing orb.

And so it was named abyss. And into its wide expanse the snake fell.

The black fruit drew down in size and remained fixed upon the branch as a swirling orb of deep green and the darkest blackness.

David understood himself now as his own fog lifted and his ego shed apart. He released Rose and reached above them to the cosmos beyond the canopy of the tree to find Flueric cascading through space and time. He grasped him, and Flueric raged to little avail. David cast him into the pit beside Leviathan with the whisper of, "Until you next wish to lay a wager."

Rose grasped David's hand, and they dropped to the branch that held their world, barren and desolate due to Abaddon's feral deed.

"I can feel their hope."

"Hope is their gift."

Rose and David held one another and spun atop their perch on the tree. Free as those with complete innocence in a moment of cosmic significance, they kissed for the last time and reveled in one another's warmth. Two parts of the same whole, being united once more.

Rose thinned and broke free of her body into a dancing cloud of primordial seeds, and the wind took her to dance around David. His tears fell as the last vestiges of humanity left him, and the tree accepted them as his fire ignited and left him a cloud of fertile ash to join her.

What once was their bodies descended upon the world and birthed new life, the likes of which humanity had never known outside Eden. Among these gifts were one thousand years of abundance earned by the likes of Chelsea, Dodd, and Leonard. And an existence outside the wiles of Flueric.

David and Rose, freed from their mortal bonds, lifted together as two choruses of the same song, and the Seraphs sang their notes, ending the silence.

EPILOGUE

Chelsea tended her garden alongside Dodd, who occasionally griped about the pain in his knees. The curse of the ifrit had been lifted from him within Eden before the angels bid them depart back to their world. Dodd was thankful to be relieved of his dark passenger even if it came with the caveat of arthritis

Lilith was granted succor within the garden, which she accepted, though she declined the subsequent offer of having a counterpart created for her. In time, she'd find herself happy enough to spend her days alongside the once-proud Princess Anastasia, who had been lost in the woods just over one hundred years ago and was found on the wrong side of Baba Yaga's temper. She was made whole once more as Rose fulfilled her promise.

Barbara and Leonard often visited Chelsea's home and discussed old stories and new hopes together. The couple had been offered the most gracious of gifts by none other than Samael himself: to stay within Eden and live everlasting.

They declined.

Leonard felt he could be of service working alongside Barbara at New Horizons, a rebranded philanthropic conglomerate version of All Century dedicated to helping the world heal. Thus far, they'd made significant progress. Leonard and Barbara continued their relationship and frequently behaved like two teenagers who had become infatuated with one another. Their human resources department eventually made them remove the blinds from their office windows. Not good for decorum, they said.

The couple still managed to find time for mischievous trysts. Many did. With less greed and more plenty, the population boom was underway. Advances in tech for carbon capture all but solved the global climate crisis, making the world rely less on the recent supernatural growth of food crops. Which was a good thing. Who knows how long that might last?

Keyana had less trouble getting her mother to eat nutritious food during the time following the great conflict. "Everything tastes better now," Lady Perez would say as she made peanut brittle for the neighborhood kids. She spent more time outside on the stoop watching and waving than in front of the television, which made Keyana happy. The young lady herself made magnificent leaps within her organization, in no small part due to Barbara's appreciation for her courage, but also largely because of her business acumen.

Grace left activism behind and settled into the pursuit of art. Her parents felt less inclined to scoff at the notion these days.

Stephen Cappodak continued his hobbies, working with kids to help them find their hidden talents. His time on encrypted message boards and inside the hotel room felt like a bad dream. He never did tell a soul about it, but the truth of his dark thoughts wouldn't remain hidden forever. All becomes revealed in the purging fogs of purgatory.

Mr. Eryn continued teaching and coaching. His rough demeanor softened some, but most of his athletes still considered him to be a prick. Can't win 'em all, can we?

The world moved on and celebrated June eighteenth as the day Rose and David gave themselves to save everything in the grand experiment we find ourselves within.

What will come of things in one thousand years, when the pit opens and Flueric is loosed upon the world once again?

The outcome is entirely up to you.

ACKNOWLEDGMENTS

I owe a great deal to a number of people for their incredible encouragement and dedication to this series. This piece of writing is very bittersweet for me. I had considered tabling it many times to pursue other projects, and for good reasons. The entire series bears the scars of a green writer. Hell, *Beneath the Veil* still has open wounds, but also because the entire story is very indulgent. I wrote this tale for your enjoyment, but I also wrote it for mine. I let fly many clichés, tropes, and broke more rules than I felt comfortable with. Though I did mold these choices to my own design, it's generally frowned upon to be so reckless. That said, this story is a fun ride. Good guys winning, bad guys being force fed a well-deserved dose of accountability. In the age of killing our darlings and yours, it feels like a pleasant reprieve.

The Valor of Valhalla began as something of a pseudo autobiographical depiction of how I felt in my young adult era; powerful, ephemeral, very idealistic, but it quickly transformed into something entirely its own. The supporting cast of characters in general feels so alive to me, and it was nice to reward most of them for their valor. To my readers who enjoy horror, don't worry. I've simultaneously punished others for their shortcomings in smaller works on the side and will release them in a collection set in the *VoV* universe for your enjoyment.

Rose remains the most delightful surprise from this experience. To me, her character overshadows David in almost every way. From her stoicism to how she banters with Dodd, she was just a delight to write.

While crafting this story wasn't easy in terms of having time and brainpower to spare for the endeavor, it was a labor of love, and I hope you enjoyed it. *VoV* came to me with a very discernible beginning and end. I had to sift through the murk to find the rest of the tale and often did so with very little sleep and many other worries in the back of my mind. They sat back there scraping their way to the surface not so unlike Dodd's ever-present ifrit.

I am indebted to my wonderful wife, Kimberly, and her endless support as I typed away during the evenings. She is always open to hearing me babble on about these tales and others, and she continues to read each book and every short story first. That means a great deal to me. Her perspective and criticisms were and are invaluable as I create, and we've had more than a little fun along the way. One early example comes to mind. "What's with your love affair with the word maw?" she'd ask, and I'd just crack a joke or two. It's a good word! I did remove about seven of them from the first draft of *Beneath the Veil*, though.

More than that alone, Kim is an inspiration to me, and Rose formed from my memories of a breathtaking twenty-something-year-old who danced to the music when everyone else stood still.

Our two boys, Daniel and Charlie, were a welcome distraction during this process and earn an honorable mention because they are adorable and I treasure them above all else. On the rare occasions when I'd try to get some writing done during the day, their laughter and ridiculous antics reminded me of an innocence this story evolved to highlight. Their lesson is to be happy, remain in the moment, and never shy away from being silly.

To my dedicated beta readers—Stephanie, Dale, Blair, John, Steve, Cyndi—and all others who touched these manuscripts before they met the printing press, thank you. Your involvement has meant the world to me, and I count on your feedback to twist these tales into the best possible ones they can be.

To my friends and close confidants who have supported the books after release—Steph, Mike, Yuuki, Erin, Derek, Jade, Charles, Luke, Rob, Justin, Morgan, Gina, Jon, Ryan, and others I may have left out—I am grateful for your support and feedback. Keep it coming.

I'm indebted to Angela Traficante for being the amazing editor she is. Her expertise is invaluable; her patience and understanding far more than merely appreciated. I swear I'll meet the next deadline we set. For those interested in reading some more of her great work, check out *The Fire Within* series by Ella M. Lee.

Many thanks to Maurice Mosqua for his alternative covers and interior artwork, and Todd Keisling via Dullington Design Co. for his outstanding formatting and cover design. Todd's work is stellar, as evidenced by his prestigious awards and nominations. I highly recommend picking up everything he's written. You won't regret it.

Most importantly, I am thankful to you for sharing this journey with me from start to finish. I hope you enjoyed it and continue to push back the dark.

Martin Kearns
Putnam County, New York
July 18th, 2024

MARTIN KEARNS is the author of *The Valor of Valhalla* series and select short fiction. He is a special education and English teacher and lives with his wife and children in the Hudson Valley. "Stories were my first love and during rare moments of quiet my mind turns toward those I've watched, read, and lived. They bring to mind possibilities, which are really where the seeds of a story begin. I truly hope to bring creative tales to readers who, like me, enjoy finding themselves lost somewhere in a world of endless possibilities."